8519

W9-ANN-842

The Dry Grass of August

**Center Point
Large Print**

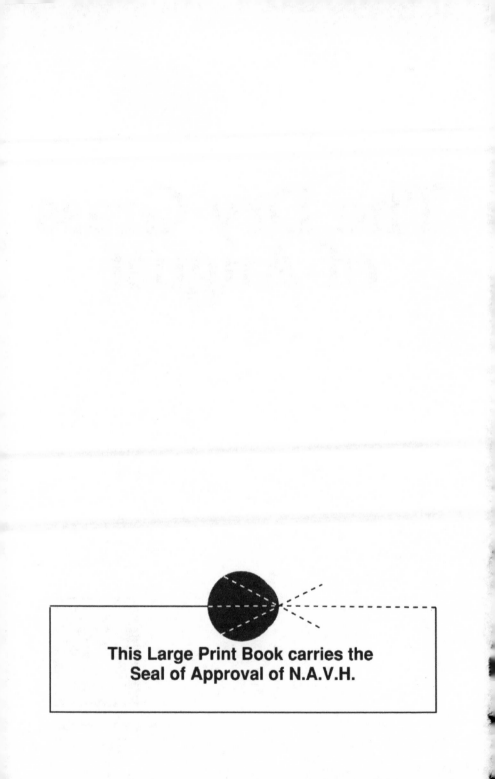

**This Large Print Book carries the
Seal of Approval of N.A.V.H.**

The Dry Grass of August

ANNA JEAN MAYHEW

CENTER POINT PUBLISHING
THORNDIKE, MAINE

This Center Point Large Print edition
is published in the year 2011 by arrangement with
Kensington Publishing Corp.

The text of this Large Print edition is unabridged.
In other aspects, this book may vary
from the original edition.
Printed in the United States of America
on permanent paper.
Set in 16-point Times New Roman type.

ISBN: 978-1-61173-124-8

Library of Congress Cataloging-in-Publication Data

Mayhew, Anna Jean.
The dry grass of August / Anna Jean Mayhew. — Large print ed.
p. cm.
ISBN 978-1-61173-124-8 (library binding : alk. paper)
1. Large type books. I. Title.
PS3613.A956D79 2011
813′.6—dc22

2011014114

for Jean-Michel

and

for Laurel

In the midnight hour
When you need some power
When your heart is heavy
Steal away, steal away home
I ain't got long to stay here.
—*African-American spiritual*

The Dry Grass of August

CHAPTER 1

In August of 1954, we took our first trip without Daddy, and Stell got to use the driver's license she'd had such a fit about. It was just a little card saying she was Estelle Annette Watts, that she was white, with hazel eyes and brown hair. But her having a license made that trip different from any others, because if she hadn't had it, we never would have been stuck in Sally's Motel Park in Claxton, Georgia, where we went to buy fruitcakes and had a wreck instead. And Mary would still be with us.

Stell and I carried the last of the suitcases to the driveway. The sky was a wide far blue above the willow oaks that line Queens Road West, with no promise of rain to break the heat. I put Mary's flowered cloth bag in the trunk and Daddy took it out. "Always start with the biggest piece." He picked up Mama's Pullman and grunted. "She packed like she's never coming back." He hefted it into the trunk. "Okay, girls, what's next?"

Stell tapped her suitcase with the toe of her size six penny loafer.

"That's the ticket." Daddy put Stell's bag in the trunk beside Mama's. He looked at the luggage still sitting by the car and ran his hand through his hair, which was oily with Brylcreem and sweat. "Ninety-five, and not even ten o'clock." He wiped his face with his pocket handkerchief and pushed his wire-rimmed glasses back in place. His hands were tan from playing golf, thick and square, with blunt fingers. On his right pinkie he wore a ring that had been his father's—gold, with a flat red stone.

The cowbell rang as Mary shut the kitchen door behind her. She came down the back walk, Davie on her hip. Puddin stumbled along beside them, struggling with the small suitcase she'd gotten for Christmas.

Daddy said to Mama, "Don't let Mary ride up front."

"I'd never do such a fool thing," Mama said. "Everybody use the bathroom one last time."

Stell stepped into the shade of the garage. "I don't need to."

I ran to the breezeway, touching Mary's arm when I passed her, letting the screen door slap shut behind me. Daddy's bathroom smelled like cigarettes and poop. I cranked open the window and sat on his toilet to pee. In the full-length mirror on the back of the door, I could see the awful welts on my thighs. I stood and yanked up my pedal pushers.

Daddy was rearranging the luggage, making one more square inch of room in the trunk. Stell Ann stood by the car, shiny in her readiness, from her silky hair to her clear lip gloss to her pale-pink nails. Polished like I could never be.

A horn honked. Aunt Rita's green Coupe deVille skidded into our driveway, stopping beside the Packard. She rolled down her window. "I found the picnic basket."

Mama said, "Great!" She asked Daddy, "Can we make room for it?"

He groaned, looking into the crammed trunk.

Aunt Rita passed the basket out the window to Mama. "It's packed with dishes, glasses, utensils. The ones in the paper bag are for Mary." She lowered her voice. "There's talk of the Klan in Georgia."

Mama handed the basket to Daddy. "We'll be fine."

"I hope so." Aunt Rita waved as she pulled out of the driveway.

Mama jingled her car keys. "Say good-bye to your father."

Daddy hugged Puddin with one arm and reached for Stell with the other, but she held herself stiffly away from him. He brushed my forehead with a kiss. "Be good, Junebug. You know you're Daddy's girl, right?"

His head blocked the morning sun and I couldn't see his face.

Mary stood in the driveway, holding Davie. Daddy poked Davie's tummy. "Say bye-bye."

Davie waved.

"Take care of my boy for me," Daddy said to Mary.

"Yes, sir." Mary didn't look at Daddy when she spoke.

We all got in the car, Mama and Stell Ann in front, Davie between them in his canvas baby seat. Puddin and I were in the back with Mary, who sat behind the driver's seat, tall and straight, her dark face already damp with sweat. She patted my leg to let me know she liked sitting next to me.

Mama's hair was curled and hanging loose, flashing red and gold. She handed me her sun hat, scarf, and gloves to put on the ledge in the back window. "Fold my gloves and put them under my hat, then cover my hat with the scarf." She watched me in the rearview mirror, making sure I did what she said.

She started the car. "Is everyone ready?"

"Ready, Freddy," I said. Stell sniffed. Slang was beneath her now that she was sixteen, was in Young Life, and had been saved.

Daddy leaned in Mama's window to kiss her on the cheek. "I'll see you at Pawleys, okay?" Mama bent to move her purse and he kissed her shoulder instead. "Keep it in the road," he said.

She put the car in reverse. Had she felt his kiss on her shoulder?

Daddy waved from the garage, looking alone already, and I remembered what he'd said to Uncle Stamos, his older brother. "While they're gone, I'm going to play golf every afternoon and get stinking drunk whenever I want." I wondered how he'd feel, coming home to a quiet house, nobody on the phone, no supper in the oven. No one to yell at when he got mad.

Mama turned onto Queens Road West, into the shady green tree tunnels formed by the towering oaks. "I hope there's not much traffic between here and the highway."

On the way out of Charlotte we passed Municipal Pool, and I saw Richard Daniels poised on the new high dive while another kid did a cannonball from the low board. Nobody was a better diver than Richard. Next time I talked to him, I'd ask him to give me lessons.

When Daddy and Uncle Stamos won the contract to build those diving boards, they had hunkered for weeks over blueprints spread on the dining room table. Huge papers that smelled like ether and had WATTS CONCRETE FABRICATIONS, INC. in a box on every page, with a caption: CHARLOTTE MUNICIPAL SWIMMING POOL, and subheadings: DECK. BASE FOR THREE-METER BOARD. BASE FOR ONE-METER BOARD.

Daddy showed me how to read the drawings. "Always check the scale. An inch can equal a foot or ten feet." He held the papers flat to keep them from curling. "If you don't know the scale, you won't understand the drawings." I learned about blueprints as I breathed in his smell of tobacco and Old Spice.

He liked teaching me things. When I was in first

grade he gave me a miniature toolbox with painted wooden tools, which Mama thought was ridiculous. "That kind of thing is for boys," she'd said.

"I don't have any," Daddy had told her. "Yet." He patted her bottom. "And girls need to know the business end of a hammer."

If Daddy wanted help, I grabbed my toolbox and ran to him, but he hadn't asked for my help in a long time. Thirteen was too old for make-believe tools.

Puddin wriggled on the seat next to me. "I want to be in front when we get to Florida so I can see the ocean first."

"That won't be till tomorrow afternoon," I told her.

She put her head against my shoulder. "I can wait." Then she sat up again. "Do my braids so I look Dutch." I knotted her skimpy braids on top of her head, knowing they wouldn't stay, as fine as her hair was.

"Do I look Dutch?"

"You look like Puddin-tane with her braids tied up." Silky blonde wisps fell behind her ears.

Davie started to fuss and Mama asked Stell to check his diaper. He was almost two but wasn't taking to potty training, so Mama had him in diapers for the trip. Stell lifted him free of the car seat and asked, "Are you ever going to let me drive?"

"Yes."

"His diaper's okay. Take him for a while, Mary." She helped Davie climb over the seat. Mary reached for him and he beamed at her, spreading his arms.

Stell asked Mama, "When?"

"At Taylor's, but not on the highway. Not yet."

"I'm qualified." Stell was pushing her luck. Mama didn't answer.

We were going first to Pensacola, Florida, to see Mama's brother Taylor Bentley, who was divorced. His graduation photo from Annapolis was in our living room in a brass frame, taken when he was twenty-one, handsome in his white uniform, his hat held under his arm. When he kicked Aunt Lily out, a judge said their daughter would stay with Uncle Taylor. I heard Mama on the phone. "Lily Bentley is a slut." My dictionary cleared up the mystery enough for me to suppose that Aunt Lily must have been caught in an affair, a word that made me long for details I was hopeless to know.

In the early afternoon, we ate pimento cheese sandwiches in the car and stopped at an Esso station west of Columbia. I dug through the ice in the drink box until my hand was red before I came up with a Coke, and stood in the sun gulping it despite Mama saying I could only have one and to make it last.

I looked around for Mary and saw her closing the

door of an outhouse behind the filling station. She took Kleenex from her pocket and wiped her hands. I went to her. "You going to get something to drink?"

She shook her head. "Don't know when I'll find another outhouse."

Stell walked up, tapping her Coke. "Want to play traveling?"

"Okay. Two bits." I guzzled my drink and belched.

"Suave. Do that for the next cute boy you see."

"I'm ready. One, two, three!"

We turned our bottles over. "Charlotte! I win!" I loved beating Stell at games.

"Atlanta," she said. "You lose."

I called to Mama, who was by the drink box, a Royal Crown in her hand, "Which is farther away, Charlotte or Atlanta?"

"Atlanta. Why?"

I slapped a quarter on Stell's outstretched palm. She smirked.

An old man popped the cap off a Seven-Up and raised it as if he were playing traveling, too. He squinted at the bottom of the bottle, where a bubble of air was trapped in the thick glass, green and sparkling in the sun. "Ever who blowed this'un had the hee-cawps," he said in a cracked squeal. When we got in the car, I told everybody what he'd said and the funny way he talked. Only Mary laughed.

We took off again, Puddin snuggling under the

18

feather pillows we'd brought along, curling herself up until just her sandals showed. She hated air-conditioning. I thought it was because she was skinny, with not enough meat on her bones to keep her warm.

I always looked out for Puddin, because before you knew it, she'd disappear. Once, on a trip to the mountains, we left her at a filling station and went twenty miles before we missed her. I'm the only one who noticed how often she hid herself away. Mama wasn't alarmed. "She's only five. She's only six. She's only seven."

Wiggles of heat rose from the highway, and the trip was long and boring, even with Mama pointing out things such as the Georgia state line and peach trees heavy with fruit. We played alphabet until I was almost to Z. Mary pointed to a calf and whispered, "Young cow," for me to use for my Y. Stell said that wasn't fair, and Mama wouldn't rule, so we quit.

In a town called Toccoa, I saw signs in people's front yards: SEPARATE BUT EQUAL IS GOOD FOR EVERYONE and SEGREGATION AIN'T BROKE. DON'T FIX IT.

"Mama, what do those signs mean?"

"It's got to do with that mess in Washington." She glanced at Mary in the rearview mirror. "Never mind; it won't happen in Charlotte."

"What won't happen?"

"Hush. I don't want to talk."

Mary took my hand. I looked at our intertwined fingers—mine slender, smooth, and pale; hers brown, thick-knuckled, and calloused. On her left hand, resting in her lap, she wore a thin gold ring. We didn't talk much in the car, and she seldom spoke except to say "Yes, ma'am" or "No, ma'am" or "Y'all leave off talking till your mama gets us back on the highway." She and Mama hadn't had much to say to each other in a long time.

We passed Davie around to keep him from getting too fussy. He fell asleep in my lap, his head on my chest, and I didn't mind him drooling on my shirt.

South of Atlanta, Mama said, "We'll be at Taylor's by tomorrow afternoon easy." She sounded excited. She told us about a town nearby called Warm Springs. "President Roosevelt went to Warm Springs because of his polio, and he died there when Stell and Jubie were little. I took y'all to the Southern Railway station in Charlotte and we watched his funeral train pass by."

Something important had happened to me and I didn't remember it.

"Girls, Taylor said Sarah can hardly wait to see you." Mama must have been trying hard to make small talk, because she didn't have much to say for her niece, who she once described as prissy. But Sarah was my only girl cousin and she wasn't particularly fond of Stell, so I was excited about seeing her again. In her last letter, she said that when I got there we'd go sunbathing, just the two of us. She never wrote anything about her mother being gone, and I wasn't sure I should ask. I remembered Aunt Lily as exotic, with her brunette hair thick and heavy on her shoulders, her passion-pink toenails, her silver high-heeled slingbacks. She was the only mother I knew who'd named her daughter for a movie star—Sarah Dolores. Mama said she did that because people told Lily she looked like Dolores del Rio. How was Sarah doing living with only her father? I couldn't imagine Daddy fixing our supper or not liking what we'd picked out to wear to school or making a grocery list. Maybe Uncle Taylor had a hired girl who did all those things.

About six thirty my stomach growled, and Mama told Stell to get the paper bag from under the seat. "There's Lance crackers, a pack for everybody, and apples. That'll hold us a while longer. I want to avoid the supper crowd."

It was after eight by the time we stopped, with the trees casting long shadows across the road. We pulled into the parking lot of a restaurant, and Mama twisted the rearview mirror to show her reflection. "Jubie, make room so Mary can change Davie."

Davie started to fuss when Mary put him down. "Gone get you some supper," she crooned. "Baby, now don't you cry."

Mama put on fresh lipstick and powdered her nose.

I felt like I'd been sitting forever. Even with the air-conditioning on, my thighs had perspired against the car seat, making the welts sting. I decided that no matter what, I would not straddle the drive shaft again. Mama had pointed out many times that I needed more leg room than most grown men. Stell had shine, but I had height.

Mama took Davie from Mary. "Anything in particular you want for supper?"

"No, ma'am, just whatever. And the restroom for the kitchen help."

"I'm sure that'll be fine." Mary got back in the car. I looked over my shoulder and waved to her as we walked into the restaurant, Mama first, with Davie on her hip. She stood beside the cash register, looking around until a waitress called out, "Y'all go on and find a table."

The men in the restaurant turned to look at Mama, but she just walked straight to the table she wanted, like the queen of England. I thought it was silly the way she always primped before we left the car, then didn't enjoy the attention she got. Aunt Rita said that it was unfair for a woman who had four kids to still be such a looker.

We sat around a green Formica table by the window, facing the parking lot where Mary waited.

Whenever we went out to eat at home, Mama or Daddy did the ordering. This time Mama said, "We're on vacation. Order anything you want."

Stell said, right away, "I'll have a salad with Russian dressing, green beans, candied carrots, and a baked potato with extra butter."

I read everything on the three-page menu before I ordered the spaghetti and meatballs, which Mama almost never fixed at home, but the plate put in front of me had an orange gloppy mess on it that looked like Chef Boyardee. Stell's dinner smelled delicious. So did Mama's pork chop, which she just picked at. While I was chewing the gluey meatballs, I heard the thump of a car door. I looked out the window and saw my own face reflected in the glass, then through it I saw Mary standing by the car, stretching, her arms raised. I was glad Mama had ordered fried chicken for her, not the spaghetti and meatballs.

Before we left, the waitress gave us a greasy paper bag. "Here's the food for your girl. Boss says she can use the bathroom off the kitchen."

There was a sign at the town limits of Wickens, Georgia:

NEGROES
Observe Curfew!
WHITES ONLY
After Sundown!

Daddy would approve of such a sign. I hoped Mary hadn't seen it. Her head was against the seat back, her eyes closed.

Mama pulled into a motor court and asked me to go with her to see about rooms. We passed a lawn jockey with a grin on the black face, white teeth gleaming. Mama told the man at the desk, "I've got four children, one of them still a baby, and I brought my girl along to help. We don't mind sharing with her, but she must have a bed to herself."

"Can't have your children sleeping with her." The man touched Mama's hand. She jerked it away. He frowned. "They's a nigger hotel downtown where she can stay, then y'all can c'mon back here."

Mama flinched. She never used that word. She said colored or darkie or Negro. Daddy said she was mired in euphemisms.

"Well?" the man said.

"I won't have her staying off by herself." Mama's voice was low and sharp. She left the office, pulling me behind her.

We found a place that would have Mary, the Sleep Inn Motel. The man who ran it walked outside with Mama and pointed to a cabin behind his office. He looked at Mary standing by our car. "That your girl?"

"Yes."

He rubbed his mouth. "She can just let herself in."

As soon as we got in our room, Mama called Uncle Taylor. "Hey! We're at Wickens, Georgia, well south of Atlanta, making good time." She said, "Uh-huh. No, no problem. We found a place that let her stay." Mama listened, then said, "I can't talk to him right now." Did she mean Daddy? Another pause, then, "We'll see y'all tomorrow; can't wait."

After I put on my pajamas, I wanted to go see if Mary was okay. Hot as it was, Mama made me wear her bathrobe so I'd be decent. When I got to the cabin, I was shy to knock on the door. Mary stayed with us when Mama and Daddy went out of town, but it was our house, and I never minded walking right in the den where she slept on the pull-out sofa. I knocked softly.

Mary called out, "Come on in, Jubie."

The door opened into a small room. The bulb hanging from the ceiling didn't give off a lot of light, making the room feel close and hot, even with the one window open. The air smelled of dust and soap. Mary was in the only chair, a wooden ladder-back like we had in the kitchen at home, but with one leg shorter than the others so that she was slightly tilted. There was a tattered white Bible in her lap.

"How'd you know it was me at the door?"

"Who else would visit me so late in the evening?"

"Might have been a gentleman stopping to see you."

"Might have."

She wore a blue chenille robe and white terry cloth slippers. Her reddish-brown curls were free from her combs. I'd heard Mama say that Mary used a henna rinse, and I liked it that Mary had vanity.

She pointed to the bed. "Sit yourself down, girl."

I sat and had to grab the footboard to keep from falling backward.

Mary asked, "You never been on a straw tick?"

I tried to find a way to sit, but the bed pulled me down. I scooted upward and put my back against the headboard, my left leg dangling off the side. "How can you sleep in this thing?"

"That's what you do with a tick, sleep in it, not on it."

"What's that squeaking every time I move?"

"Got ropes underneath, not springs like you used to."

"That would keep me awake." I swatted at a mosquito that buzzed my ear.

"You doing okay, Jubie?"

"Except for being crowded in with everybody, our stuff all over, and here you are with a whole room to yourself."

"Sometime it pays to be a darkie." She rocked on the uneven chair.

I hooked my toe through a hole in the rag rug. "Where's your bathroom?"

"What you think this is, a castle for colored folks? There's an outhouse, little ways into the field, and the pitcher and bowl there."

"Got any water in it?"

"The lord of this here moe-tell let me fill it from a tap outside. I'm better off than I might've been."

"This room has nice ambience." I tripped over the word. I hadn't said it out loud before.

"Another new word, huh? What's it mean?"

"That your room has a good feeling to it." I struggled off the bed. "Is that a family Bible?"

"It was my grand's. Got our dates in it."

"Could I see?"

She opened the front cover of the Bible and handed it to me. "Be gentle. It's got more'n seventy years on it."

I held the book carefully. In many different hands, there were records of births and deaths, marriages and baptisms. The dates in Mary's Bible went back much further than what Stell had recorded in ours. One entry said, "Mary Constance Culpepper, born September 20, 1906. Married Pharr Lincoln Luther, May 18, 1925."

"That's you."

"It is. Got a birthday coming. Be forty-eight."

I'd never thought about her age. Her caramel skin was smooth. "I didn't know you were so old."

She threw back her head and laughed, showing

her front tooth that was framed in gold. "I like you more and more, June Bentley Watts, more and more."

I looked back down at the Bible. "Your husband died in a wreck, right?"

"Yes, one night coming home from work. Doctor say it was his heart."

"A heart attack while he was driving?"

"Might be. Never know for sure."

"Is that your wedding ring?" I pointed to her left hand.

She nodded. "Pharr got it engraved, our initials and date."

I touched the next page of the Bible. "Do you have two brothers and a sister?"

"Only got my one brother left now that I know of. Sister died having her fourth child. And my baby brother, we hasn't heard from him in twenty years; I s'pect he's gone." I couldn't imagine not knowing what had happened to Stell or Puddin or Davie.

"You were the second oldest, too, the same as me."

"That's right. My mama had two born dead before Sister, but I don't reckon they count."

I handed her the Bible. "I'd better be going so everybody can get to bed." I touched her shoulder. "Night, Mary. Lock up behind me." I sounded like Mama.

"No lock on that door. If it had one, I'd use it."

She had the Bible open and was looking down at it when I left.

In our room, everybody was asleep but Mama. She was brushing her teeth, standing in the bathroom with the door open. Her hair was pulled back to keep it out of the cold cream she used to cleanse her face, her skin glistening in the light over the sink. She looked at me in the mirror. Her mouth was all foamy, and she held her dental bridge in her left hand while she brushed with her right. She rinsed and spat. "Get to bed now, Jubie, and don't make any noise." The words lisped out through the hole where her front tooth was gone. Stell told me Daddy knocked it out. Mama never talked about it. "You need to tinkle before you climb in?"

"No, ma'am." I draped her bathrobe across the footboard of her bed and lingered there. I tried not to look at her, but I didn't often get to see her without her tooth.

"What is it?" Mama asked, her bridge back in place.

"Mary has an outhouse instead of a bathroom, and a pitcher and bowl like Aunt Rita has in her living room, only the ones in Mary's room are for using."

"I paid more for that cabin than I did for this room, and it's just fine. Get on to bed now." Mama reached to turn off the light as I climbed in next to Stell.

I lay there in the dark, listening to my family breathe. Somebody made a throat noise, Puddin, or maybe Mama. Way off, a dog barked over and over. I wondered if Mary heard it.

CHAPTER 2

Five days before we left for Pensacola I was
sitting on my bed, listening to the sound of our
neighbor's mower. I peeked out the window.
Carter Milton was naked from the waist up, his
muscled shoulders red, his back broad. He looked
like a man working in his yard, not the boy next
door. Why was he so crazy about Stell? That
morning she'd told Mama I was hiding in the tree
house when Mama wanted me to go grocery
shopping. That was a lie, but no matter what Stell
says, Mama always believes her.

I opened the window. Carter stood in his
driveway, drinking a Coke. I called out, "Meet me
by the hedge."

The house felt empty. Mama still shopping,
Puddin out back with Davie, and Stell at a
planning meeting for the cheerleading squad. I
could hear Mary in the kitchen. I tiptoed
downstairs, hoping to slip out the front door. I was
in the foyer with my hand on the doorknob when
she said, "Hey, Jubie." She stood in the hallway,
holding a dish towel. "You gone go out?"

"Just for a minute."

"Your mama want you here to put away
groceries when she gets home."

"I need to tell Carter something."

"Stell Ann's boyfriend?"

I shrugged and ran out to meet Carter by the boxwoods that separated our front yards. His eyes were topaz in the sunlight. I snapped a twig, stripping the leaves into my hand to make a bracelet. "You want to hear stuff from Stell's diary?" I popped the tip from one of the leaves.

He wiped his forehead. "You think there's something in it about me?"

"You can find out for a dollar."

"Okay, sure, Jubes. When?"

I liked him calling me Jubes. "Half an hour, the tree house."

While I was looking for Stell's diary, I found her piggy bank hidden in a cardboard box on the floor of her closet, behind her summer shoes—white ankle straps, black patent pumps, bone flats. I turned her piggy bank slowly. I could hear paper money rustling, the clink of heavy coins. My bank never had anything but pennies in it.

I used a bobby pin to pull a dollar bill through the slot in the bank. After my next babysitting job, I'd put a dollar and a quarter back. Stell would never know. With the loan from her bank and the dollar from Carter, I could go to the Manor Theatre with Maggie, my best friend, to see *Gentlemen Prefer Blondes*, which Mama said was racy. She hadn't seen it, but she didn't trust anything with Marilyn Monroe in it, not to mention Jane Russell. I'd buy the latest *Space Cadet* comic, get popcorn and a grape Charms at the movies, and ride the bus home.

Before I put the piggy bank back in its box, I stretched out on the floor and stared up into her skirts, all hemmed to fall exactly two inches below her knees.

Her diary was not in her closet, not in her dresser, her bedside table, or under her bed. I finally found it on a shelf in the sewing room, behind a box of patterns. She'd written on the front, *Estelle Annette Watts. Her Diary. 1954.* I noticed exactly how it was hidden before I took it so I could be sure to put it back the same way. Stell Ann had radar for things out of order.

A few minutes later I stood on the island of trees that divides Queens Road West, waiting for a car to pass. The tree house, in the middle of a stand of oaks on the last vacant lot from Selwyn Avenue to Kings Drive, was built by kids from several blocks around with lumber they swiped when our house was under construction. Carter was lying on his back, staring up through the leaves. His crew cut was thick and blond, curling back from his forehead like Tab Hunter's. There was a line of fuzz on his cheek above where he shaved.

He sat up. "Hey, little squirt."

"Call me that again, the deal's off."

"Right. There's nothing little about you anymore."

My cheeks burned.

"Did you bring it?"

I nodded and climbed through the doorway, sitting down with my legs folded on the rough boards so I wouldn't touch him. I pulled the diary from under my shirt, where I'd stuck it inside the waistband of my shorts. "I'll read you two pages for a dollar. You got the money?"

He jingled some coins in his pocket. "How'd you know which two pages?"

"Geee-e-e-e-ez, it was really tough."

"So read it."

A breeze carried the scent of aftershave. Maybe he was wearing it for me. I sat back against the tree trunk and opened the diary at a scrap of newspaper that marked the place. "Okay, here goes." I thought about Stell.

"Well?" He reached into his pocket and brought out two quarters and a half-dollar.

I began reading.

"Friday, July 30, 1954. I went to the club dance tonight with Carter and we had a perfectly wonderful time. He brought me a corsage of blue carnations. How did he know the exactly right shade to go with my dress? Probably Mrs. Milton asked Mama. I wore my new silver sandals. My dress has these darling off-the-shoulder sleeves, and Carter didn't know where to pin the corsage, but Mama did it. Daddy

took five pictures and I thought I'd die, because Carter probably thinks I asked Daddy to take the snaps. He was drinking, but not drunk, and he was really nice."

"Holy cow." Carter sat up. "I hadn't had a thing to drink."
"Daddy. She means Daddy."
"Oh."

"Carter held my hand in the car all the way there. Chappie Barrett was green over my dress. She didn't say so, but I could tell. Hers was all the way up to the neck with long tight sleeves and was putrid yellow. I think it's the white one she wore to the prom, renewed with Rit."

I turned a page.
"Is that a whole page already?"
"Yes."
"And I'm paying for this?"

"I danced a lot with Carter, once with Reid Henderson, and Ross—"

"She has his name underlined, with no last name."
"I know who she means. Go on."

"—and Ross asked me three times but I only danced with him twice. I could tell Carter didn't like it. We went to Papa's Kitchen after with a bunch of kids, and Carter kissed me when we got home. I thought I would die of rapture."

I snapped the book shut.

"That's all?"

"Yep. Gimme the money."

"There's nothing else in there about me?"

"Not a word. I've read the whole thing." He handed me the coins, warm from his hand. I wanted to touch the curly hair on his arms. He stood and grabbed a limb, swung away from the tree, and jumped to the ground. "Later, gator," he hollered, taking off toward his house. I called back, "While, dile," too low for him to hear, and stretched out in the tree house, holding Stell Ann's diary and the coins.

She *had* mentioned Carter again, in a passage where she said sometimes she thought about dating other boys. In May she'd heard that he went out with another girl. Stell and Carter had a fight about that.

"I'm gonna tell." A loud whisper startled me. Puddin climbed into the tree house. She kneeled next to me, hands on her hips, her lower lip stuck out. A shaft of sunlight turned her hair into a cap of gold.

"You're gonna tell that I'm in the tree house?"

"About Stell's diary." She twisted her arm and picked at a scab on her elbow.

I shoved her. She fell over, howling. I jumped on top of her, straddling her waist. "I'll smack you if you say that again."

"You won't." Her face was red, but she wasn't afraid.

I crumbled beside her. "Daddy'll whip me."

"Did Carter kiss you to make you read Stell's diary?"

"He gave me a dollar."

Puddin sat up, her hand out. "Gimme it and I won't tell."

"The whole dollar? I'll take the whipping."

"Seventy-five cents?"

I slapped a half-dollar on her knee. "Fifty cents. That's all."

She crawled toward the door, the money in her fist. "Okaa-ay."

"Promise you won't tell."

"I promise." She scrambled down the ladder and ran off through the trees.

Maggie and I talked about the movie all the way home from the theatre, walking because I didn't have enough left for the bus. "Couldn't you just die over Marilyn Monroe?" she said.

"She's not a natural blonde."

"How do you know?"

"She's a brownette. Her real name is Norma Jeane. I saw pictures in *Photoplay*."

We turned onto Westfield. Reid Henderson passed us on his bicycle, tossing newspapers onto porches. I tried to picture him dancing with Stell Ann. I waved. "Hey, Reid, neat bike." But he didn't turn around. I raised my middle finger to his retreating back. "He's so spastic."

Maggie snickered in that fake way she has when I say something she thinks might be clever.

"What name would you have, if you were a movie star?"

"Anything besides Margaret Elizabeth," Maggie answered, imitating her mother's British accent. "What about you?"

"Loretta. I don't know what last name, but my first name would be Loretta." I loved the sound of it rolling off my tongue.

"That's a colored name."

"Maggie!"

"Well, it is."

"I'm keeping it." But I wasn't as crazy about it as I had been.

We passed Mrs. Gibson's house and I saw Daddy's car parked in our driveway.

Maggie turned to go home. "Bye, Loretta."

"Bye, Margaret Elizabeth. Oh, hey, Mags, wait!"

"What?"

"Don't forget. *Seven Brides for Seven Brothers*, not *Gentlemen Prefer Blondes*."

38

"Natch! I'm no dumb blonde."

We linked arms and swung in a circle before she spun off for home.

I opened the den door to a shaded silence that made me want to go back through the breezeway into the sunlight. Mama heard me walking through the den. "June? June Bentley, come here."

Mama was standing by the stove when I got to the kitchen. "Hey, Mama. Maggie and I went to see *Seven Brides* again. Where's Mary?"

"She'll be back in a while." She stared at me, then looked out the window over the sink. "Your father's in the bedroom. He wants to see you." As I left the kitchen, she said, "What you did is unforgivable."

Puddin had told.

I knocked on the bedroom door, my mouth too dry to answer when Daddy called out, "Come in."

He sat in the upholstered lady's chair in the corner, sunlight streaming in the windows on either side of him, bouncing off the drink in his hand. He took a sip and set his glass on the bedside table with a clink that made me jump. My punishment was always worse when he was drinking. He crossed the bedroom in two steps, grabbed me by the upper arm, steered me into the hall. With his other hand he unbuckled his belt. It slithered through the loops as he took it off.

"Daddy, I'm sorry, I'm so sorry." My voice

squeaked. I looked at Mama as Daddy opened the basement door. She turned her back.

Daddy shoved me ahead of him down the stairs. At the bottom, he said. "You've broken your sister's heart." He took off his glasses.

"I didn't think about what I was doing. I'll never do it again."

He put his glasses in his shirt pocket. "You won't?" His voice was soft, reasonable, but I knew what was coming. My confessions never stopped him.

"No, sir, and I'll carry out the trash for a month with no allowance, and I'll—"

"Take off your jeans." His words made me shiver. I smelled bourbon.

"I didn't mean any—"

"You didn't mean to read your sister's diary?"

I was still clearing one foot from the leg of my jeans when the belt hit my bottom. I gasped so hard I couldn't cry, and fell to the concrete floor. I scrambled with my feet caught in my jeans, trying to get away. He struck out again and the tip of the belt stung my belly below my T-shirt.

"Get up." He strapped me across my thighs.

"Don't, Daddy," I cried, my back against the cinder-block wall.

He reversed the belt, wrapping the end of it around his hand, then whipped me again. The buckle bit the inside of my left leg.

"Daddy, the buckle!"

He raised his arm, his red ring sending out shoots of fire. I got to my feet and he kept hitting me. I tried to run to the laundry room. He caught me by the arm, shoved me against the wash sinks, and raised the belt. I fell against the folding table. A bottle of bleach turned over and the lid popped off. The belt wrapped around my legs and the buckle bit my knees and thighs. I thought: *He's killing me. This time he's going to kill me.* I began to scream.

"Mr. Watts!" Mary's voice, sharp and shocked. "Mr. Watts, you stop that now." She stood beside Daddy, still in her street clothes, holding a new uniform on a hanger. She hung it on a nail and touched Daddy's arm. "You're all het up, Mr. Watts."

Daddy jerked away from her.

I sank to the floor. Bleach stung my legs. I pressed my hot face to the cold concrete.

Mama came down the stairs. "William."

"Paula, leave this to me." Daddy sounded tired.

"She's had enough."

Mary was going to say something, but Mama shook her head. Mary got the uniform and headed for her bathroom under the stairs. Mama said, "Leave us. You can change later." Mary hung up the uniform and climbed the stairs.

Mama bent over me. "You did a truly awful thing, Jubie, but you've paid for it." She touched a cut on my right calf. "I'll get you some cream.

Ye gods, William, what did you hit her with?"

But Daddy was gone. Mama tried to put her arms around me. I pushed her away, sobbing and hiccupping. "If Stell—if she read my diary, he wouldn't beat her."

"Stell would never do what you did." Daddy's heavy steps pounded over our heads. He stomped around their bedroom above us, opening and closing bureau drawers. Then his footsteps went off toward the kitchen, and the cowbell jangled as he slammed the back door.

Mama stood. "He's gone to the club." She straightened her back. "Just think how Stell felt when she heard what you'd done."

Standing over me, Mama looked as tall as Daddy. She had never beaten me, never even spanked me, and she never would, not as long as Daddy was around to do her dirty work.

"There's a basket of diapers by the dryer. Dampen one and wipe your legs. Come up to my bathroom and I'll give you something to take the sting out. Is your white skirt clean?"

"Huh?"

"Your white circle skirt. If it's dirty, we need to wash it, then you can iron it for church tomorrow. You can wear your loafers and crew socks, so your legs—"

"Socks and loafers to church?"

"Or you can stay home. Maybe that would be best." She sniffed. "Why does it stink of bleach?"

42

She spotted the overturned jug of Clorox. "I suppose that happened in the tussle."

I nodded.

Mama went up to the kitchen and said, "Mary, there's a mess on the basement floor."

I pulled myself up the stairs, one hand over the other on the rail.

Mary was standing at the bar when I walked into the kitchen, tears on her face. She opened her arms wide and pulled me to her. I sobbed against her shoulder and she whispered into my ear, "That was a mean, wrong thing for your father to do." She held me tight, rubbing my back. "You're a good girl, Jubie. Sometime you do a bad thing, but you're a good girl. You remember that."

Mama called from the hallway, "Hurry up, June."

"Your mama got something to help." We both looked down at my legs. The red stripes and cuts were swelling into angry welts.

In her bathroom, Mama gave me a jar of cream to put on the cuts. She turned to leave.

"Would you do the back of my legs?"

She dabbed half a dozen places, then handed the jar to me. "You can get the rest. It's greasy. Put a towel under you when you sit." She looked at my underpants. "Why are you all wet?"

I had peed myself. "I think it's Clorox."

"Take off your panties before it burns you." She closed her bedroom door behind her.

After I put the cream on my legs, I climbed the stairs with a towel wrapped around my hips. When I passed Stell's room, I saw her lying on her bed, her head in her arms. Puddin was sitting beside her, patting Stell, her back to the door.

I screamed at them, "Look at me!"

Puddin turned. Stell raised her head. "Get out," she said, her voice hoarse.

I dropped the towel. "Look what Daddy did."

Stell stared.

"I gave Puddin half the money Carter paid me to read your diary. She took it, fifty cents, then she told anyway."

Stell pushed Puddin away. "You took money not to tell?"

Puddin nodded. Stell shoved her. Puddin fell on the floor, sobbing, "I'm sorry! I'm sorry!"

Stell turned her back to me. "Get out, both of you. Leave me alone."

I sat on the edge of my dressing stool, careful so the cream wouldn't stain the flowered print seat. The first time Daddy spanked me, I was seven. I'd spilled a bottle of ink on a stack of Mama's clean white sheets. He never laid a finger on Stell or Puddin, only me.

I looked at myself in the mirror. My cheeks were splotched, my eyes swollen. But the beating didn't show on my face. There was a tube of Revlon lipstick on the dresser. Stell had thrown it out because it was too bright, what she called floozy lipstick. I twisted the tube until the slanted top stuck out a half inch, then applied it, going outside the lip line. I read the label on the bottom and mouthed the words at the mirror, my lips full and pouty like Marilyn's, *Fire and Ice*.

CHAPTER 3

Mama stood in the courtyard of the Sleep Inn Motel, smoking and looking at her watch while Stell held Davie, and I helped Mary pack the car. Then we lit out like somebody was on our tail, Mama half awake and so nervous you'd think we were going to be arrested for spotting a mattress that was already stained. We were even more crowded in the car because Mary hadn't been able to fit the picnic basket back into the trunk. Mama said for me just to hold it, that we'd need it when we ate breakfast on the road. I sat behind Stell, the basket on my lap, the wicker scratching my legs through my jeans.

We passed a sign: WICKENS TOWN LIMITS. Y'ALL COME BACK NOW! Mama said, "Not likely." I looked through the back window to see if there was a curfew sign on this side of town. There was.

Mama smoothed her hair, which she'd put up with a tortoiseshell barrette. "We'll have breakfast as soon as I see somewhere to pull over. Watch for picnic tables." She kept glancing into the backseat and smiling at Davie, trying to make up with him after smacking his hand for wetting the bed. He sat on Puddin's lap, holding Mary's arm and sucking his thumb.

We'd only been in the car a few minutes when

46

Mama wrinkled her nose. "What's that stink?" Mary had washed Davie's soiled pj's in the motel sink, and I'd spread them in the shelf over the backseat to dry. They gave off a sour smell in the morning sun. I pretended I was dozing.

I peeped at Mary through my half-closed eyelids. What did she think of Mama? I'd heard Mary talking with her daughter when Young Mary came to our house before we left Charlotte, telling her how to take care of Daddy while we were gone. "He wants a light starch in his shirts, and you got to iron them while they still damp." Mary's voice was soft and low. "And white vinegar on the table for his greens." She put her arm around her daughter's shoulders as they stood in the pantry. "This Boston brown bread is good with baked beans and pork chops."

"Bread in a can?" Young Mary's voice was high-pitched and timid. She'd jump if Daddy asked her the time of day. What was she doing as we traveled across Georgia?

I said, "I wonder how Young Mary's going to get along with Daddy."

Puddin looked at Mary. "Your daughter?"

Mary nodded. "She doing the cooking and cleaning a couple days a week."

"Your father'll be just fine," Mama said. "He always could get someone to take care of him."

Mama wasn't calling Daddy anything but "your father." She had always called him Bill or William

47

or, when she was teasing, Willie. She hadn't called him Willie in so long I could hardly remember. Maybe not since we'd lived in the house off Selwyn Avenue.

In Alabama we passed towns named Opelika, Loachapoka, Notsaluga. I said the odd names to myself. I couldn't remember seeing signs back home like the ones we saw in Tuskegee: SOME THINGS DON'T MIX! OIL AND WATER. COLOREDS AND WHITES! and, in front of a school, FOR WHITES, NOT BROWNS!

In Andalusia Mama pulled up to a café for us to have lunch. We'd just passed a grill with colored people standing in the doorway and on the sidewalk. Mary said she'd walk back there to eat. Mama was fixing her face in the rearview mirror when Mary asked for the keys to the trunk. "You mind if I freshen up before lunch?"

Mama rolled her eyes but handed Mary the keys.

"Jubie, get the keys when Mary's done." Mama took Puddin's hand and Stell carried Davie into the café.

Mary got her flowered bag from the trunk and took out a rose knit hat I'd never seen. She unfolded it, fluffed it, and pulled the brim over one eyebrow, checking her reflection in the car window. In quick strokes she put on glossy lipstick, then reached in her bag for red earrings and a matching necklace. She changed her navy

Keds for red patent leather heels, making her snazzy, even in her ordinary blue cotton dress. With her handbag dangling from her fingertips, she started down the street, click-clacking on her heels. I watched her go, my mouth hanging open.

She looked over her shoulder and winked. "Feels like Sunday."

Before Mama pushed her plate away and reached for her cigarettes, I worried that Mary wouldn't be back on time, that Mama would be mad at her for dillydallying. For once in my life I didn't ask for dessert, but Mama didn't notice. I excused myself and went to the car. Mary was coming down the sidewalk, humming, her pocketbook swinging at her side. "Hey, Jubie girl, you glad to see me?"

"I am, Mary."

She had already taken off her hat and earrings and was removing her necklace. She scrubbed her mouth with a Kleenex the way I did when I came home from school after wearing Tangee all day. I unlocked the trunk, and Mary scuffed off her heels. In a minute she had on her Keds. Mary again, as if she'd never left the car. Mama came out of the café carrying Davie, with Puddin and Stell behind her.

"How was your lunch, Mary?"

"Just fine, Miz Watts, just fine."

"Not too expensive?"

"Not too bad." Mary squeezed my hand as we got in the car.

49

● ● ●

Mary came to work for us when I was five, the first colored person I'd ever known. I studied the tall woman who occupied our kitchen, busy at the sink or the washing machine or the ironing board. Her thick-fingered hands, brown on top and light underneath, wove lattice crusts on apple pies, diapered my new baby sister, and hefted baskets of wet wash. When she caught me peeking at her from behind the kitchen door, she waved.

I observed her from the queen chair when she vacuumed, or through the window as she pinned my pajamas to the clothesline. One morning while she mopped the kitchen, she hummed "Twinkle, Twinkle, Little Star," adding words to the tune as she rinsed the mop: *"Little mousy, are you there? Watching from a fine old chair?"* She turned and caught me staring.

I broke my silence. "Why are your feet so big?"

"To keep me from falling over."

It pleased me that an adult took me seriously.

Once, when I asked her what she thought of me when we met all those years ago, she said, "Seem to me you were struggling to give up being the youngest."

I touched her arm and she turned to me. "Hm?"

"Do you remember the little house in the woods off Selwyn Avenue, where we lived when we first moved back to Charlotte?"

"I remember."

"That's where you started working for us. I was five."

"Uh-huh. You had a head full of blonde curls. Always following me around."

As we drove through Pensacola I tried to take in everything about the town where we'd be spending the next week. We whizzed by a sandwich-board sign with a shimmering, come-hither eye in the middle of it. The only words I caught were "Three-Legged Girl."

"Ye gods," I said, "did y'all see that sign?"

"Watch your tongue, young lady," Mama said. "We're almost to Taylor's."

We were passing an amusement park, Joyland by the Sea. A Ferris wheel turned in the afternoon sun, and lively music filled the air. "Oh, Mama, look. We've got to go while we're here. It's fabulous."

"They are always fabulous from the car."

Stell Ann read directions from a map Uncle Taylor had sent. "Take ninety-eight over Pensacola Bay and Santa Rosa Sound."

We rode in silence across the water. It only took a few minutes, but I looked out on the wide expanse of sparkling blue, no land in sight, and pretended our car was a ship, skimming the waves. I glanced at Mary. Her eyes were large in her solemn face.

At Uncle Taylor's, Mama set the brakes and said,

"Three thirty! We made good time. Grab something to carry, and be sure . . ." We scrambled from the car and ran up the front walk. Only Mama knew what she wanted us to be sure of.

Nobody answered the bell, and Mama went right on in. There was a note on the table in the shadowed foyer:

> *Pauly, we're at the beach. Ring the brass bell on the back porch so we'll know you're here.*
> *Welcome!!!*
> *Taylor*

The *Welcome* was scrawled across the note. Beneath it, Uncle Taylor had signed his name in neat script. Puddin ran through the house to the back porch and rang the bell, which sounded like ships' bells I'd heard in movies. "We're here!" she yelled. "We're here!"

I went back out for the luggage. A strong wind lifted my hair, smelling of salt and sun and far-off places across all that sparkling water, so much bluer than the Atlantic, the only other ocean I'd ever seen. Ocean? No, not an ocean, I remembered from my geography lessons. The Gulf of Mexico.

I brought in Mary's cloth carryall, Mama's vanity case, and the paper bags of stuff that wouldn't fit into our suitcases, piling everything in the front hall until Uncle Taylor could tell us where we'd be sleeping.

Was his house always so neat, or had he straightened up because we were coming? No toys, no books on the coffee table or newspapers on the sofa, none of what Mama called clutter. How would it feel to live in such a neat house?

Mama cleared her throat. "Mary, please get me a glass of water. I'm parched."

Mary looked uncertain where to go, but she went.

In the living room, I sat in a sloping green chair with no arms, low and comfortable. The room was filled with angles and circles, blond wood and pastels. Had Aunt Lily decorated it from a picture from *House Beautiful*? A beige sofa with a curved back was more inviting to lie on than Mama's burgundy velvet Sheraton. The end tables with slanted legs looked like robots, and a chrome floor lamp near Mama seemed to make her jittery. She walked back and forth with Davie on her hip, the vertical blinds moving in her wake.

I thought of our living room, the baby grand, the oriental rug and brocade drapes, the queen chair by the mantel.

Stell said, "This is a delightful home." She'd been talking that way ever since she got saved.

Mama shifted Davie from one hip to the other. "You girls are going to have to mind your p's and q's. Taylor keeps things shipshape."

Mary came back to the living room and handed Mama a glass of water. Mama took a long sip and wrinkled her nose. "Beach water, such a horrid taste. I'll drink tea the whole time I'm here."

Puddin ran into the living room. "Uncle Taylor and Sarah are coming up from the beach. That bell works great."

Mama handed Davie to Stell and pushed at her hair, smoothed her skirt. "I'm going to fix my face."

I hadn't noticed Mary going out, but I saw her through the blinds, walking in the front yard. "I'll get Mary."

She was standing by the walk.

"What are you doing?" I asked.

"Looking at Florida. A strange place, seem to me. Almost no trees, just scrubby things bended down by the wind. And them," she said, pointing at the palm trees that lined the street, "looks like somebody took good trees and gave 'em a shave."

"Those're palm trees. You remember Palm Sunday, in the Bible?"

"Course I do. Hosanna and praise Jesus. The hour has come to sing His—" She stopped. "You mean like the palm branches they waved at Jesus?"

"Same thing."

"What you say," said Mary. "What you say."

The front door opened and there was Uncle Taylor, smiling, his arms held wide.

I hadn't seen him in over a year, not since he and

54

Aunt Lily came to visit us before Davie started walking. But he was as handsome as I remembered, his hair bleached by the sun, his blue eyes sparkling. He grabbed me up, swinging me off the front walk.

"Jubie! How's my favorite niece?" Even if he said that to Puddin and Stell Ann, too, which he always did, I knew he only meant it to me.

"Hey, Uncle Taylor." I hugged him back. He smelled like lemons.

He put me down and held me out, squinting, studying me. "You've grown, girl. What have you been eating, spinach and baked vitamins?"

"Too much of everything, if you ask Mama." I reached for Mary's hand. "You remember Mary, Uncle Taylor?"

"Of course I do. How are you, Mary?"

"Just fine, Commander Bentley, just fine."

"I've got a nice room for you upstairs. Y'all come on in and let's get you settled, then we'll go down to the beach. Jubes, where's that good-looking mother of yours?"

"She went to the bathroom."

He opened the front door for me and Mary. "We'll find her."

Mama was in the entry hall. Uncle Taylor wrapped his arms around her. "Hey, big sister, I've been looking for you!"

Mama buried her face in his chest. She said his name over and over. She started to laugh. "Oh,

Taylor, I'm so glad to be here." The laughter turned to crying, first like tears of joy, then like her heart was breaking. I knew that kind of crying, the hiccupping sobs that wouldn't stop. I was embarrassed for her.

"Pauly-Wauly." Uncle Taylor held Mama close. "You've had a rough time, old girl."

CHAPTER 4

There was a time in my life before Mary, a time when Mama and Daddy weren't fighting, when they still called each other Pauly and Willie. Maybe if I'd never known them happy, the trouble between them wouldn't have bothered me so much. But I remember Shumont Mountain and the four-room log cabin next to Rainbow Lake where Mama and Daddy had spent their honeymoon. We moved there in the summer of 1944, a few months after Grandmother Bentley died, leaving Mama and Uncle Taylor a tidy sum. Daddy said we'd stay there till the war was over and he could start his business in Charlotte. While we lived on Shumont, he was home at night and almost never got drunk.

Our cabin was on a flat place between two peaks reached by a road of twenty-one hairpin curves that Daddy and I counted out loud whenever we went up or down the mountain, stopping at least once to let Stell throw up. The road was something that didn't change. Years later when we went back for summer vacations, we had to go around the same twenty-one curves between Bat Cave and Shumont.

Stell was seven that summer and I was almost four, with Mama and Daddy all to ourselves in the years before Puddin and Davie. There was no electricity or running water in the cabin by

Rainbow Lake, and Mama still says hell isn't hot, it's cold like Shumont Mountain in the dead of winter. But it was also a place of light and cattails, of tomatoes growing in the front yard, going on horseback with Daddy to pick apples, swimming together in the lake that left us smelling faintly of rust. When I remind Mama, she says, "Yes, it was those things, too."

We arrived on Shumont just as the blackberry vines were drooping with ripe fruit, and the blueberry bushes soon would be. Mama pointed them out and said, "We could have great fun making jelly, if we just knew how." The next time we went down to Black Mountain for groceries, she bought a book—*Fruits of the Appalachians: Legends and Recipes*—and read it after supper, by the light of our kerosene lamps, making a list of what she needed: pectin, Mason jars, wax, sugar, cheesecloth.

The day we made jelly, Daddy was stoking a fire in the front yard when Mama came out on the porch. He said, "You're mighty fancy for someone who'll be up to her elbows in berries."

She twirled in her cotton print dress and sandals, the skirt flaring around her as she danced down the steps, her hair tied back in a pink satin ribbon.

Mama's gold hoop earrings and bracelets flashed in the sun as she stirred the pots over Daddy's fire, while Stell and I strained the hot berries in cloth bags, the juice running down our arms onto our shirts. Mrs. Straley, a neighbor who'd come to help, said, "You'uns is more the color of berries than girls." I brushed at the stains covering my shirt and shorts. Stell smiled, her teeth white in her purple face.

Daddy sampled the jelly. "Tastes great! But will it jell?"

"Sure it will," Mama said, but she sounded uncertain.

When we'd finished, two dozen pint jars sat on the porch rail, sparkling like amethysts and sapphires. Mama gave us a cake of Ivory soap. "Get in the lake and scrub the stains off. Stell Ann, watch your sister."

I was standing waist deep, my arms covered with lather, when Mama raced down the path from the cabin. She kicked off her sandals, ran out on the pier, and dove into the lake in her berry-stained dress. When she came to the surface, she let out a whoop that echoed off the mountains. Stell sat on the end of the pier, watching Mama, who went under again, stayed down a long time, and came up out in the middle of the lake. Daddy was on the opposite shore, his shotgun slung in the crook of his arm, grinning.

"C'mon on in, Willie, the water's great!"

He put down his gun, stripped to his underwear, and dove in. Mrs. Straley, who'd walked out on the dock, said, "Yore daddy's gone crazy."

"He's done that before," Stell said.
"Gone crazy or gone swimming?"
Stell didn't answer.

The jelly we made turned out just fine. Daddy's favorite was the spicy brown apple butter Mama put up in the fall, which he ate with hot biscuits and fried frog legs, after Mr. Straley taught him how to gig. Daddy let me stand in the marsh grass at night and watch as Mr. Straley beamed a flashlight steady on a frog to blind it while Daddy impaled it on his gig, an old broomstick with tenpenny nails in the end. They tossed the frogs into a sack that hung from a tree limb. The bag kept on wiggling, which made me feel bad. Mama cooked frog legs at least once a week, but I never would eat them. I made do with everything else, snap beans and limas, corn on the cob, tomatoes and green peas, collards boiled with fatback, new potatoes, and leathery dried apples.

Our bathroom was an outhouse across a creek, and Mama wouldn't let us use it at night. So Stell and I, who slept together in a single bed, peed in an enamel pot that was cold to my bottom, summer or winter. When I had to get up in the night to squat over the johnny, I'd crawl back in next to Stell and try to stay awake to listen to Mama and Daddy. Sometimes they laughed so loud it shook the wall between our rooms.

In the winter, when the front room smelled of

kerosene and wood smoke, Stell and I played Parcheesi and Chinese checkers to the shuffling and snapping of Bicycle cards as Mama and Daddy played gin rummy. There was an old piano with pump pedals and perforated rolls of music. Mama and Daddy harmonized to "The Darktown Strutter's Ball" or "A Bicycle Built for Two" or Daddy's favorite, "Wait Till the Sun Shines, Nellie."

Stell asked Daddy why he liked that song so much.

"Your mama knows."

Stell looked at Mama. "Is it because you fell in love?"

Mama shook her head. "Not right away."

"Speak for yourself," said Daddy. "The first time I saw you, I fell for that mess of curls and those gorgeous hazel eyes."

"Then you got married and had two little girls," I said.

Mama smiled. "Something like that."

That night, Daddy stood at the kitchen sink pumping water, singing, *Wait till the sun shines, Pauly.*

Even before they married, there were problems with Daddy's mother, Cordelia Watts, who thought that a college girl like Mama would never appreciate a country carpenter like Daddy. In Mama's opinion, Meemaw wouldn't have approved of anyone her baby boy took for a wife.

And right off, they disagreed about religion. Meemaw asked Mama what church she went to, and Mama said, "Methodist, of course," which was well known of girls who attended West Virginia Wesleyan.

Meemaw said, "The Watts're full-immersion Baptists. Always have been."

Mama told us she went to one baptism and never saw anything so primitive. She stayed what Meemaw called a "city Methodist," and eventually Daddy became one, too.

When I think of Shumont, I remember a June morning after Puddin came along. We'd gone back to the mountains for a vacation. Mama was nursing Puddin in one of the wooden porch rockers, a scarf around her shoulders against the chill. Daddy was splitting kindling, and Stell and I were helping Mrs. Straley churn butter. Daddy had his shirt off, and in spite of how cool it was, he was puffing and sweating.

Mama hummed while she rocked. Mrs. Straley let us churn until we got tired, then she finished, moving the plunger up and down as if there were nothing to it. She poured off a glass of buttermilk for herself and spread fresh butter on a slab of homemade bread for me and Stell. That morning is what I remember when I think of the log cabin on Shumont, and it's hard to understand how bad things got between Mama and Daddy after that.

CHAPTER 5

Stell stood by a building between Uncle Taylor's house and the dunes. She shouted over the roar of the surf. "We're staying in here—with Sarah."

The cabana reminded me of the breezeway at home, filled with light, catching the wind, with bamboo blinds to lower if it rained. Straw mats covered the floor, and strings of Japanese lanterns crisscrossed the ceiling. Three bunks with plaid spreads, summer blankets folded across the end of each. Our suitcases on luggage racks. Stell pointed to a door. "Our own bathroom."

"Cool! And where's—" Then I saw her, plain and quiet, sitting on the third bunk. "Hey, Sarah."

"Hey." She was all bony angles. Her brunette hair, tied back with a green ribbon, was thick and glossy. Like her mother's. Her eyes looked fuzzy and sad behind the thick lenses of the horn-rimmed glasses she nudged with her finger. Nothing fit my memory of my pleasant cousin.

"How you doing?" I asked her.

"Okay."

The screen door banged open and Puddin came in. "Y'all come to the beach! It's great—oh, hey, Sarah."

Sarah looked at Puddin.

Puddin said, "I saw your daddy. Where's your mama?"

"Gone."

"When's she—"

Stell said, "Puddin, hush."

Puddin looked at Stell, startled.

Mama should have explained things to her.

Sarah brushed past me. She was long-legged and skinny as a rail. Mary would be after her to eat. The screen door slammed behind her.

Puddin asked, "What's the matter with her?"

"Don't ask about her mama, okay?" I said.

"Why?"

Stell said, "Just leave it be."

I went after Sarah as she headed for the house, catching up with her. "I'm sorry."

"Everybody asks about Mother." Again she pushed at her glasses. Her fingernails were chewed to the quick. "She's gone. There's nothing to say." She went through the back porch toward the kitchen. Her shoulder blades stuck out under her blouse. I stood on the path, looking down at the sandy soil.

Sarah and I had so much fun when they'd visited us in Charlotte, riding our bikes to Freedom Park, lying on our backs in the grass, finding elephants and rabbits in the clouds, talking and laughing until it was past time to go home. Except for Maggie, I'd never had such a good friend.

Where *was* Aunt Lily? Did Sarah ever get to see her?

I went in the house. The kitchen and dining room

were empty, but I heard Mama and Uncle Taylor's voices coming from a room at the end of the hall. A door stood open onto a narrow, steep staircase leading to the attic. I looked up and saw Mary. "Hey!" I climbed the stairs.

Her room was long and narrow, hot and stuffy, with a single bed near the only window, a short chest of drawers under the eaves, a metal folding chair with a torn vinyl seat. The roof pitched sharply downward on both sides of the bed, and we couldn't stand upright except in the middle of the room.

"You okay up here?" I asked.

"A bit warm." She stood by the open window, her face glistening with sweat.

Uncle Taylor appeared in the hole in the floor where the stairs ended. "Mary, here's a fan. Is everything okay?"

"Yes, sir," Mary said.

I said, "It's really hot up here."

Uncle Taylor plugged in the fan. "This'll help." He switched it on and set it to oscillate. A strong breeze blew through the room.

"Thank you," said Mary. "Makes a difference."

Uncle Taylor said, "Jubie, get your suit on. The water's great."

"I'll be right down."

"Okay, and Mary? We need to keep the hall door shut. The air-conditioning . . ."

"Yes, sir."

After he left, I asked, "Is it really all right?"

She put her flowered bag on the bed. "Only be up here maybe twice a day."

"Did you bring a bathing suit?"

She shook her head. "Can't swim."

"You're not going in the gulf?"

She looked out the window. "That's not likely."

In the cabana, I changed into my new one-piece suit, hoping there'd be boys on the beach who might notice how well I filled it out. Just before I left I tied a towel around my waist to cover the welts on my thighs.

I'd never seen sand so white and water so blue. The waves weren't as fierce as on the South Carolina beaches, which made the surf seem friendly. Board fences ran from Uncle Taylor's house, across the dunes, and down to the high-tide mark, fencing off the property. That seemed strange to me. Owning the beach is like owning a mountain or an island, putting your name on something that belongs to the whole world.

"Hey, Jubes!" Puddin ran over the dunes. Mary was behind her, carrying Davie, who had on his bathing trunks. Mary was still in the dress she'd traveled in. She put Davie down and sat on a dune behind us.

"Mary!" I beckoned her. She shook her head.

"Yoo-hoo!" A woman puffed through the sand, waving her arms. She was round and fat in the middle with skinny legs, a barrel on broomsticks. She gasped her way to me. "You are Taylor's niece."

"Yes, ma'am, June Watts."

"It's a pleasure to meet you, June Watts. I'm Lula Willingham, your uncle Taylor's neighbor. I knew y'all would be here today. I've lived next door for four years and Taylor tells me everything. I want to meet your mama and all her babies." She pointed at Mary. "Is that your girl?"

"Yes, ma'am," I said, glancing back at Mary, who I knew could hear us.

Mrs. Willingham's two-piece was tight around her stomach and thighs, with stripes of sunburned skin above and below—the most uncomfortable-looking suit I'd ever seen.

"Must be nice to travel with help. I know your mama needs it with all you children. Five or six of you, right? Taylor was worried about having enough of everything to—"

"Four."

"Four? That's not so many. Still and all, having a girl lets it be a vacation for your mama. Else she'd have to fetch food and carry wet suits and haul that toddler around. Those your brother and sister?"

"Yes, ma'am, Puddin and Davie."

"I'll be back in half an hour and I want to meet everybody. Ev-ree-body."

"Bye, Mrs. Willingham."

"Bye-bye," she called over her shoulder. "I'm off

for my daily walk; makes me feel not so old. Not fifty yet, even if the years do keep racing by." She was still talking when she got to the fence.

Sarah came down to the beach and walked right past where Puddin and I were sitting on our towels. She shook out a beach blanket, put her sandals and glasses on it, and went into the water up to her waist. Her somber silence was ominous. I ran down to the water and waded in. "Hey," I hollered over the noise of the waves, "you okay?"

She jumped. "I was till you scared me." She started for the beach.

"Huh-uh, you weren't." I followed her.

"Just leave me alone."

"I will if you'll tell me what's wrong."

"You want to know what's wrong? Ask your daddy!" She snatched up her glasses and ran.

I was still standing there when Mama and Uncle Taylor came over the dunes, Stell Ann behind them. Mama was in her black latex one-piece and she looked happy. Cheeks pink, red-gold hair on fire in the late afternoon sun, hand in hand with Uncle Taylor. She stopped where Mary was sitting and said something. Mary got up and headed back toward the house.

"You been in the water yet, Jubie?" I could see Uncle Taylor looking at the welts on my legs.

I nodded. "Sarah was with me. She went for a walk." I pointed. She was way up the beach.

"Is the water cold?" Mama asked.

"No, it's great. Where's Mary going?"

"To fix supper."

Uncle Taylor spread a beach towel, and Mama dropped her sunglasses on it.

I said, "Mrs. Willingham was here—the next-door lady? She said she'd be back."

"Oh, Lord," Uncle Taylor said to Mama. "Lula's the one I was telling you about. Everybody's business is Lula's business." He grabbed Mama's hand and pulled her toward the gulf. "Last one in's a sand crab." I hadn't heard Mama laugh so hard in a long time.

I walked over to where Stell was spreading out her towel.

"Mama's having fun."

"Uncle Taylor's good for her. Isn't this a sublime beach?"

"Uh-huh." I looked around while Stell settled herself. "You talked to Sarah yet?"

"Just hello. Why?"

"She's acting weird. She said I should ask Daddy if I wanted to know what was wrong with her."

"Daddy? Our daddy?"

"That's what she said."

"How on earth could Daddy know what's wrong with Sarah?"

"She said it like it was his fault she's unhappy."

Stell looked at Mama and Uncle Taylor playing in the water. "I don't know how I would feel if Mama and Daddy got a divorce."

"Do you know why Aunt Lily left?"

"I think she had a boyfriend." Stell opened her beach bag and took out her homemade suntan lotion—baby oil mixed with iodine.

"You mean adultery?"

She rubbed her shins with the lotion. "Maybe. I'm guessing, because of what Mama says about Aunt Lily."

"I can't imagine Mama leaving us."

"Me, either. Or us living with just Daddy."

CHAPTER 6

I was not yet seven the first time I heard Daddy fire his handgun. The war had ended, we'd moved from the mountains into a new house in Charlotte, and Mary had come to work for us. Mama and Daddy began to bicker a lot, but they were nice to each other when Mary was around. I was alarmed if she didn't show up when she was supposed to, on days when the Number 3 bus was late.

Meemaw visited us for weeks at a time, and Mary had a way with her, fixing her coffee or helping her tune the radio to her stories or getting aspirin if Meemaw complained of a headache. When Mama heard them talking, she told Mary, in a voice loud enough for Meemaw to hear, "Don't let Cordelia keep you from your work." She and Meemaw didn't get along, even with Mary as a go-between, disagreeing about little things such as the cowbell Mama hung on the kitchen door to remind her of Shumont. It clanked whenever anyone came or went. When she heard it, Meemaw frowned and said, "Dang cowbell." But Mama was adamant and the cowbell stayed. I paid attention to Mary about such things, like when Mama said to Aunt Rita, "Life is good, except for Cordelia," and Mary shook her head as if to say I shouldn't notice.

Meemaw sat on the sofa all day with the radio on, listening to her programs and crocheting. Mama told Daddy she felt like a prisoner in her own home. "Cordelia sits there like a Buddha, with fuzzy things growing in her lap, watching me. She's so suspicious."

"How do you know she's suspicious?"

"By the look on her face. A suspicious look."

"You're being paranoid."

"I heard what she said to Rita. 'Paula thinks she's too good for us.'"

"That was two sentences. She really said, 'Paula thinks. She's too good for us.'"

Mama tried not to smile, but Daddy always got around her.

Aunt Rita and Uncle Stamos came over to visit Meemaw and play bridge. The two men sat in the living room, shuffling papers and talking about Watts Concrete Fabrications, which they'd started with ten thousand dollars of Mama's inheritance. They worked hard but didn't agree about the need for putting in long hours. "Rita's not happy with all the work I bring home," Uncle Stamos said.

Daddy rolled a blueprint. "It's a postwar boom. We've got to strike while the iron is hot."

"We're juggling too many jobs and cutting corners."

"We're coming in under budget and the work's not suffering. We'll be millionaires in ten years."

Mama called from the kitchen, "Sounds good to me."

"Some things matter more than money," Meemaw said, looking up from her crocheting.

Mama closed the kitchen door.

Uncle Stamos got the card table from the hall closet and set it up in the middle of the living room. "Ready for bridge, my love?" He and Aunt Rita were never far apart, always touching each other. Mama said one time that Rita could stand to lose a few pounds, but I could tell Uncle Stamos thought she was beautiful. Maybe she wasn't as pretty as Mama, but she made me feel important and was always giving me small things. That night it was a brooch of red stones. "For when you get older." She'd folded my fingers over the pin. "If I had a daughter, I'd want her to be just like you."

Mama walked in, drying her hands. "What do y'all want to drink?"

"A highball for me," Uncle Stamos said. He was as skinny as Fred Astaire, in spite of how much he ate, and when he sat down he looked like he was folding up.

Meemaw asked Aunt Rita, "Did you bring Carlisle's—I mean, his letter?"

Aunt Rita pulled an envelope from her pocket-book. "He's doing so well. Here, you can read it." I loved hearing Aunt Rita and Uncle Stamos talk about their only child, Carly, who was fifteen, in military school, and hoping to go to West Point.

Mama said, "Time for bed, Jubie. Tell Stell and Puddin I'll be there in a minute."

My sisters and I shared a room that had two windows, fluffy curtains, and single beds with wooden headboards that were in the shape of apples, red with brown stems. Daddy and Uncle Stamos made them for us when Puddin got too big for a crib.

After Mama said good night, Stell and I lay in bed whispering.

Daddy filled the doorway. "You girls are supposed to be asleep. I'm going to separate y'all. Jubie, let's go."

That was a fairly regular turn of events, putting me in Mama and Daddy's bed so Stell and I wouldn't talk late.

Their room was twice the size of ours, with the bed facing a big front window. They had a bedroom suite that Mama bought after Daddy began making money—a cherry bed, with two tall chests and a matching dressing table. I had fun going through their things, especially Daddy's. His top drawer smelled of cedar, lighter fluid, Doublemint gum, and the oil he used to clean his handgun, which he kept under a jumble of socks and handkerchiefs. Just the sight of it scared me. I never touched it when I rummaged through his stuff for a piece of gum. He told me he couldn't get Doublemint during the war, and that no other gum was as good. It was my favorite, too.

The sheets on their bed were fresh and crisp from sunshine. I fell asleep on Daddy's pillow and woke to the sound of glass breaking, a loud crack above my head. I screamed.

The bedroom door hit the wall. "What's going on?" Daddy turned on the light and I squinted against the brightness. "What'd you do to the bed?"

"Something scared me." I started to cry.

Mama, Aunt Rita, and Uncle Stamos crowded into the bedroom.

Aunt Rita gasped, "The window!"

There was a hole in the front window, the wooden frames hanging loose.

Daddy said, "Sit up, Jubie, real careful."

The cherry headboard was cracked down the middle. I began to sob. "I didn't do it. A noise came . . ." Daddy lifted me off the bed and set me down by Aunt Rita, who put her arms around me.

He climbed onto the bed and ran his hand over the headboard, then pulled something up from behind the pillows. "By God, look at this." He held a white sock stuffed like a Christmas stocking, bulging at the toe. "A rock. Pitched through the window."

Uncle Stamos picked me up and held me close. "Could have hit June." I put my head on his bony shoulder. He said, "It's all right now, you're safe."

Mama said, "I'll bet it's those kids who shot firecrackers at the house down the street."

"Are you okay, Junebug?" Daddy touched my cheek.

"Yes, sir." Him calling me Junebug made me feel better.

He opened his top drawer and got his gun. "I'll find the hoodlum thinks he can get away with this."

"Bill, no," Mama said. "Call the police."

"You call them. I'm going to catch a punk."

"Calm down, Bill." Uncle Stamos put his hand on Daddy's shoulder.

Daddy shrugged it off. "Don't tell me what to do." He stomped out of the bedroom and down the hall. The front door slammed behind him. There was a loud bang in the front yard. Daddy yelled, "I'm gonna get you!"

Mama called through the broken window. "Bill, please. There's a better way to handle this."

Blam. Another shot.

Meemaw hurried in, her long white nightgown billowing around her. She pushed past Mama and shouted, "Billy Watts, you get in here right now. This minute." There was no response and Meemaw said, "I mean it, Billy. Acting a fool."

The front door opened. Daddy's footsteps clumped through the foyer. "Whoever it was, they're gone."

"Now let's call the police," Mama said.

But someone else had called them and they pulled into the driveway.

Uncle Stamos put me down next to Stell, who

stood in the hallway in a corner, pale and quiet. I took her hand. We went to our room and got in bed together. "Where's Puddin?" I asked.

"She was here a minute ago." Puddin was only two but was already hiding herself away.

A sound like a kitten came from under her bed. I got on the floor and lifted the bed skirt. "Hey, Puddin-tane."

She crawled out, dust in her blonde curls, her face splotched. "Daddy scared me." She got into bed with Stell and me.

Loud voices came from the living room.

"Got a license for that gun? We *can* put you in jail if you fire it again."

Meemaw came into our room. Her flowery smell made me think everything was going to be all right. "Your daddy's—he's just upset. You girls should be in your own beds—I mean, company helps when you're scared. Night." She left. In the dim light I saw her thick gray pigtail hanging down her back.

Mama checked on us after the police left. "I hope the neighbors don't think we're crazy, the way your daddy carried on." She lowered her voice. "Thank God Cordelia—well, for once I'm glad she was here."

Puddin and I got in our beds. Mama pulled the covers up, turned off the hall light, and closed our bedroom door. Every time I'd almost drift off, I'd remember: Daddy had been ready to shoot somebody.

CHAPTER 7

Uncle Taylor was throwing a party so his friends could meet Mama. Mary spent the whole day in his kitchen, making gallons of ice tea, baking biscuits and apple pies. I helped her put the leaves in the dining table and cover it with a white cloth that fell to the floor. She tugged one side, then the other. "It got to hang just right," she said.

Mama set six tapers on the table in the middle of flowers she picked from her brother's garden. They were expecting forty people. I was uncomfortable at big parties and felt wobbly just thinking about this one.

Two guests came early and stayed late. One was Mrs. Lula Willingham, the neighbor I'd met on the beach. She settled herself on a step stool in the kitchen, seeing to it that dirty dishes were washed as soon as they came through the door, ordering Mary around, telling her to watch the serving platters, keep them full. When Mrs. Willingham took over, Mama left the kitchen to enjoy the party. I thought she was relieved not to have to be in charge of Mary.

The other early arrival was a war widow Uncle Taylor had met at church, Mrs. Kay Macy Cooper. She had a soft voice and wore her blonde hair tied back with a coral ribbon that matched her dress.

Every time she was introduced, it was with her whole name, because she was related to somebody who owned a department store in New York City. Mama said Macy's made Ivey's look piddling. In Charlotte, Ivey's covered its display windows on Sundays so good Christians wouldn't be distracted on the Lord's day, and some said that put them a step ahead of Macy's.

Mary was at the kitchen sink, drying her hands on a dish towel when Mrs. Cooper tapped her on the shoulder. "I don't believe we've met."

"I'm Mary Luther. I work for Miz Watts."

Mrs. Cooper said, "It's nice to meet you, Mrs. Luther." She glanced at Mary's wedding ring. "It is Mrs., isn't it?"

"Yes, ma'am."

"I'm Kay Macy Cooper." She held out her hand. Mary looked startled, then took it.

"Pleased to meet you, Miz Cooper."

Mrs. Willingham handed a platter of sliced ham to Mary. "I believe there's a place on the dining room table for this." Mary left the kitchen with the heaping platter.

"Kay Macy, Taylor will be needing you in the living room," Mrs. Willingham said, smiling as always. The smile didn't reach her eyes.

Mrs. Cooper left the kitchen without answering.

I sat in a chair in the corner of the dining room with my supper plate balanced on my knees. If anybody spoke to me, I mumbled something and

79

looked away. The party voices sounded like turkeys gobbling, nonsense noises punctuated by snatches of music, the tinkle of ice in glasses, the clink of silverware. When the record player quit, somebody called out, "Flip the stack, flip the stack." A hazy cloud of smoke formed at the ceiling, drifting with the movement of people walking in and out.

Uncle Taylor's voice boomed from the living room, "Everybody gather around. I want to introduce my big sister."

The dining room cleared as people went to meet Mama. She'd chat with everyone she met. She loved parties.

I was going to duck out the back door and go to the beach, certain nobody would miss me. But something shiny caught my eye under the hem of the tablecloth. The toe of a patent leather shoe. "Puddin!"

"Don't tell, Jubie." I scooted under the tablecloth and drew in my feet, giggling with my little sister in our dusky cave.

"How long have you been under here?" I whispered, sitting back against one of the table legs.

"For the whole party." She handed me a cookie. "I've got a lot. You can have more."

"Thanks."

Mama was making a speech about how happy she was to be in Pensacola, how nice everybody was, how she didn't know where Puddin and I'd gone. The chatter started up again as people crowded the dining room, their feet showing under the tablecloth.

I heard Stell say, "Why, thank you, a gift from my boyfriend." Her gold cross. "Our next-door neighbor." How she met Carter. "Together we formed Charlotte's first Young Life group." Together, ha! She'd had to drag Carter into it.

"Young Life?" a woman asked.

"A club for Christian teens." Stell's voice was full of pride.

Mrs. Willingham said to someone, "Paula's lucky to have her, that's what I told one of her kids." Her voice faded into the others as she walked away.

Mary came into the dining room. I recognized her black lace-ups. "Commander Bentley, reckon it's time for the apple pies?"

"What do you think, Kay?" Uncle Taylor asked.

"They gobbled up your biscuits, Mrs. Luther, and I'm sure your pies will be delicious. Yes, it's time."

I couldn't get over her saying "Mrs. Luther." I'd never heard anybody call Mary that.

Mrs. Willingham, who was standing by the table, said, "Calling a colored gal by her last name is making a show of being broad-minded. Kay Macy's a Yankee, you know. Maybe she'd be good for Taylor and Sarah, but maybe not."

"Thank goodness that's not your decision," Mama said.

"Oh, Paula, I didn't see you. Well, I do have opinions."

"Perhaps you should keep them to yourself."

"I've never been good at that. Just come right out with what I think."

Mama's heels clicked across the foyer into the living room.

Things got quiet. Puddin and I crawled out from under the table.

Mrs. Cooper stood in the kitchen doorway. "There you are. Your mama's been looking for you."

Puddin said, "Jubie found me under the table."

"Cocktail parties aren't a lot of fun for kids." She took Puddin's hand. "Sit on the stool and let me fix your barrettes." She gave me a hug. "Nobody's in the kitchen. If you scoot out the back door, you won't have to help with the dishes."

As the screen door closed behind me, Mrs. Cooper said to Mama, "Mrs. Luther must be worn out. Why don't we let her go to bed and I'll finish up in here."

"Another half hour won't kill her," Mama said. "I brought her along to help."

CHAPTER 8

In the fall of 1952, Daddy announced that the house he'd built for us on Queens Road West was ready. The day we moved in, Mary got Mama settled in Daddy's platform rocker in the den. "Too bad," Mary said, "a new house and a new baby at the same time."

"A lousy coincidence," Mama said. She sat by the breezeway door, smoking and drinking coffee from a thermos, telling the movers where to put things. She took the cowbell from her cloth carryall of last-minute stuff—toilet paper, bar soap, the magnets she'd taken from the refrigerator—and gave it to Mary to hang on the kitchen door.

Mary hung the bell, and the familiar jangle echoed through the empty rooms.

"Now it's home," Mama said.

The house was so big we didn't have enough stuff to fill it—five bedrooms, three bathrooms— four floors including a full attic, a basement, and a two-car garage with an efficiency apartment above it. Mama said she'd have a good time shopping for new furniture after the baby was born. Her belly was huge and I thought she'd fall over every time she stood. She wore nothing but tennis shoes or bedroom slippers on her swollen feet.

I commented on being way taller than Mama, so Mary measured me, making a pencil mark on the bathroom doorjamb. "Five foot seven," she said, "and you not yet twelve. I s'pect you got even more growing to do." That was fine with me. I liked looking down on Mama and Stell Ann. I wasn't crazy about having big feet, but Daddy pointed to his own size fourteens and said that came with the territory.

In the new house, I had a room to myself for the first time in my life, with a double bed I felt lost in. The walls were painted in what Mama called mauve rose, with a white quilted spread, floral print curtains, and a matching dust ruffle. Mama sold our beds with the apple headboards to a woman with triplet daughters.

"Aren't they just the cutest things!" the woman said.

"My husband designed them and his brother cut and painted them," Mama told her.

"Oh, no," the woman said, "I mean your daughters. They're just adorable."

"Oh."

"So why are you selling the beds?"

"The oldest's fourteen."

"But you might have another girl." The woman looked at Mama's stomach.

"I certainly hope not. Check or cash?"

Sometimes I didn't want to hear what Mama said.

• • •

A week after we moved in, Mama began having labor pains while she and Mary were putting shelf paper in the pantry. Mama said the pains didn't amount to anything, but Mary convinced her to lie down, and they spent the afternoon in Mama's room. Stell and I could hear the mumble of their voices, their laughter, Mama's occasional moans.

Daddy woke Stell and me at three o'clock in the morning. "I'm taking your mother to the hospital. Change the sheets on our bed. Her water broke." He said that as if we knew what it meant. "This one won't take long." Daddy sounded excited. He wrapped Mama in a quilt and carried her to the car, the way fathers do in the movies.

Before noon we had a brother. The only thing Daddy told us when he called was that it was a boy, that his name was David William, he weighed over eight pounds, and he had a big head.

Immediately I went to the den and took the King James Bible off the bookshelf. Several years ago Stell had started recording our family history, beginning with our great-grandparents—as many names and dates as she could piece together, including the death of Mama's sister, Hanna Eudora Bentley, in 1932. Then Mama and Daddy, their birth and wedding dates, and the birthdays of their children. I added *David William Watts, born September 27, 1952*. Stell would frown when she

85

saw my handwriting, but she didn't own the Bible.

Mama and her fourth baby stayed in the hospital two extra days because Mama had her tubes tied. I overheard enough of what was said between Aunt Rita and Mary to learn that Mama and Daddy were through having children, and that it was good Mama already had four or the doctor wouldn't have fixed her.

Right from the first time I saw Davie, I couldn't get enough of holding him, smelling him, rubbing his silky head, letting him grab my fingers with his tiny hand. Mama taught me and Stell how to change his diapers when he was only a few days old, and I got enough of that right away. The first time I saw his thing, I wanted to puke. It looked like raw meat. How did boys walk with all that stuff hanging down?

Davie didn't hold his head up until he was six weeks old, and Mama worried about it. She also thought it might mean he was a genius with a big brain. I didn't understand what Daddy told Uncle Stamos: "That boy's head ruined the best thing a man ever had."

When Davie was six months old, we had our picture taken by a man who photographed all the best families. He posed us with Mama in the queen chair, holding Davie, and with Puddin perched on the arm. Daddy, Stell, and I behind them. My blonde hair, my blue eyes, my tawny skin were so like Daddy's. I stood a head taller than Stell, who had Mama's freckles and hazel eyes. The portrait had been enlarged, tinted, and framed in mahogany to hang over the mantel. I studied it, wondering what people thought about the happy family in the picture.

We had to be quiet when Davie was napping, and sometimes I felt I'd bust from my need to make noise. When it got too much for me, I went out to the garage and climbed the stairs to what Mama called an efficiency apartment and Daddy called the recreation room. I thought it was heavenly, and had suggested more than once that somebody ought to live there full-time to discourage burglars. I spent hours by the windows that overlooked Westfield Road, watching people walk their dogs or ride bicycles or push strollers on the sidewalks. Our neighbors acted friendly, but I didn't think I would ever really belong, being so plain and awkward. When we joined Myers Park Country Club, I felt we could be members and still not have the right to be there. Mama wanted us to get into Charlotte Country Club, but not enough people nominated us. Daddy said that was just as well, because Charlotte Country Club was too far away. Mama said, "Sour grapes." She tried to join the Junior League. When that didn't work out, she told Aunt Rita she'd rather be in the Junior Woman's Club any day. I couldn't help thinking about sour grapes.

Stell was upset that Mama hadn't gotten into the Junior League. "I'll never get to make my debut."

"What's that?" I asked.

"Coming out in society. It's really important."

"What's Junior League got to do with it?"

She wiped Pond's off her face. "Charlotte's funny that way. If your parents aren't in, you aren't, either."

"In what?"

"Leave me alone."

She was a freshman in high school and had started ironing her clothes on Sunday evenings, lining up five outfits in her closet for the coming school week. I said to Mary, "I guess she doesn't think your ironing's good enough."

"She want it the way she want it."

Mary would hear nothing bad about Stell but didn't hesitate to point out my flaws. "Close that book, Jubie, and help your mother. You got to be quiet, your brother's sleeping. Put things away when you're done with them."

"Why don't you ever boss Stell?"

"When she needs it, I will."

Daddy was at a dinner meeting at the club, and Mama told Stell and me it was time to watch *The Family at Home*. The commercial for it said, "The Henry Roberts family solves their problems with love, laughter, and help from their dog Woofers." The joke was that Woofers was never seen, was only heard barking from somewhere behind the camera.

Stell kicked off her shoes, curling her stocking feet under her while Mama fiddled with the vertical hold. By the time she got a good picture, the show had begun.

Tom Roberts, a tall, skinny teenager, was in the kitchen with his sister, Milly.

"What a cute outfit she has on," Mama said. I missed something Tom said. He was sitting on a bar stool that looked just like one of ours, and I wondered if the seat was red Naugahyde. He sat with his long legs stretched out, looking at the floor, his scalp showing through his crew cut.

"Even if you don't make the team," Milly said, "the important thing is you tried." If he believed that, he was a real jerk.

Mr. Roberts came into the kitchen. He took a pipe from his mouth. "Hello, Sonny, Princess. What's up?" He only called them Milly and Tom when he was being stern.

"Hi, Pops," said Milly. I could never call Daddy "Pops."

Tom said, "Aw, Milly's got this way-out notion that I'll make the football team."

Mr. Roberts sat on a stool, stuck his pipe back in his mouth, and reached for a cookie jar. He had black-rimmed glasses and his ears stuck out like Clark Gable's. "So, son, are you going to make it?"

"No sweat," Tom said, but his voice was sad.

What did Mr. Roberts do when he got mad at Milly and Tom? I tried to picture him angry.

Mrs. Roberts walked into the kitchen in heels and a shirtwaist dress.

Mama smoothed her skirt.

"Hello, children." Mrs. Roberts grabbed a cookie from her husband and put it back in the jar. "Henry, you'll spoil your appetite. The roast is almost ready." She tied her apron and adjusted her pearl necklace.

"Oh, Louise, I was only going to have one."

"After supper."

"Ha!" Stell jeered. "Try snatching a cookie from Daddy."

Mrs. Roberts tucked a strand of blonde hair back into place. If they were going out for the evening, she wore a ribbon around the bun at the crown of her head, and once she'd worn flats on a picnic. She looked sweet and kind, never smoked or had too much to drink, and didn't say a cross word to anyone. I knew this was just TV, but I wanted it to be real.

"Jubie?" Mama said. "Why are you scowling?"

"I'm concentrating."

The dog barked offscreen.

"What's up with Woofers?" Mr. Roberts asked.

Milly said, "It's time for the evening paper. How does he know?"

"He checks his wristwatch." Mr. Roberts jabbed the air with his pipe. The audience laughed and the screen faded to a commercial for Camay, the soap of beautiful women.

Mama said, "You can learn a lot from Milly about grooming and makeup."

"She wears costumes, and her hair's a wig," said Stell.

Mama sniffed. "She's chic and a smart young lady." She went to the kitchen. The garage door screeched open, then slammed down.

"Daddy's home," I called to Mama. She came back in the den with a glass of ice tea as the door opened from the breezeway.

"Hey, y'all." Daddy sailed his fedora through the den to the dining room table. His hair was messed up from his hat.

"Shush," Mama said, "we're watching our program."

"Oops!" Daddy tiptoed past us, grinning. He'd had just enough to drink to make him happy, and I hoped he'd go right to bed.

The stiffness between Mary and Mama started the last time the bridge luncheon met at our house. I don't think the extra work is what made Mary act so strange. But maybe getting ready for the bridge club had her on edge, so when she heard what Mrs. Feaster said to Mama, that was the last straw.

The house never got so clean as the day before Mama's bridge club, and it was impossible to know, with a refrigerator full of food, what was okay to eat and what was special for the ladies. Mama was in a tizzy, looking into the refrigerator every ten minutes at the food she'd fixed, with at least two other things set aside to substitute in case the tomato aspic didn't jell.

The cowbell rang when Carter Milton came through the kitchen door.

"Hey, Mrs. Watts," Carter said. "I'm here to help."

Mama's face lit up. "Hey, Carter."

Stell and Carter were hosting a Young Life meeting the same day as the bridge luncheon, like there wasn't already enough going on.

Of all Stell's friends, Carter was Mama's favorite. He always looked dressed up. Today he had on a madras plaid shirt and sharply creased slacks. He was particular, which I guess is what appealed to Stell. Carter had recently gotten a flattop, after having a crew cut for a long time. A definite improvement, as far as I was concerned.

Mama handed him a tray of glasses. "These are for your meeting. Stell's in the rec room setting out the other things."

Stell got Young Life going in Charlotte after she'd been saved by Leighton Ford, the brother-in-law of Billy Graham, who is like God's brother-in-law as far as Charlotteans are concerned.

When Stell announced that she'd been saved, Daddy had asked, "Is that the same as being born again?"

Stell had beamed. "Yes, Daddy. I'm reborn in Christ." From the expectation on her face, I guess she thought Daddy would tell her how great it all was. But he just said, "Okay," and went back to reading his paper.

"Jubie," Mama said, after Carter headed for the rec room, "get the fluted bowl from the top shelf. Mary, are you sure Rita didn't call?"

"I hasn't talked with her."

Mama frowned. "It's not like Rita."

"My friend Reese, she sometime hard to find. Goes a spell without calling, then I see her at church and she act like it's nothing wrong." Mary dumped a bag of russets into the colander and washed them. She popped out sprouted eyes with her thumbnail, her long, knobby fingers lost among the potatoes, so much the same color. "Reese—you know Reesy, came here last year to help, the party you had for Mr. Stamos and them— she doesn't think you got to return calls. But calling back is just decent."

Mama handed the fluted bowl to Mary. "I know they're not out of town."

"I has to call Reesy two, three times." Mary put soap flakes in the bowl.

"I need to ask Rita if they found a yard man," Mama said. "I got a name from the girl who sweeps up at the beauty parlor. Do you know a Bobbo Scott? Would he be a good yard boy for Rita and Stamos? Bobbo, is that right?"

"That's his name. Not much of a name, but he not much of a man."

"Oh?" Mama's voice arched like her eyebrows.

"He carries a bottle."

I knew that was it for Bobbo.

Mama said, "Rita got a name from Safronia. Woodrow Addison. Do you know him?"

"Uh-huh." Mary wiped the bar. "He falls out. Has blood sugar. All his people do."

Neither Mama nor Aunt Rita would approve anybody colored until they'd run the name by Mary. If Mary didn't know them, she knew somebody who did.

Mary picked up a basket of wet sheets and went out to the clothesline. Mama never let Mary put sheets in the dryer because the sunshine made them smell good.

"Jubie, have you swept the walk?" Mama asked.

Mrs. Feaster, a lady from Mama's bridge club, pulled up while I was sweeping. "Hello, June," she called out. "I'm here to help your mother."

"Yes, ma'am. Mama said you were coming over. She's in the kitchen." I followed her into the house.

Mama handed me the colander of potatoes. "Hey, Susie, thanks for coming over. Jubie, peel these, please."

Mrs. Feaster hung up her hat and coat. "Glad I can help."

"I thought Mary was going to peel them," I said to Mama. The potatoes smelled like damp dirt.

"When she finishes at the clothesline, she has to do the ironing." Mama handed me the peeler.

"That plastic cloth on the table in the den," Mrs. Feaster said, "has how to bid printed right on it. Diana Sawyer always stares at the place that means what she's bidding. She might as well pass notes to her partner."

"My linen cloths have to go on the tables in the living room. I can't leave the den table bare. And I won the plastic cloth at the club last fall."

"If you have to look at a tablecloth to know how to bid, you shouldn't be playing." Mrs. Feaster carried the fluted bowl into the dining room and came back with two silver trays that she put beside me on the kitchen table. "Wish I had your head of hair, June, so thick and blonde. Mine's getting grayer every day and I'm always at the tail end of a perm. That's a lot of potatoes."

"Yes, ma'am." I looked at the colander.

"How many people are y'all feeding tonight?"

"Carter's eating with us, and my friend, Maggie Harold, but that's only eight."

"Only eight," Mrs. Feaster said. "I swear, Pauly, I'd go crazy with so many people around all the time."

"Sometimes I do."

Water came on full blast in the sink, dishes rattled. Mrs. Feaster said, "Speaking of crazy, will Brenda be here tomorrow?"

Mama sighed. "Eventually she will. About the

time I'm serving dessert, she'll come in, all short of breath and full of excuses."

"Maybe she was an hour late being born and never got caught up."

"Brenda doesn't function very well these days," Mama said. She didn't add, "Bless her heart," the way she usually did when she criticized another woman.

"Paula, you're too kind. Brenda Simpson'd make a nigger look smart."

"Susan!" Mama sounded shocked, but she laughed. Her laugh broke off and she gasped.

Mary stood in the doorway, the laundry basket at her hip. "Miz Feaster, you ought to know better than to say such a thing." She didn't sound like herself, didn't sound like a maid.

"Mary!" Mama said. "We didn't know you were standing there."

"That is no excuse for talking trash."

"Mary"—Mama's voice went quiet and cold—"you're forgetting your place."

"No, ma'am." Mary left the kitchen, came back in her hat and coat. She didn't look at me.

Mama followed her. "I'm so sorry."

"I be here in the morning. Wouldn't leave you with all your ladies coming." Mary closed the den door hard behind her.

CHAPTER 9

At Joyland by the Sea, just outside Pensacola, only a few cars were parked in the roped-off grassy field. Stell said, "There's not a lot of joy in Joyland." The sky was low, overcast, not at all what I'd imagined the weather would be for our afternoon at the amusement park.

Mary stood by the car, Davie on her hip, as I took the stroller from the trunk. "Lord's day. Maybe folks just stays in church."

We walked past the sandwich board I'd seen from the car the day we arrived in Pensacola:

BRYSON McCURDY'S
TRAVELING CARNIVAL!!

THE SNAKE MAN
THE WILD DOG OF THE EVERGLADES
THE THREE-LEGGED GIRL
and MORE!!!! No Gate Charge!

"Yay!" Puddin shouted. "There's a carnival, too."

A wide midway of sand and sawdust ran through Joyland, with booths and rides to either side. Calliope music played somewhere ahead. Signs pointed the way to the carnival that had hooked up with the amusement park.

The stroller was hard to push. Every time I freed it from the sawdust, I had to shake out my sandals, too. But I was glad I'd worn them, even if there was dust on my toenails, which I'd polished a dazzling red for our outing at Joyland.

Mary took over the stroller. "No need for us to slow you down." She looked hot, and I wished she could have worn shorts like Stell and me, but Uncle Taylor had advised her to wear her uniform so it would be clear she was there to help with the children.

Stell and I walked ahead, past an old woman in short shorts who sat on a stool at a lemonade stand, her skinny legs streaked with bulging veins, grinning at people who walked by. If most of my teeth were gone, I wouldn't smile.

I wasn't paying attention to where I was going, and bumped into a fat man strolling along with his family.

"Excuse me." I tried not to stare at the enormous stomach hanging over his belt.

"That's okay, young miss." He touched my shoulder.

A skinny girl about my age spoke to him. "Hey, Daddy, let's go on the merry-go-round." Why would a teenager want to do such a childish thing? But I thought it was neat that she wanted to ride with her father. Her knobby knees and black hair made me think of my cousin. When I had asked Sarah to come with us to Joyland, she said she'd rather go out to the base with Mama and Uncle Taylor.

As the family walked by, a woman in green coveralls called out, "Ri-i-i-ide the rolly coaster!"

Stell nudged me. "You and I can do that later."

A man with a gleaming bald head winked at Stell and beckoned, waving a pennant. "Penny pitch, ring toss! C'mon, girly-girls, give it a try!"

Ahead of us a man pulled a woman between two tents. I looked at them as we passed. They were kissing hard, his hands on her back, moving up to her shoulder blades, down to her bottom. Stell caught me looking and yanked me by the hand. "That's disgusting." She sounded like Mama.

Four sailors crowded around us, their white bell-bottoms flapping. "Hello there," said the tallest one, who was redheaded and skinny.

A short brunette boy swept off his sailor hat and bowed to Stell. "Can we treat you to the Ferris wheel?" He was a Yankee, I was sure.

"I have a boyfriend," Stell stammered.

A sailor grabbed my hand. His thick blond curls bushed out under his cap. "Howdy, ma'am. I'm Tucson Tom from New Mexico. You might think Arizona, but you'd be wrong." His hand was strong and warm. How would it feel to see the circus with this cute boy, to walk the midway holding hands?

"So where is he," the first sailor asked Stell, "this famous boyfriend?"

Stell snatched me away from the blond boy. "Y'all stop bothering us."

Mary came up, pushing Davie, Puddin hanging on to her skirt. "What you boys doing?"

"And here's their mammy," said the third sailor.

The first one saluted Mary. "We want to take these nice girls for a ride."

"Just leave us be," Mary said.

Three girls passed by in a cloud of perfume, arm in arm, smiling at the sailors. They all had bows in their hair, white blouses, and red lipstick. I was disappointed when the boys ran after them.

"Thank goodness," Stell said. Did she really mean it?

Everything tempted me—the freak show; the Enchanted Castle Boat Ride where a couple waited, the boy feeding cotton candy to the girl; the Tilt-A-Whirl, kids staggering as they left it. The warm air carried delicious smells that made me hungry—corn dogs, peanuts, candy apples.

"The merry-go-round!" Puddin shouted.

I asked Mary, "You want to ride with Davie and Puddin?"

She frowned. "Ask the man."

I walked up to the ticket window and saw a notice: MERRY-GO-ROUND, TEN CENTS. And in larger print below that: WHITES ONLY EXCEPT MONDAYS.

I looked at Mary.

"Hey, young lady, you wanna ride?" The man in the ticket booth talked around the cigar in his mouth.

"Yes, but—I mean not me, just my sister and my baby brother. And our girl, to hold him."

He took his cigar from his mouth and pointed it at the sign.

"What if I pay double for her and she doesn't sit down?" I put four dimes on the counter.

He put his cigar back in his mouth. "I'll let her go if she just stands there, holds him on the horse."

As I gave Mary the tickets, a clown standing nearby smiled at me and tipped his hat.

Mary, Davie, and Puddin spun in a whirl of music from the calliope. The fat man I'd bumped into stood by his daughter on the merry-go-round, his hand on the neck of her pony, waving to his family as the carousel turned. Davie laughed every time he saw us, and Mary stood beside him, beaming, tapping her foot to the tooted notes, the skirt of her uniform rippling. It was worth the extra dime.

"Whew! Now that was fun!" Mary said as she got off, carrying Davie, holding Puddin's hand. She shifted Davie to her other hip. "You girls leave the little ones with me. Go have some fun your own self."

Stell and I ran to buy tickets for the World's Biggest Ferris Wheel. Soon we were at the top, swinging forward and backward as the wheel stopped to load the bottom baskets. The redheaded sailor and one of the girls from the midway were in the car in front of us. The sailor said something close to the girl's ear, and I wanted to be in her place, smelling of perfume, wearing a bow in my hair, flirting with a boy who might go off to war any minute.

We were so high I could see the gulf, blue and smooth under the cloudy sky, looking cool and clear beyond the tattered carnival tents billowing in the wind. Mary, Puddin, and Davie were toys on the ground far below us. Mary waved at me. A boy Puddin's size walked up to them, handing out papers. He was dressed all in glittering red, and even from our great height I thought there was something odd about him. Puddin pushed him away and ran behind a tent where I couldn't see her.

"Mary!" I yelled, but the wind carried my voice away.

"What?" asked Stell.

"Puddin's running off." The Ferris wheel began to turn, and the sailor put his arm around the girl. Down on the ground, Mary turned in a circle, looking for Puddin, who came from behind the tent, waving.

"There she is." I sat back and let the wind hit my face.

After the ride, the clown who'd tipped his hat

waltzed over to me, his outsized shoes slapping the ground with each step. He reached out and plucked a red rose from my ear. The sweat running down his painted face looked like tears, which went with his sad orange mouth. He handed me the rose, bowed, and danced away, trailing a scent of cigarettes.

Stell asked, "What was that all about?"

"My natural beauty." I touched her cheek with the rose. It was the color of my toenails and smelled like Meemaw's toilet water.

The boy in the sequined red suit handed Stell one of his papers, and when he turned I saw a cigar in his mouth, the stubble of a beard—no wonder Puddin had run from him. He wasn't even four feet tall, but he was old.

"A dwarf," said Stell. She gave me the paper he'd given her, with pictures of the freak show attractions. The Three-Legged Girl. The Python Charmer—a man wrapped in snakes. Madame Capricorn, the Eastern Mystic—a colored woman with a towel around her head.

"The carnival freak show. I'm going."

Stell grabbed my arm, her mouth set. "I'll tell Mama."

"I'm going."

"Not by yourself," said Mary.

Another group of sailors passed. One of them winked at me. "I'll take you."

Stell took my arm, ignoring the sailor.

"There it is." I pointed to a sign for the freak show and went to the ticket booth. "Two, please."

The man stared at Mary.

I dropped three dimes in the change tray. "She can stand in the back."

The man took the money.

Inside the tent, no more than a dozen people sat in rows of folding chairs, fanning themselves in the heat and dust. I took a seat on the last row so Mary could stand behind me without blocking anybody's view. A drum roll sounded. A tall colored boy wearing a yellow satin coat and black trousers pulled the curtain open. He had on a top hat that teetered as he moved.

The three-legged girl sat in a wheelchair, her legs under a pink afghan, three feet sticking out. Yellow curls framed her face. Circles of rouge matched her red lipstick. What with her having three legs, I wanted to see her walk. But she just sat there, wiggling, moving her legs so we could see they were real. She had on patent-leather pumps with bows on them, two lefts and a right. I thought about what a problem underpants would be for her.

The boy crossed the stage again, closing the curtain. Mary grabbed my shoulder and yelled, "Leesum!" The boy jumped like he'd been shot, giving the curtain such a jerk that the whole thing came down. The three-legged girl stood by her wheelchair on two good legs, the third one in her arms. She dropped the false leg and ran.

104

Mary yanked me with her as she headed toward the stage. "Leesum Fields," she said, "you stay right there."

The audience screamed, "Fake! Money back!" The ticket seller crossed the stage, waving his arms. "Sit down, sit down. The show will go on in a minute. Believe me, it's worth seeing—"

"Boo," yelled a man. "We want our money."

Mary had me in one hand and the boy in the other, pulling us outside, where even the overcast day was too bright after the dim tent. Mary let go of me and took the boy's hands. "Leesum Fields, what in the name of the Lord are you doing in this carnival?"

"Hey, Miz Luther. I got me a job." The boy's voice was deep and rich.

"Your mama's been in her bed with grief over you."

"Huh, I bet." He didn't look at all concerned about his mama.

"You show some respect for your mother, boy."

"She nothin' but a ho, smokin' tea an' sniffin' coke."

I strained to understand him.

"She still your mama."

"Yeah, and she still a ho."

The ticket seller came out and yelled, "What in hell you mean, boy, jerking the curtain down?"

"Couldn't help it."

The man shook his fist in Mary's face. "Girl,

you cost me a dollar and thirty cents in refunds."

"I wanted to talk to Leesum." Mary didn't seem one bit afraid.

"You owe me a dollar-thirty."

"I don't reckon I do."

"Watch how you talk, girl."

"You running this here fake show. Got this boy working for you, which probably's not legal. And I has these white children with me and they uncle is a commander out to the Navy base."

The man's face twisted. I tried to pull Mary back, but she didn't need my help. The man stomped his foot and turned to Leesum. "You're fired, boy. Weren't that good anyway. Get the hell out of here 'fore I throw your pecker to the wild dog." He snatched the top hat off Leesum's head. Snaky ropes of hair sprang out in all directions. "Gimme back my costume."

Leesum took off his yellow coat. "Can't take off the pants, Mr. McCurdy, ain't got nothin on under 'em."

"Get your clothes, then. And don't let me catch you 'round here again."

The boy ran toward a metal trailer that looked like a tin can on wheels, his pigtails bouncing. Mary hollered after him, "We'll wait right here, Leesum."

Stell Ann walked up with the kids. "What's going on?"

Mary shook her head. "That boy, he been in

106

trouble for a year. He only fifteen and he ran off from home last spring. His mama been beside herself. They in my church."

"What boy?" Stell Ann asked.

"The boy pulling the curtain in the freak show," I said.

"Where is he?"

"Putting on his clothes."

"He didn't have any clothes on?"

"He was fired. Had to take his costume off."

Leesum walked up, carrying a paper bag and wearing a filthy shirt and shorts, his bare feet dusty.

Stell stared at his hair.

"What you plan now, Leesum?" asked Mary.

"Get me 'nother job."

"And how you gone do that?"

"Go into town."

"Wouldn't you rather go home?"

"Ain't got money for a ticket, and Mama'd whup me till I couldn't walk."

"What if I bought you a bus ticket, and what if you stayed with Reverend Perkins for a while?"

Leesum looked at the ground.

"Be easier to get a job in Charlotte, where your church family is, than in Florida, don't you reckon?"

"Yes'm."

"Then come on out to Commander Bentley's. I'll see what we can do."

"Mama is going to have a duck," Stell said.

"Leave your mama to me."

As we left Joyland, we passed an open tent where a clown was sitting in front of a mirror, rubbing his makeup off. He saw me in the mirror and waved. It was the clown who gave me the rose. Under the makeup, his skin was darker than Leesum's.

We'd planned to stay at Joyland for supper, but Stell said we were leaving. "Mama's going to be mad enough when she sees that boy. If anybody who knows Uncle Taylor saw him having hot dogs with us . . ." She walked toward the parking lot. "I'll pick you up at the front gate."

Mary and Leesum got in the back with me. Puddin climbed into the front seat with Stell and helped put Davie in his canvas seat. We hadn't gone more than a couple of miles before I regretted my decision to sit so close to Leesum. He smelled like a wet dog. Mary cranked her window all the way down. I did the same thing.

"You gone get a bath, boy, soon's we get to Commander Bentley's," said Mary.

"Yes'm."

"Too bad there's no colored beach out where we staying. I'd dip you in the ocean first. Wash off the top layer of dirt."

"Yes'm." He looked at me, ashamed. I wanted Mary to be easier on him.

"Hmph." Mary grabbed at his hair. "A nappy-head boy with bobo tails."

"Mr. McCurdy wouldn't let me cut 'em."

"How come?"

"At the end of the show I takes a bow and lifts my hat. My tails pops out. Folks laugh." He stared out the window.

Mary touched his hand. "I can cut your hair nice, Leesum. Always did it for Mr. Luther and Link."

On the way home I kept thinking about the boy at the Enchanted Castle Boat Ride, pinching off pieces of blue cotton candy and putting them in his girl's mouth, her red lips closing on his fingertips.

At Uncle Taylor's, I put the limp rose in a glass of water and set it on the dinner table, hoping to revive it. Stell looked dubious.

Mary took Leesum's paper bag and dumped it on the kitchen floor by the washing machine. She pushed Leesum down the hall to the bathroom. "Hand me your clothes out the door and run that tub full of hot water."

"Yes'm."

She went up to her room, returned with her long chenille robe, and dropped it outside the bathroom door. "Here's a dressing gown for you."

After his bath, Leesum came into the kitchen wearing Mary's robe. It was miserably small, but it covered him so he'd be decent till his clothes dried. I tried not to stare at him, but he didn't seem to care. I had thought he was fairly dark, and was amazed how the bath had lightened him. His ropy hair looked dry, but water ran from it down his golden bronze face. His eyes were a hypnotizing pale green, his lips full, his teeth gleaming white. I was surprised that a colored boy was so good-looking.

Mary put Leesum's clean clothes in the dryer, then fixed supper: tuna salad sandwiches, potato chips, ice tea. None of us was crazy about tuna fish, but nobody complained. When it was ready, we all sat around the kitchen table, Leesum and Mary, too.

"How long were you with the carnival?" Stell asked.

"Leff school an went with 'em end of May." He tightened the belt on the robe.

"Where-all did y'all go?" I asked.

"Knoxville, Chatt'nooga, 'Lanta, M'gomery. Other towns we hooked up with places same as Joyland."

"How much money'd you make?"

"Fifteen dollars a week, my bed and food thrown in."

"What kind of bed and food?" asked Mary.

"A pallet in one of the wagons. When it rained I slep' on the sofa in Mr. McCurdy trailer. All the carny food I wanted."

"Ham biscuits and Co-Colas," said Mary. "That right?"

"Cotton candy," said Stell.

"Weren't so bad." He sounded like he thought we were making fun of him. "Least it was regular."

"Where Leesum live in Charlotte," said Mary, "his mama isn't working every day, money's not coming in steady."

"She do the best she can."

I wondered again about the words *ho* and *tea* and *coke*. I asked Mary, "Didn't you say Leesum could stay with reverend somebody?"

"Reverend Perkins and his wife. They take in folks who down on they luck." Mary started clearing the table. "Jubie and Stell Ann, y'all get this kitchen straightened up. Puddin, go read something to Davie. Leesum, get your clothes out the dryer and come upstairs."

We were putting the last plates in the cupboard when the front door opened.

"We're home," Mama called out. "Where's everybody?"

"The kitchen," I hollered.

Mama, Uncle Taylor, and Kay Macy Cooper came to the kitchen. Mama lit a cigarette and filled the coffeepot. Sarah walked through without saying a word and closed the back door behind her.

"Have a good time at Joyland?" Uncle Taylor asked.

"Yes, sir," Stell and I answered at the same time.

Mama pursed her lips. "What's up?"

"Nothing," we said.

"Nothing, my fanny. You two are into something."

Mrs. Cooper said, "Paula, do you have radar?"

111

"They look like they robbed Fort Knox." Mama put an ashtray on the table. "What is going on?"

I was about to speak when Mary came into the kitchen. "Good evening," she said, just as cool as could be, like it was perfectly normal that a colored boy was in the attic.

"Mary," said Mama, "what's with Jubie and Stell Ann?"

"They has done nothing wrong. It's all my doing and I can fix it, don't need no help; just want to keep him here till we can get him a ticket home and—"

"Whoa," said Uncle Taylor.

"Coffee?" asked Mama. She was planning to cope. No matter what Mary had to say, Mama would have a cup of coffee with her cigarette and she would be calm.

CHAPTER 10

M ary came to work the day after Mrs. Feaster said what she did, acting like everything was fine, but she and Mama were stiff around each other, saying only what had to be said for Mary to do her work. At first I wished they could get back to laughing and joking, but after a while I got used to their cool politeness.

Meemaw was coming to visit us in our house on Queens Road West, which she'd never seen. The night before her arrival, Mary worked late, starching the rec room curtains and rolling them to be ironed later. She hung the throw rugs over the clothesline and beat them with a broom, then went back up to the garage apartment with her cleaning supplies.

The next morning, the Electrolux cord lay coiled on the living room carpet like a snake, and the freshly ironed ivory sheers were laid out on the sofa. Tarnished flatware covered Mama's heart-of-pine dining table. Grandmother Bentley's silver service gleamed on the tea wagon in the morning light. The tang of silver polish hung in the air, mingling with the smell of pies baking. In the kitchen, Mary was kneading bread dough. "It's half past nine. How come nobody rousted you earlier?"

"I'm lucky. Where's Mama?"

"Beauty parlor. Get yourself some cereal." She nodded toward the pantry. "When you're done, I need you to fetch stuff from the freezer."

"You're bossier than Mama this morning."

"I reckon I am." She sounded pleased.

I sucked in my stomach and inched between the bar and the ironing board, where Mama's best tablecloth spilled onto a sheet spread to keep the white damask spotless. I fixed my cereal and sat at the bar. The percolator hiccupped on the stove.

"I want some coffee," I said, just to see what Mary would do.

"Your growth need stunting." She gave me a mug of half coffee, half milk.

I shook sugar into it. "When'd you last see Meemaw?"

"Year or so, when she stayed over to your aunt Rita's."

"Because she and Mama were fighting, right?"

"Where you hear that?"

"Everybody knows it." I took a sip of the coffee, added more sugar.

"I can't say if they was or not, but one didn't see much of the other, not the whole time your grandma was here. She hasn't been back since, that I knows." Mary looked out the window, shaking her head. "He this one's son and that one's husband. Womenfolks is bad not to get along."

"What you need from the freezer?"

"A quart of strawberries, another pound of

bacon, two boxes of cream corn. You want to write it down?"

"A quart of bacon, another pound of cream corn, two boxes of strawberries."

I returned to the kitchen, my arms full. Mary handed me a paper. "Your mama says you got to do these things."

I groaned. "Windex rec room windows. Sweep breezeway rug and front walk. First vacuum, then dust living room and den." I stuffed the list in my pocket. "She always reminds me to vacuum before dusting, like I'm a moron."

"My mama always said dust first. Chicken and the egg."

"You know why Meemaw has to stay in the rec room?"

Mary raised her eyebrows. She knew my question was loaded. "You reckon you know why?"

"So Mama won't have to share her bathroom."

"Hmph. You just get to the things on that list."

I looked at the clock over the kitchen sink. "Stell sure knows how to get out of work."

"She got all that silver to polish when she gets done her Bible study."

"She's better at polishing apples."

"Uh-huh." Mary handed me the Windex. She wasn't taking sides this morning.

Up in the rec room, I tuned the radio to WGIV, a jive station Mama hated. With the volume turned all the way up, I washed the windows to the Chatty Hattie Show. Leaves and grass were matted into the straw rug on the porch, and before I'd finished sweeping it, Mary came out to inspect.

"I know it's hard, but you got to go over it again. Your mama'll want every speck of red mud off that rug."

I did it again, pretending I was a parlor maid for a rich family in Boston in 1850. I wore gray uniforms with long skirts and ruffled white aprons. When I spoke to my mistress, I said, "Yes, ma'am," and curtsied. She didn't know I was going to be a mail-order bride for a silent handsome cowboy in the untamed West.

Mama came home from the beauty parlor smelling of crème rinse. She had a bouquet of mums and gladiolas in her arms. "Gee, Mama, you're gorgeous."

"Thank you, Jubie."

"What'd you get done besides your hair?"

"Got my legs waxed, a pedicure, a manicure . . ."— she put the flowers on the bar and waggled her glossy nails—"and a facial. This morning I saw dimples in my thighs. They'll sag more each day for the rest of my life. I can feel them shaking with every step." She took her cigarette case from her purse, pulled out a Camel, and tamped it on the bar. "I thought I'd never get done." She exhaled a puff of smoke with every word. "A dryer was broken and they had us stacked up, taking turns on the other two." With her thumb and ring finger she plucked a piece of tobacco from her tongue, flicked it away, and looked at her watch. "I'll go get changed. The porch and the walk look good. Is the rec room done?"

"Yes, ma'am."

"Better get going with the vacuum. It's getting late."

"Ugh."

"No sense complaining, young lady. Finish everything on that list or you'll do without supper."

I was under the sofa, trying to plug in the Electrolux, and hoping Mama didn't know about the dust bunnies, when she called from the kitchen, "Jubie, before you start, bring me the blue vase from the dining room."

I took the vase from the top shelf of the corner cabinet, blowing dust off the cobalt crystal, which shone like the sapphires in Mama's dinner ring. She had never let me pick it up and I hadn't known how heavy it was. I cradled it in my arms and took it to Mama.

With the vacuum running, I sat on the Sheraton and pushed the nozzle back and forth across the rug, jumping up when Mama came into the living room. "Let that go and help me take things to the rec room." She carried the blue vase full of flowers. I followed her with an armful of thick terry towels and our best percale sheets.

Stell came in the den door. Mama said, "Silver needs polishing, and the tablecloth has to be ironed. How was Bible Club?"

"Reverend Coonts has bad breath."

"That's a terrible thing to say about a preacher."

Stell looked at her nails, which she'd spent an hour manicuring the night before. "I'll ruin my nails if I polish silver."

"Use rubber gloves. Get to it, young lady."

Stell gave Mama a look I would have been smacked for and left the den.

"Where are you going?" Mama asked.

"To change my clothes." Stell didn't turn around.

"Estelle Annette!"

Stell stopped, her back to Mama. "What? I don't want polish on my good blouse."

"Oh, all right. C'mon, Jubie, we've got to finish."

Mama put the vase in the middle of the breakfast table in the rec room and arranged the flowers. She refolded the bath towel and hung it over the bathroom rod, then walked around touching things.

"What's that?" I pointed to wineglasses and a carafe of liquid on a tray in the kitchenette.

"Sherry." Mama wrinkled her nose. "Your grandmother wants a nip before bed." She inspected the windows. "They'll do. The room looks good, don't you think?"

"If Meemaw doesn't like it, she can stay in my room. I'd be glad to sleep here."

"Well, I'm glad we can give Cordelia her own private place." Mama stood in the middle of the room, chin in hand. She snapped her fingers, went to the closet, and tossed a lumpy bed pillow at me. "Go get your pillow. Cordelia won't sleep on anything but goose down."

When I got back with my feather pillow, Mama had moved the flowers to a table by one of the windows.

"It catches the sunlight," I said.

"It's too elegant for the rec room, but Cordelia will know we made things special for her." She nudged a gladiola into place. "Your father can't complain. I even remembered the sherry."

We went down the stairs. Mama sniffed the air. "Take a shower before you dress."

"I had a shower this morning."

"June, you do not smell like a lady."

I took the shower but didn't use soap. I put on my gray wool skirt, my white blouse with the Peter Pan collar, the red belt that matched my shoes. Then I got out the fab brooch Aunt Rita had given me and pinned it at my neck. The red jewels twinkled.

I was sitting in the queen chair when Stell came downstairs, looking just right, as usual. The den door opened. Puddin ran in. "They're here! Daddy and Meemaw."

I followed Puddin to the garage. Daddy had just opened the car door, and there was Meemaw, her face hidden by a low-brimmed brown hat. She put out her hand for Daddy to help her from the car. She was much fatter than I remembered and the top of her hat didn't reach my shoulder. "Why, June, how you've—and Carolina—you girls, you girls." She squeezed my hand. Puddin hugged her, and her skinny arms didn't go halfway around Meemaw's middle.

"My word, Carolina, you're not a baby any—so where is my grandson? Estelle, you standing there quiet—I mean, a lady. Last time, I was dizzy with your chatter." They put their arms around each other briefly. They were the same height, though I'd never thought Stell was so short.

Daddy put his hand under Meemaw's elbow and said, "Come on, Mother, let's go in the house." It was strange to hear Daddy calling someone Mother.

Meemaw waddled through the breezeway, her body swaying from side to side.

Mama met us at the den door and said, "Hello, Cordelia. It's so nice to have you." They touched cheeks.

"I'll take your coat and hat, Miz Watts." Mary stepped from behind Mama. She had on a black uniform, a starched apron, and a stiff little hat like a dollop of whipped cream plopped on her head. A maid from the movies.

Without the felt cloche and wool coat, Meemaw looked soft. Her gray hair swirled into a thick bun near the crown of her head, wisps curling around her face. In the den, she sat in Daddy's platform rocker and put her feet on the ottoman. Her leather lace-ups were doll shoes on Daddy's big footstool, and her ankles were so puffed out over the tops of her shoes I wanted to poke them.

Meemaw sighed loudly.

Daddy cleared his throat. "Paula, how about some coffee?"

Mama called over her shoulder, "Mary? Coffee, please. The service."

"Where's David?" Meemaw asked. "Thought you'd—I mean, got to be getting big."

"He's asleep," I said.

"Takes good naps, does he?"

"Usually," I said. "He's a great kid."

Mama focused on the brooch glittering at my neck. She closed her eyes and looked pained, smoothed the skirt of her amber silk, touched her gold necklace.

Mary came in carrying a tray with the silver service on it. She put everything down on the coffee table and backed out. I wished she'd stay.

Mama poured a cup of coffee and asked Meemaw, "Cream and sugar?"

Meemaw shook her head. "Don't drink it this late in the day."

Mama handed the cup to Daddy. "How was your trip, Cordelia?"

"It'd be nice if we got what we paid—I mean,

bumping along in a train car since early this morning."

Nobody said anything while Meemaw sat and rocked slightly, the reading lamp behind her, her hair shining.

Daddy said, "Was your compartment okay?"

"Might have been. Wish I'd been left in peace."

"We booked a private compartment."

"You couldn't know they would—I mean, people just barge."

Everyone waited for her to finish, but she sat there with her hands clasped across her stomach.

Mama asked, "Cordelia, are you saying somebody shared your compartment?"

"Three of them. Came in and made theirselfs comfortable."

"Why didn't you report them to the conductor?" asked Daddy.

" 'Twas his idea. Train was crowded. He asked if I'd mind sharing—a woman and her two children. Her daddy had died from his heart—so a mercy trip, you know. What can you say, if you—I mean, they gave me a voucher for when I go home." She reached to the floor, where she'd set her pocketbook, fished around in it, and held up a paper.

Daddy took it from her, "A free ticket. Mother, that's really nice."

"I couldn't nap or read. Stared out the window and cried, paid them no mind."

"You were crying?" Mama said.

Meemaw snorted. "The mother, not me."

"Did the kids behave?" I asked.

"Boy sat next to me. She just put him—kicked his feet against the seat. The girl—about your age, June—hummed 'Tennessee Waltz' and 'Some Enchanted Evening'—not a tune in a bucket, neither."

"You must be worn out, Cordelia," Mama said. "Why don't we get you settled before dinner." She turned to Daddy. "Are your mother's things still in the car?"

Meemaw cleared her throat. "I just got the one. Travel light, always have."

Daddy started to rise. "I'll get it."

Mama put a hand on his knee. "No need, William. Stell, you and Jubie show your grandmother to her room. Carry her bag up for her and help her get settled. It'll be an hour and a half until dinner, Cordelia, which will give you a nice rest."

Puddin jumped up. "I'm going, too, Meemaw. All your granddaughters can help."

Stell put out her hand for Meemaw to stand. I ran ahead. "We'll get the suitcase. C'mon, Puddin."

I got Meemaw's bag from the car, ran up to the rec room, and put it on the luggage rack.

At the top of the stairs, Meemaw held her hand to her chest. "Where's the ladies—I mean . . ."

"The door in the corner." I pointed.

"Got to take—my arthritis. Should have before now." She closed the bathroom door behind her.

"What's arthur-itis?" Puddin sat on the sofa.

"Her joints don't work right," Stell said.

The bathroom door opened and Meemaw swayed into the room, trailing the scent of rosewater cologne. She opened her suitcase and handed each of us a gift-wrapped package. "Here you are, girls." Meemaw sat down next to Puddin.

"How nice," Stell said, opening the envelope that was Scotch-taped to her gift. The word *Granddaughter* was printed in glitter on the front of the card. Inside Stell's package was a silver charm bracelet. "Oh! I love it." She jumped up to hug Meemaw.

"I'll give you charms—Christmas and your birthday."

"I'm next!" Puddin pulled at the wrapping paper and Stell said, "The card, Puddin."

"Oops." Puddin read her card, mumbled, "Thank you," and ripped the package open. Pastel hair ribbons spilled onto the floor. "Meemaw! How'd you know my hair was long enough?"

"Asked Rita. Tomorrow I'll weave one into a braid for you." Meemaw sat back. "Now you, June."

I read the plain note card first. On the front was a verse in Meemaw's spidery handwriting: *Roses are red. Violets are blue. Flowers are sweet. You can be, too.* Inside she'd written, *This is something to help.* I wasn't sure what that meant, but I said, "Thank you, Meemaw."

My gift was a tin of deodorant powder and two metal sticks with hooks on the end. "What are these?"

"Crochet hooks. I'll teach you while I'm here. And the powder tin has directions."

"I know how to use talcum."

"Read it, you'll see." Meemaw settled into the sofa cushions, her eyes closed, sighing, "Oh, Lord." She said, "One of you—I mean, my shoelaces . . ."

Stell and Puddin kneeled and untied the leather shoes and I helped Meemaw stretch out. I got the plaid blanket from the ottoman and spread it over her. I think she was asleep before we were halfway down the stairs.

I sat at my dresser and read the back of the powder tin. "Use liberally under arms and in intimate areas to stifle body odor and prevent alarming rashes. Contains essence of gardenias for discreet allure." Did Meemaw think I had BO? I put the tin in my dresser drawer, thinking about all the fuss people made over body smells. Mama sometimes told Mary to use more deodorant, but I liked all the ways Mary smelled—whether of soap or sweat or her Cashmere Bouquet talcum.

I was combing my hair when Mama's voice floated up the stairway, calling Puddin, Stell, and me to her bedroom. She shut the door and sat on the side of the bed, tapping a cigarette into an ashtray on the nightstand. "Be on your best behavior. Use your manners. Remember about the forks; we put out all three. The spoon at the top of your place setting—"

"For dessert," Stell said.

"That's right. And don't get mad at Davie if he spills something. Jubie, where in God's name did you get that brooch? Come here."

"Aunt Rita gave it to me."

She unpinned the brooch. "Get my short pearls from my jewelry box."

I handed Mama the pearls and watched in the mirror as she fastened them. I looked like Stell Ann had dressed me.

"Be as good as you can be." Mama jabbed the cigarette out. Puddin crawled into her lap and said, "I'll be the goodest girl in the world." Mama kissed Puddin's blonde curls. One of the new ribbons was tied in a bow and bobby-pinned to Puddin's hair.

Mama said, "I know you will, Puddin-tane." I couldn't remember Mama ever kissing me and holding me that way.

Mama scooted Puddin onto the floor and reached for the Sen-Sen she kept in the drawer of her nightstand. She popped one of the mints in her mouth and sucked on it. "Cordelia knows I smoke, but she doesn't approve, and I want her to think about it as little as possible." She was spritzing herself with Old English Lavender when Daddy opened the door. He had a drink in his hand.

"How many is that, Bill?"

"I'm just having a toddy before we eat. Let's get along, okay?"

"Okay, Billy Boy. How can I be rude to your mother when I have no idea what she's saying?" She smirked at Daddy and said, *"I mean,"* in perfect imitation of Meemaw.

Stell motioned me with a jerk of her head. I took Puddin's hand and pulled her out the door.

In the hallway, Stell said, "Lord, help us make it through the night."

We went to the living room. Stell sat on the sofa and crossed her legs at the ankles, adjusting her skirt so it covered her knees, just the sort of prissy thing she did when she was nervous. She had on her new bracelet. I sat in the queen chair, and Puddin squeezed in with me. She leaned against me and asked, "Why does Meemaw call us June and Carolina instead of Jubie and Puddin?"

"Old ladies don't use nicknames."

Mary lit the candles on the dinner table. "The other Miz Watts, she hasn't showed up yet. Somebody better fetch her."

Mama came to the living room. "Jubie, run tell your grandmother supper's ready."

I knocked on the door to the garage apartment,

and Meemaw called out, "Come on up," in her whiny old voice.

"Hey, Meemaw. Supper's ready."

"Why don't you all begin without me?"

She was on the sofa, plaid blanket spread over her, exactly as we'd left her, except for the half-empty carafe on the coffee table.

"We'd rather wait for you."

"Maybe you'd better bring me a tray. I'm worn out from traveling and climbing those stairs."

"Mama thought that you'd rather have this apartment all to yourself, with your own bathroom. I'll help you with the stairs. We could work out a signal—"

"June, I believe I'm too tired to—just fix me a tray. I'm an old woman."

"Yes, ma'am."

"And not much food—delicate appetite."

As I went through the garage, I wanted to go on out to the street and cut through backyards to Maggie's house and hide under her bed. When I walked into the dining room alone, Daddy said, "Where's Mother?" at the same time Mama said, "Well?"

"Meemaw asked if we'd fix her a tray. She doesn't feel well."

"I do not believe this," Mama said.

"She told me the stairs were too much for her," I said.

"Her bedroom's on the second floor at home."

Daddy pushed back his chair and got up. "Is she sick?"

"I knew she'd pull something," Mama said.

"She's old and tired. She's not pulling anything."

"She's only sixty-seven. And she has never liked me. You know it."

"Oh, come on, she's just—"

"She never calls me by name; have you noticed?"

Davie clinked his silver cup on the tray of his high chair.

Stell looked down at her plate.

Daddy stood in the den doorway, holding his linen napkin. "I really think I should go up and see—"

"That's exactly what she wants." Mama's voice was sharp. There were tears in her eyes.

Daddy threw his napkin on the buffet. "I'd rather have a crust of bread in peace than a feast in strife." He stormed out.

"Where are you going?" Mama called.

"In search of tranquility." The breezeway door slammed shut.

Mary walked into the dining room. "You want me to carry a tray to the other Miz Watts?"

Daddy's car door slammed.

"I don't care." Mama stood. "I just don't care." She left the dining room.

"Oh, Lord," said Stell softly.

Out in the street, Daddy's tires squealed as he turned onto Queens Road West.

I looked at Mary. "Meemaw said she didn't want much."

"Much? Hmph." She went to the kitchen.

"I'm hungry," said Puddin.

Davie banged his high chair.

I moved to Daddy's place and sliced the ham. Stell ladled pineapple sauce over the slices as I passed the plates around. I put a heaping spoonful of creamed corn on Puddin's plate, knowing how she loved it, and Stell dished out the Kentucky Wonders that Mama had cooked especially for Meemaw. We ate our supper by candlelight, droplets of water making tracks down the crystal goblets and pooling in the sterling coasters. The flames flickered when Mary walked through the dining room with a tray covered by a linen tea towel.

CHAPTER 11

Mary came into Uncle Taylor's kitchen with Leesum. He was dressed in his own clothes again, which were in pretty bad shape, even clean. He was barefoot, and his hair, now that it was dry, stuck out from his head worse than ever.

"This Leesum Fields, from Charlotte," said Mary. "I will cut his hair in the morning."

Nobody said anything.

"Or this evening."

"That would be nice," said Mama. "Now. What is he doing here?"

"He in my church family back home. He a boy with trouble and we come on him and I wouldn't leave him to fend for hisself and we got to let him sleep here till—"

"Mary!" Mama took Mary's hand. "Calm down. What are you talking about?"

"At that carnival, we—he the son of a lady in my church. He got no place to stay nor nothing to eat. He only fifteen. Can sleep on a pallet on the floor. . . ."

"Y'all please have a seat," said Kay Macy Cooper.

"Not you two," said Mama to Stell and me. "Go watch TV. Or put Puddin and Davie to bed. Something. Just stay out of here."

An hour later, Mama went to her room and closed the door. I looked for Mary. She had Leesum on a stool on the back patio, a sheet tied around his neck.

"Wisht you'd let me see what you doin'," Leesum said as Mary cut off the snaky ropes of hair.

"And I wisht I had me a pick and some barber shears. Pomade would be real nice, come to it."

Stell walked past, toward the cabana.

I asked Mary, "Do you mind if I stay and watch?"

"Not if Leesum don't mind."

"S'okay." He tried to look at me, but Mary grabbed him by the chin to keep him still.

She had a rat-tailed comb and a pair of kitchen scissors. She stuck the rat tail into a rope of hair and pulled it as far from Leesum's scalp as she could before cutting. His eyes followed the pieces of hair to the flagstone patio.

"You snatchin' me bald?"

"I'll even it out. I believe you'll be right pleased."

"I be pleased to be done with them locks, that's for sure."

Mary took the cloth from around Leesum's neck and snapped it in the gulf breeze.

I had little hope for the recovery of his hair, which stuck out from his head in short prickly points.

Mary pulled a nylon hose from her pocket. "Before bed, damp your hair good. Then slip this stocking over your head and sleep in it."

Leesum nodded like he knew all about nylon nightcaps.

"I'll get a broom so's you can sweep up this mess." Mary went through the back porch to the kitchen.

Leesum looked toward the gulf, a deep blue-green in the dusk. "I'm gone get up before anybody tomorrow so's I can go in that water. Been wantin' to, but Mr. McCurdy never gave me time off, said they wasn't no colored beach nohow. But I'm goin' in it." He stared out at the gulf the whole time, not talking to me.

I heard Mary coming through the back porch. "Scratch on my screen." I pointed at the cabana. "I'll go with you."

At six thirty in the morning Leesum scratched on the screen. I grabbed my bathing suit, waved to him, and went into the bathroom. When I left the cabana, Stell and Sarah were still sound asleep. Leesum was waiting, a tall silhouette in the early light.

"Hey," he said. His curly hair was smooth and neat. Mary had done a good job.

"I'd still be sleeping if you hadn't waked me."

"I'm a mornin' person."

I couldn't think of such a grown-up thing to

say about myself. I ran ahead, over the dunes. "C'mon!"

Before we got to the water he stopped. "I'm a good swimmer." His eyes were large and round, his skin tawny. "Ain't never been in no ocean."

"It's smooth this morning. Easy to float in, once you get past the whitecaps."

"What're them?"

"The foamy water where the waves break."

He studied the surf. "You go on. I'll watch a bit."

I dove through the waves, coming up on the other side of the breakers, and stood in chest-deep water, beckoning him. He ran toward me, doing exactly as I had done, pointing his arms above his head and diving into the breakers. He came up beside me, sputtering. "You dint tell me 'bout no salt."

I grinned and swam away from him. He came right after me and I saw that he'd told the truth about being a good swimmer. I flipped onto my back. "See how easy it is to float in salt water?"

He spread his arms and legs. "That's really sumpin. Can't never float in the Catawba, where I goes swimmin' back home."

Silence settled on us while we floated. I could have hung there in the water with Leesum forever. He broke the spell. "Miss June?"

"Ye gods, call me Jubie."

"That don't seem right."

"Because I'm white?"

"Yes'm."

"Don't ma'am me. You're older than I am."

"Some things matters." He treaded water, facing me.

"Call me Jubie when we're alone, okay?"

"Okay, Miss—okay, Jubie. Can I ax you sumpin?"

"Sure."

"Why's you legs so banged up?"

His question surprised me as much as my answer. "My daddy whipped me."

"How come?"

"I read Stell's diary to her boyfriend."

"What's a diary?"

"A book where she writes her private thoughts. It was a terrible thing to do."

"Ain't like you broke a commandment."

I laughed. Leesum was saying what I did wasn't all that bad.

"What's so funny?"

"Just nothing. Is Leesum your nickname?"

He dove under. I felt him brush by my feet and he came up on the other side of me, blowing like a whale. "My mama gave me that name. She say I was the nearest thing to heaven so she call me Leesum, get it?"

"No."

"Leesum Fields. Another name for heaven. Paradise. Sumpin like 'at."

"You told Mary your mama was a hoe."

His face got hard. "What of it?"

"I—well—it doesn't make sense. A hoe is a garden tool."

"We been in different places, Miss June—Jubie. I been right here on earth and you been on the moon." He dove underwater again and was gone for quite a while, long enough for me to get worried. He surfaced fifteen or twenty yards away, kicking his feet and blowing spray into the air. He swam hard using several different strokes before he turned a wide circle and swam back to me in a strong, rhythmic butterfly with a double-dolphin kick. His muscular shoulders gleamed in the sunlight. When he got to me, he was breathing hard.

"Where in the world did you learn the fly?"

"Boy where I worked at Rozzelle's Ferry House . . . he were a student at J. C. Smith . . . the college . . . he showed me." He caught his breath. "Say I were a natural." I put out my hand to touch his oddly dry-looking hair. He jerked back.

"I wanted to see if your hair was as dry as it looks."

"Course it ain't dry. It just don't slick down the way yours do."

"May I feel it, please?"

"Yeah, since you ax me so nice."

It was wet and soft. I'd thought it would be wiry, like a Brillo pad. "So what's a hoe?"

"You know what a prostitute is?"

I felt a tingle of shock. "A whore. So your mama—" I couldn't finish the sentence.

He shrugged. "I was born when she was seventeen, and she ain't but thirty-two now. She has took care me best she could; wouldn't never put me in a orphanage."

"And the tea and coke?"

"Marijuana and cocaine. You ever done 'em?"

"No." I shook my head. "No, no, no-no-no-no, NO!"

"And what would your daddy do if he found you smokin' tea and sniffin' coke?"

"He'd kill me!"

"He the one bad." He went under again and came up a few feet away.

I heard Davie and saw him playing in the surf with Mary, who was dunking him up and down in the shallow water. Every time a wave came in, they whooped and jumped over it. She had kicked her shoes off. Her uniform was wet halfway up her thighs.

"Hey, Jubie girl!" she said when I got to them. "We gone make us a sand castle." She looked past me. "You and the boy been swimming."

I glanced over my shoulder. Leesum was walking toward us in the shallow water.

"We came out early."

"Uh-huh. Don't reckon nobody else would've gone with him."

Davie grabbed Mary's hand. "Mary! Shell."

Leesum and I started gathering shells. We all got outside of Uncle Taylor's beach. Mary was at the edge of the water, bent over and digging at the wet sand with her hands when Mrs. Willingham walked up. "Be careful, Mary. This is a white beach, you know."

Mary straightened and left the water. "Yes, ma'am." She looked up and down the beach. There was no one else out.

"Not that I mind," said Mrs. Willingham, "not one bit. But others'd get mighty upset if they were to see you or that boy."

"Yes, ma'am."

"And he needs to get some clothes on. Almost naked." She looked at Leesum like he was a bug she wanted to step on.

"I'll tell him."

"I understand Taylor's sending him home today."

Mary looked at me. "We making arrangements, yes, ma'am."

"Well, that's good." Mrs. Willingham smiled her fake smile. "The law's the law. We've had troubles here with folks forgetting who they are, so it's better if we just keep things separate." She looked at the shell in Mary's hand. "Now that's real pretty."

"For the castle." Mary put her shoes on. I didn't see her outside the fences for the rest of the week, and not once again did she take her shoes off.

138

CHAPTER 12

Uncle Taylor and Mama were talking about Leesum as I came up from the cabana.

"He can't stay here, Taylor."

"I know, but I want to help him."

"How? Adopt him?" Mama's lighter snapped open, clinked shut. "Mary's going to call her pastor—preacher, whatever he is. It's all arranged."

Mama wouldn't believe how sad I was that Leesum was leaving. All summer I'd wanted to meet a nice boy, and the ones I'd seen were creeps or stuck-up. Now there was Leesum, with those mystery green eyes, golden skin, and curly hair that looked dry in the gulf.

After breakfast Uncle Taylor took Leesum to the naval base to buy him clothes and a bag for the trip to Charlotte. We didn't have a chance to say another word to each other. I went to the kitchen and asked Mary, "Is Leesum going back to Charlotte?"

"He is. I'm going to talk to Reverend Perkins. The boy'll be just fine, don't you worry."

"Okay." I left the kitchen and went to Uncle Taylor's den, where I'd seen a thesaurus. I sat in his easy chair with the heavy book in my lap and looked up synonyms for *heaven* and *paradise*.

I was sitting in the damp sand, dribbling it through my fingers into cone-shaped towers that became shapeless mounds when waves washed over them. Sarah came over the dunes and said hey. She shook out her blanket next to my towel and took a pair of binoculars from around her neck.

I got up and went to her, startled by her friendliness. "Hey."

Her hair was pulled up into a knot, and her ears stuck out above her skinny neck and knobby shoulders. She had on a bathing suit and voluminous Bermuda shorts that enveloped her matchstick legs.

I said, "I don't remember you wearing glasses."

"I've only had them six months."

"Did your eyes get bad all of a sudden?"

"I've been nearsighted for ages. Nobody figured it out until Mrs. Cooper."

"How'd she know?"

"I kept bumping into stuff. Daddy thought I was just awkward, but Mrs. Cooper . . ." she pushed at her glasses. "Sorry I've been a pill."

"That's okay." I smoothed my beach towel.

"I just don't want to talk about it." Her voice had the same final tone Mama used. "Look over there." Sarah handed me the binoculars and pointed at Mrs. Willingham in her canvas beach lounge.

I focused the binoculars. "What's she eating?"

"Candy."

I couldn't think of anything more boring than watching a fat lady eat candy. I handed the glasses back and told Sarah how mean Mrs. Willingham had been to Mary and Leesum that morning.

"She can be horrible, but Daddy always takes up for her."

I'd left out the part about me swimming with Leesum. Sometimes I didn't want to talk, either. I put my head down on my arms, letting the sun soak into my back, thinking about him.

"She's reaching in her bag for a Coke," Sarah said. "You should see her lounge. Stains all over it."

A voice thundered, "Sarah Dolores!"

I shaded my eyes against the sun and looked up. Uncle Taylor loomed over us. He took the binoculars. "Spying on Mrs. Willingham?"

"We were watching her eat candy," I said.

Uncle Taylor held the binoculars to his eyes. He was in uniform—a short-sleeved khaki shirt and trousers—standing like an officer on the deck of a ship, fiddling with the focus ring, making a sweep of the beach. "Trash patrol."

Sarah groaned.

"What's trash patrol?"

"Sarah will show you."

"How much?" Sarah asked.

"Ours, hers, and theirs," Uncle Taylor said, pointing west.

"We weren't hurting her."

"You were stealing her privacy."

"She's sitting right out there on the beach, for all the world to see."

"Tell you what. Go sit right next to her and watch her."

"Jubie just told me what Mrs. Willingham did to—"

Uncle Taylor cut her off. "We'll talk about it later."

"What if she asks me why we're doing her beach?"

"Tell her it's neighborly love."

As Uncle Taylor turned to leave, I said, "I thought your uniform was white."

"I have a white dress uniform. Where'd you see it?"

"We have a photo in the living room at home."

"From my graduation, I guess."

"I like the one you have on, too."

"Thank you, Miss June." He took off his hat and bowed to me. I watched him walk back to the house, taking high arcing steps to keep sand from getting in his shiny shoes.

"Dad'll do an inspection when we're done. If he finds a toothpick, we'll have to add another chunk of beach."

We went to the kitchen for grocery bags to put the trash in, and I looked around for Leesum but didn't see him.

Cellophane from Nabs, cigarette butts, soda

bottles, a bloody Band-Aid. I put a candy wrapper over my fingers to pick it up and put it in the bag.

As we picked up trash, I asked Sarah, "Will you get a spanking?"

"What for?"

"Spying on Mrs. Willingham."

"Trash patrol is for that."

"Doesn't your daddy spank you?"

"He says he's going to, but he never does."

Yellow plates were set around the white kitchen table for lunch. Ham sandwiches on rye bread filled a platter next to a bowl of slaw. A plate with slices of cantaloupe and honeydew sat on the lazy Susan with a basket of potato chips, a dish of tomatoes, and yellow salt and pepper shakers. A perfect picture of a lovely lunch. I put ice in glasses while Sarah called everybody to eat, and Mary came along behind me, pouring tea.

Uncle Taylor switched on the attic fan, propping open the door to the screen porch, and the paper napkins fluttered as we sat down. Mary and Leesum took their plates to a table on the porch. When we bowed our heads for Uncle Taylor to say the blessing, I squinted through my eyelids at Leesum. His eyes were closed, his hands together under his chin. He took praying seriously.

Over lunch nobody said much. As we finished, Sarah asked her father, "Now can I tell you what Mrs. Willingham did?"

"You may." Uncle Taylor turned to Sarah, giving her his full attention. Daddy wouldn't listen to me for more than a minute.

"All Mary was doing was walking on the beach, and Mrs. Willingham told her to stop, and for Leesum to get dressed, and things have to be separate."

"When was this?"

Sarah asked me, "When, Jubie?"

I looked at my plate. "Early this morning."

Uncle Taylor asked me, "Were you there?"

"Yes, sir. We were gathering shells for a sand castle."

"You and who else?"

"Me and Davie, Mary and Leesum. Mary walked in the water on Mrs. Willingham's beach."

"And what was Leesum wearing?"

"Shorts."

Uncle Taylor turned in his chair to speak to Leesum. "Is that right, Leesum?"

"Yessuh."

"And did you go in the gulf?"

"Some." Leesum looked at me.

"Did Mrs. Willingham see you in the water?"

"Don't think so. Leastways she dint say she did."

Uncle Taylor turned back to me. "What did Mrs. Willingham say?"

"That Mary shouldn't be in the water, that it's against the law."

He took his napkin from his lap and wiped his

mouth. "Mrs. Willingham is a lonely woman with too much time on her hands. Negroes scare her. She worries about her property value." Daddy never explained things the way Uncle Taylor did, speaking to us as if we were adults.

Uncle Taylor turned in his seat and spoke to Leesum and Mary. "I'm sorry for what happened. She's right about the law, but most people are pretty relaxed about hired help." He cleared his throat. "Uh, Mary, what did your minister say when you called?"

"He be happy to have Leesum stay with him for a while. They's a bus at five this evening that gets to Charlotte tomorrow night. Reverend Perkins'll be there to meet it."

So it was decided. I hoped Leesum knew how sorry I was that he was leaving.

Mama, Uncle Taylor, and Kay Macy Cooper were going for bridge that afternoon at the officers' club with Mrs. Willingham. "She's an incredible bridge player," Uncle Taylor said. Mama groaned.

Mrs. Cooper said, "Taylor, you're too kind. She's lucky. That double finesse she pulled last week . . ."

"She counts cards. That's skill."

"Why do you defend her?"

"Skipper Willingham saved my hide more than once. His widow's a narrow-minded biddy, but I watch out for her."

Uncle Taylor wanted to take Leesum to the bus

station, but the schedule would've messed up their plans, and Stell was dying to drive the Packard. Uncle Taylor said, "You'll be fine, Stell Ann. It'll be broad daylight. Take Mary and Jubie with you, and let Mary get out with Leesum to buy his ticket. You and Jubie lock the car and stay in it. If you have any trouble, look for a policeman, an MP, anyone in uniform. Everybody knows me."

I spent a lot of time getting ready for the trip to town. My yellow cotton sundress was great with my tan, and for once my hair did exactly what I wanted it to. When I looked in the mirror, I knew I was pretty. I ached to ride in back with Leesum, but that couldn't be. I knew the rules and I hated them. On the ride across the bay and into Pensacola, I kept sneaking glances at him, catching him looking at me. He liked me as much as I liked him.

At the station, there were sailors everywhere. When Stell pulled up in front of the bus station, I got out and she shrieked, as I knew she would, "Where are you going?"

"Inside with Mary, to say a proper good-bye to Leesum."

"You are not! I'll tell Mama."

Mary said, "Estelle Annette, I'll take care of her." When Mary used our full names, we listened.

Inside the station, Mary told us, "Y'all go over

by the door to the buses. I'll get the ticket."

Leesum and I walked to double doors marked DEPARTURES. Next to the doors was a sign, NEGROES BOARD LAST. We stood there, the backs of our hands touching like everything was okay, looking at each other. I said, "Your name does mean heaven. Elysium or elysian fields. I looked it up."

"Wonder where my mama heard that."

"Maybe at church."

He said, "You the prettiest girl I ever knowed."

I couldn't think what to say.

"I probably ain't never gone see you again, but I ain't never gone forget you."

"Me, neither."

"If you want, you could write me a letter sometime."

I tried not to show how happy that made me. "Where?"

"McDowell Street Baptist Church, McDowell Street, Charlotte."

"Okay."

"You know I can't write you back."

"Yes."

"I can write. Just you can't be gettin' no letters from me."

"I know."

Mary tapped my shoulder. "Bus leaves in ten minutes. We better go." She handed Leesum his ticket.

As Mary and I walked through the crowded station, I looked back at Leesum until I couldn't see him anymore.

That night Uncle Taylor took us all down to the beach to lie on blankets under the stars. A steady breeze blew in from the water, bending the sea grass, and jazz music drifted over the dunes. Lights from a ship moved slowly across the gulf.

I lay back under the stars, thinking about the kind of music Leesum listened to. In my mind I was already writing him a letter.

"Oh, Taylor, how delightful this is," Mama said. "If I lived here, I'd be on the beach every night."

"Lucky there's a gulf wind," said Uncle Taylor. "Otherwise you'd be cursing the mosquitoes."

"Look!" Stell cried. "A falling star."

"Star," said Davie.

I made a wish about Leesum.

"A meteorite, actually," Uncle Taylor said. "There are a lot of them in August."

I smelled the lemony scent of his aftershave.

"I could sleep here," Mama said.

"Polaris, the North Star!" Sarah said. "And Ursa Major, the Big Dipper."

"The Milky Way." I gazed at the cloudy trail of stars across the sky. Where was Leesum on his long trip back to Charlotte? Did he have a window seat? Could he see the Milky Way, too?

Uncle Taylor was saying, "That's right, our galaxy. Visible from dusk to dawn."

"Taylor's always been able to read the sky," Mama said. "Ever since he was your age, Sarah."

"And my big sister's always bragged on me."

I loved the sound of his voice. What would it be like to be his daughter?

CHAPTER 13

Every spring Mama brought out the hand-cranked ice cream freezer and had Mary take it apart to make sure the wooden paddles hadn't rotted over the winter. In June, when strawberries appeared at the A&P, we began our weekly trips to Jackson's Ice House for rock salt and bag ice so Mama could make ice cream. When we got there, I looked across McDowell Street at the House of Prayer for All People, and the place where Daddy Grace stayed when he came to town—a red, white, and blue mansion with music floating from upstairs windows . . . a choir, a piano, tambourines, drums.

At Jackson's, men wearing heavy gloves used tongs to lift the dripping frozen blocks from a conveyor belt, stacking them into walls of ice in the delivery trucks lined up at the loading dock. Sweat ran down their faces, summer or winter. Puddin pestered the workers for slivers of ice and I shivered nearby, staring at the House of Prayer parsonage. Colored people dressed in their finest went up stone steps to a wraparound porch. I thought about climbing those steps, knocking on the door, being the only white person going into such a place.

One Saturday when we were at Jackson's, I saw a gray-haired Negro in a cream-colored suit in a rocking chair on the porch of the mansion. People milled around him, visiting with one another, overflowing onto the steps and into the front yard. Boys fanned the man as he rocked. He had a thin mustache, black curved lines that started at his nostrils and flared out over his top lip. From time to time he raised a knuckle to his face and nudged the tips of the mustache, first one side, then the other.

Daddy came to get me and he looked across the street. "What a mess." On the way home he said, "The niggers donate their hard-earned money, and it's not even a real church. Daddy Grace, what kind of name is that? He's Daddy Give-Me-All-You-Got. I hear he's got a belt buckle made of solid gold."

Stell was fascinated with the House of Prayer. When she read in the paper about the annual parade for Daddy Grace, she begged Mama and Daddy to let her go. "I want to learn about other religions. Jubie can come, too. Mary can take us." She talked about it for days.

Mama said Stell was worse than water wearing away a rock. "I guess there's no harm in just a parade. Let me tell your father."

I was ready early, sitting in the kitchen, drinking a Coke, when Mary walked in, cloth violets on the lapel of her purple dress, her chestnut hair pinned up under a pillbox hat of flowers—mauve,

151

scarlet, lilac. Her eyes shone and rhinestones twinkled at her ears. She smelled of Cashmere Bouquet.

"You look beautiful," I told her.

"Thank you. Where's Stell Ann?"

"Here I am." Stell had on her pink cashmere cardigan, draped over the shoulders of her beige linen dress. She wore wrist gloves and carried a pocketbook that matched her beige heels.

"You a fine young lady," said Mary. "And you looking good, too, Jubie."

I was a mud hen in my brown corduroy jumper and white blouse. I stared down at my patent leather Mary Janes. They made my feet look bigger than ever.

We got on the Number 3 bus to ride downtown. Stell and I sat on the bench seat behind the driver, and Mary walked to the back. Her skinny calves and big purple shoes made me think of Minnie Mouse. A yellow line across the floor of the bus separated the front from the back. Farther toward the rear, the faded remains of an earlier line crossed the rubber floor mat. When the bus company realized there were lots more coloreds riding the buses than whites, they moved the line forward a few feet. Even so, the back of the bus was packed. A boy stood so Mary could sit. Stell and I, the only whites, were alone among the empty seats in front.

We got off the bus at McDowell and East Third,

near the House of Prayer. Mary led us through a crush of people to a place she said would be the best for watching the parade. A few white spectators stood out in the sea of dark faces, and on every corner, white policemen watched the crowd.

Mary stopped. "This is good." She looked up, squinting her eyes in the sunlight. "Hardly ever rains on Daddy Grace."

I'd never seen so many colored people in one place, and all of them in their Sunday best—men in suits and ties, women in dresses, hats, and heels. They lined up along the curb, two and three deep, with children closest to the street so they could see, and older people sitting in chairs.

Mary leaned out. "Here they come!"

Colored girls in white dresses walked down the street, dignified, their faces solemn, tossing what I thought were scraps of paper. Little girls toddled alongside teenagers. One of the scraps fell at my feet. A flower petal. A group of boys followed, clapping their hands and dancing to the rhythm of the band behind them. "His Eye Is on the Sparrow," fast, loud. From around a corner, seven men playing trumpets and trombones joined the parade, dancing as they played, their horns swinging wildly in time with the music.

Across the street a policeman was putting handcuffs on a colored man who talked over his shoulder, shaking his head.

"What's happening?" I asked Mary.

"Probably drunk, but maybe not. Sometimes they just takes them."

The street filled with people dancing, singing, jumping off the curb and back up again in twos and threes on the sidewalks, in yards, on porches, clapping and swaying to the music.

I saw a man pull a bottle from his suit jacket and pass it around. A woman behind him tapped his shoulder and shook her head. He pushed her aside and took another drink.

I felt a sudden wetness in my panties. I tugged at Mary's sleeve. "I got the curse and I don't have anything with me."

"My goodness. Stay here. I be right back." She walked away, looking around, then called out, "Sister Coley?"

Stell asked, "Where's Mary going?"

"To find a bathroom."

Mary came up behind me. "This Miz Coley; she live right there. You go on with her. Sister Coley, this Miss June Watts."

A tiny woman said, "How do. Come right with me." I followed her, hoping I'd be back in time to see Daddy Grace.

Mrs. Coley took me up tall brick steps, across a porch. What would Mama think if she could see me going into a colored person's house? Mrs. Coley was so dark-skinned that in the dim hallway her eyes and teeth seemed to jump out of her face.

154

"The bathroom's just down the hall. I'll bring what you need."

The door she'd pointed to opened into an enormous, sunny bathroom, filled with light that bounced off tile walls and floor. A photo of a white-haired colored woman hung over the toilet. Violets in ceramic pots sat on the sills of the windows to either side of the sink. A fresh, sweet odor. Mama would love this bathroom.

"Miss Watts?" Mrs. Coley held a paper bag through the doorway. "I brought you what you need. You can use the bag for your panties."

"I'm sorry you're missing the parade."

"I'm going right back out. Take as long as you need."

The underpants Mrs. Coley brought were a little big, but the sanitary belt and napkin were the same as what I had at home. I left the house, closing the door behind me, carrying the paper bag. Two colored girls, teenagers, stood at the bottom of the steps.

The taller girl was all in lime green—hat, dress, and pocketbook. She teetered on green high heels. Her hands were on her hips and she glowered from under the floppy brim of her hat. "What you doin' in Miz Coley's house?"

The other girl, shorter, with a red hat and a mass of black curls, stepped forward. "What you got in that bag?"

I backed up a step or two, looking around for Mrs. Coley. "I had to use the bathroom."

The tall girl said, "And the bag?"

Mary stepped between the girls. "Hey, June."

The girl in the red hat said to Mary, "You know her?"

Mary took my hand. "This Miss June Watts."

"What she been doin' in Miz Coley's house?" the girl in green asked.

Mary looked at her. "Is Valora okay these days?"

The tall girl said, "You know my mama?"

Mary held out her hand. "I'm Sister Luther from McDowell Street Baptist. Your mama's a friend from when I were at the House of Prayer."

The girl looked down at the sidewalk.

"I believe everything all right now." Mary took my arm and we walked back to the curb.

I looked around for Mrs. Coley to thank her again but couldn't see her in the mass of people.

"You okay?" Mary looked at the paper bag.

"Yes." I wadded up the bag and stuffed it in my purse.

Two yellow convertibles came down McDowell side by side. Colored men sat across the tops of the backseats, with more men in front, all waving.

"Fathers of the church," said Mary. "Yessuh, Deacon McHone," she shouted, waving to one of the men. He waved back.

I almost didn't recognize George McHone. He had on a navy suit, a green bow tie, and a white shirt. It didn't seem possible he was the same man who cut our grass.

A group of women in choir robes marched down the street, singing slow and mournful, *"Shall we gather at the river?"* I heard someone right behind me, and turned. People had filled the space between us and the stone wall, and were pressing forward to see the parade. A woman tapped Mary on the shoulder. "Afternoon, Sister Luther."

"Sister French," Mary said. "You looking good." The air smelled of tobacco and perfume.

How many people who belonged to Myers Park Country Club would ever get to see such a sight as the Daddy Grace parade? This was Stell's idea, something I wouldn't have thought of, and I was glad to have her as a sister. I looked at her. Her cheeks were red, her hazel eyes shining, her honey-brown bangs plastered to her forehead. She snapped her fingers, moving her feet to the music, utterly happy.

Another band marched by, all brass, playing "When the Saints Go Marching In" as if it were a trumpeted announcement from God.

"Here he come," said Mary, "Bishop Grace." A white Cadillac convertible, trimmed in gold instead of chrome, went by so slowly I could see the crowns on the hubcaps. Daddy Grace sat in the backseat, his arms raised, the same as Jesus blessing the multitudes. I recognized him as the man I'd seen on the front porch of the House of Prayer. His hands tapered off to fingernails so long they curled under at the end. How did he dial the telephone or button his shirts? There was no way he could pick his nose. The driver and two other men in tuxedos sat in the front seat, looking back and forth at the crowd.

"His bodyguards," Mary said.

I asked, "Why's he got bodyguards?"

"Not everybody favor him. In Philadelphia somebody tried to stab him."

"You were there?" Stell said.

"Sister Vellines was. She told me."

A wave of excitement swept through the crowd as Daddy Grace went by.

"You like Daddy Grace, don't you?" I asked Mary.

"He all right."

"Colored people are emotional about religion," Stell told Mama and Daddy when we got home. "We should show more feelings in church."

"Ha!" Daddy said. "That'll be the day."

"Stell makes a good point, Bill. We really are sedate."

"I loved the music," I said, "and the way people danced, clapping and singing."

"Did you see the man himself?" Daddy asked.

"We did," said Stell. "Daddy Grace and his bodyguards."

"Bodyguards?" Daddy said. "Ye gods."

I said, "His fingernails are so long they curl under."

158

"Really?" Mama looked astonished.

"Uh-huh," said Stell. "It's sort of freakish."

At supper I asked Mama, "If a colored girl needed to use our bathroom, what would you do?"

"I'd let her, of course."

That made me feel good.

Mama put down her napkin. "We have Mary's toilet, downstairs."

Stell said, "Jubie used a colored family's bathroom."

"You went inside a Negro house?" Mama asked.

"Yes. A friend of Mary's. The bathroom was huge."

"Was it clean?"

"Yes, ma'am, and beautiful."

"Hmm." Mama shook her head as though she couldn't imagine such a thing.

CHAPTER 14

The morning sky was clear, with a strong breeze from the gulf. I didn't have to get into the backseat of the car again for three more days, finally on a real vacation. Mary knocked on the cabana door while I was putting on my bathing suit. She handed me a bottle of Coppertone. "Your mama says to put plenty of this on so you won't get burned."

I took the bottle. "She's the one gets burned. I never do."

"You got a nice tan, that's for sure." Her face was damp, even so early in the day.

"Do you use suntan oil?"

"No, and I been burned once or twice."

I touched her arm. "You get sunburn?"

"Sure I do. Just doesn't show on me the way it does on your mama." She got our dirty clothes from the hamper. "Going to run a couple loads. You go on down to the water. I know you're itching to."

I held the screen open and she headed for the house, her arms full of laundry. I went to the beach to lie in the sun and think about Leesum. I'd tried writing him, but what I put on paper looked stupid. I kept coming up against a fact: He could never be my boyfriend.

Footsteps squeaked in the sand. "Hey, kiddo."

I didn't look up. "Hey, Mama."

She spread her beach towel beside me, dropping her cigarette case, a book, sunglasses. "Let's get wet." She stepped out of her sandals.

We stood in the damp sand, letting the water lap at our feet. Mama hadn't put on any makeup and her freckles stood out. She looked sleepy. "You sure are somber this morning," she said.

"Where's everybody else?"

"Mary's going to bring Puddin and Davie down in a bit."

We walked into the water, jumped an incoming wave. Mama yelped and took my hand for balance. I dove into the next breaker and came to the surface. When Mary, Puddin, and Davie shouted to us, Mama was breaststroking toward deeper water. She turned. "There they are."

We treaded water, side by side. "This is a great vacation." Mama shook her head, her wet hair sending out brilliant drops.

I let the waves rock me up and down. "Mama, I asked Sarah why she was moping and she said Daddy could tell me."

Mama's eyes narrowed. "What are you talking about?" She grabbed my shoulder. "June?"

"Ow." I pulled away.

Stell and Sarah came over the dunes, carrying beach chairs. Mama waved to them. She said, "That is the silliest thing I ever heard. Let's go in and play with the kids." She called out, "Hey, girls!"

161

I went to the cabana to use the bathroom and saw Mary at the clothesline, struggling with a wet sheet. I grabbed one end of it, and together we pinned it to the line, where it flapped in the wind. Uncle Taylor, like Mama, insisted on sun-dried sheets. "Your mama still down to the beach?"

I nodded.

"She enjoying herself."

"I guess." I rubbed my feet in the St. Augustine grass Uncle Taylor was so proud of, thicker and pricklier than our lawn at home. We hung another sheet and I asked Mary, "Are you going to call your preacher tonight to be sure Leesum got there okay?"

She fastened a pillowcase with a clothespin. "I gave Reverend Perkins your uncle's number. He'll call if Leesum hasn't showed up. Any reason you think he won't?"

"No." I turned to go to the cabana.

"You probably not gone see that boy again."

"I know."

After supper I wound up lying on the floor in the den with Puddin and Davie, listening to Jack Benny, while Stell and Sarah went for a walk on the beach.

What was Leesum doing—did he listen to Jack Benny?

When Puddin and Davie went to bed, I walked

162

down to the beach. I loved having it there, morning, noon, and night, a place where I could go and imagine things being different than they were. I followed the sound of the gulf, looking at the stars, and almost fell over my sister and my cousin sitting in the light of the half-moon.

The three of us sat in the sand, looking out over the water to lights that blinked far away, a ship on the horizon.

"I got to tell y'all something," Sarah said. "I don't know where to start."

"At the beginning," I said.

"I don't know the beginning." Her voice got quiet. I had to strain to hear her over the waves. "Mother had an affair with Uncle Bill."

Waves pounded the beach, sending misty spray into the night air. I dug my hands in the sand.

"But—" Stell's voice cracked.

"It happened," Sarah said.

I felt lost and sure.

"That's why Daddy got a lawyer and divorced Mama. Why I have to stay with him and can't see her."

"Ever?"

"Never. Uncle Bill came to Pensacola and took Mama to a motor court. Somebody told Daddy." She pulled the rubber band from her ponytail. Her glossy black hair, so like her mother's, fell around her shoulders. "It started after Davie was born. Daddy thinks I don't know."

I looked out at the waves crashing on the beach, not wanting to see the shadowy certainty on Sarah's moonlit face.

Stell said, "Mama and Daddy have been mad at each other for a long time, but I never thought—" Her voice stopped, her words snatched away by the wind.

I asked, "How'd you find out?"

"I overheard something when I was supposed to be asleep."

"Maybe they met at the motel just to . . ." I couldn't think of anything.

Stell said, "I don't know why Mama stays with him."

The wind lifted my bangs off my forehead. "You stayed with Carter when he cheated on you."

Stell gasped. "He never cheated on me."

"He took another girl to a party. Y'all fought about it."

"We're not going steady. We can date other people."

"*You* never do."

"You're being so mean." I thought Stell might start crying.

"If you're not going steady, why do you wear his cross?"

"It's not his!" Stell cried out. "It's mine. He gave it to me."

The surf pounded, the breakers intense in the moonlight. I hated my family, all of them. Davie, who got attention because he was a boy. Puddin, who made me crazy, running off all the time. Daddy for beating me, Mama for letting him. Stell for . . . I had no reason to hate Stell. "I'm sorry." I reached for her.

She stood, taking Sarah's hand and pulling her up. "You should be."

"Do you forgive me?" I scrambled to my feet.

"I'll think about it."

She'd get over it; she always did. This wasn't the first time I'd been mean.

Stell said, "Daddy and Aunt Lily."

CHAPTER 15

Two weeks before Christmas of 1953, Meemaw's doctor called Daddy and said that somebody needed to come to Kentucky to take care of her. Daddy told Mama what the doctor said. "She's got arthritis, high blood pressure, and dropsy."

I imagined Meemaw strewing things behind her.

"So what does she need?" Mama asked.

"Complete bed rest for ten days, maybe longer. And she's got to take her medicine. Apparently she hasn't been."

Uncle Stamos and Aunt Rita agreed to go to Kentucky if Carly could stay with us for the holidays.

I couldn't wait to tell Stell Ann. We'd hardly seen Carly since he left for West Point three years earlier, but I remembered him so well. He'd always acted as if we were younger sisters, not just cousins.

The afternoon he arrived, Carly stood at the den door in his West Point uniform, a duffel bag at his feet, his hat in his hand, his brown eyes shining. Daddy clapped him on the back. "Good to have another man around the house."

"Yes, sir."

Mama hugged him. "My goodness, such broad

shoulders! The army has put some muscle on you."

"Playing football has, that's for sure," Carly said.

Mary stood in the door to the dining room. "Supper's almost ready. I'm gone be leaving now."

I said, "Carly, you remember Mary."

"Yes." He picked up his duffel bag. "Where am I sleeping?"

Mary went back to the kitchen and Daddy said, "C'mon, son, let's get you settled in the garage apartment." Even from his height of six-one, he had to look up to Carly, who was several inches taller.

Later, Carly returned to the house in what he called civvies—a plaid shirt, slacks, loafers.

The dining room table was set with Grandmother Bentley's silver flatware, which Mary had polished, and Mama's good china. Did Carly think we ate this way all the time?

When we got seated, Puddin asked Carly, "Why's your hair so short?"

"A lot of folks wonder what happened to my curls." Carly rubbed his hand over the black bristle on his head. "It's an army cut."

"Oh." Puddin looked puzzled.

Davie clapped his hands. "Milk!"

Mama said, "I forgot."

Carly pushed his chair back. "Let me get it."

"No, no, Jubie will do it."

I returned with Davie's cup and heard Daddy ask, "So what's next for you, Carly?"

"I go active as soon as I graduate."

"It's a dangerous time for soldiers, if Korea heats back up."

"The army's a great career."

Mama picked up a platter of fried chicken. "Help yourself, Carly, then pass it down to Bill." She said to Daddy, "Four breasts, dear. Have all you want."

"Thanks, honey." Daddy took two pieces and said to Carly, "Pauly knows how I love white meat." He got up to refill his drink and leaned over Mama to kiss her cheek. "Wonderful meal, sweetheart."

Stell raised her eyebrows at me. I wished Mama and Daddy would be lovey-dovey all the time.

Over dessert, Daddy explained to Carly about the hot water heater in the rec room. "It's only thirty gallons, but it's gas, so you should have enough. And when you shower, don't stand on the drain or you'll flood the bathroom." In the shower, Carly would be naked.

After supper Stell and I began to clear the table, and Carly picked up serving platters.

Stell whispered, "He's helping with the dishes."

He wiped the table and asked, "Where's the broom?"

I opened the pantry door. "Do you do this at home?"

"Dad would skin me if I left everything to Mom." He started sweeping.

"Give you a whipping?"

He looked at me. "He'd take away my car keys."

"He never whips you?"

"No."

I turned back to the sink. I could feel him staring at me.

Half an hour after we'd gone upstairs, I walked out of the bathroom and saw Carly on the landing.

He said, "What y'all doing?"

"Getting ready for bed. Where've you been?"

"Talking with your parents. You know, 'What are you going to be when you grow up?' "

"I'm so glad you're here." I touched his arm. "C'mon, let's go bother my big sister."

Stell was sitting cross-legged on her bed, brushing her hair. She had on her long-sleeved flannel pajamas, white with blue flowers, and she looked about ten.

"Hey," said Carly. "Long time since I've been up here."

Stell asked, "What's West Point like?"

He sat on the rug, leaned back against the dresser. "Uniforms, drills, reveille at dawn, that sort of thing."

"Do you like it?" Stell began brushing her hair again. It snapped and gleamed in the overhead light.

"Yeah, I do."

I sat on the bed. "Are you scared? What if there's a war?"

"I've been training to be a soldier for three years."

"Girls?" Daddy's voice boomed up the stairwell.

"Sir?" Stell and I answered together.

"Where's Carly?"

"I'm here," Carly called down to Daddy.

I heard Daddy on the stairs and there he was. "What's going on?"

I stood. "We're talking."

Daddy looked at Carly. "It's best if you don't visit the girls in their bedrooms."

Carly jumped to his feet. "Yes, sir."

I was too embarrassed to speak.

Stell said, "Good grief, Daddy, we're cousins."

But Daddy was clumping back down the stairs.

Carly's face was red. He opened his mouth, looking at Stell and me. "Jesus!" he said. He closed the door when he left.

The next morning before breakfast, I sat on the floor in my room, looking through the Venetian blinds at Carly's window over the garage, watching him shave at a mirror he'd hung over the sink in the kitchenette. I hated the tiny, moldy bathroom in the garage apartment and was sure he did, too. His shaving was the only personal thing of any interest that I learned, but knowing just that one private thing made me feel I was the closest to him of anyone in the family. Once he and his parents had gone blackberry picking with us, back when Carly first got his license. Stell and Puddin and I rode with him in Uncle Stamos' car, and

Carly had asked me to sit up front with him so he could show me how the clutch worked. Stell was ticked off about that. She tried everything she could to get his attention that day. But he liked me better.

I was at the kitchen table when he came down for breakfast with a full laundry bag he dropped on the floor. "Tell Mary I want a heavy starch in my shirts. If she has any questions, she can call Safronia." He poured himself a cup of coffee and came to the table. "Where's everybody?"

"Stell's at Bible Club, Mama's at the store with the kids, and Daddy's at work. I think Mary's—"

He interrupted me. "Would you hand me a banana?"

I reached for the fruit bowl. "Do you have any studies to do or is this a total holiday?"

"A total holiday. I've got stuff lined up with friends, but otherwise it's loaf city."

The next few days we hardly saw him. He left after breakfast and got back in the late evening, and Mama was so busy that I think she was relieved not to have anyone else to be concerned about.

Early in the morning on the Saturday before Christmas, she gave me boxes of decorations to unpack. "Before Carly leaves for the day, ask him if he'll test the strings of lights. There's always one that won't work, and I'm sure he can fix it."

I sat on the sofa in the den with the boxes of

ornaments and tuned the radio to a station playing carols. I thought Daddy was in his shower, and I turned up the volume to drown out the noises from his bathroom. The water ran, then stopped. The shower curtain rings squeaked. When the door opened, I looked up to see Carly wrapped in a towel, his chest wet. He jumped back into the bathroom, called out, "I forgot my robe."

I ran into the dining room, shouting over my shoulder, "Coast's clear." A while later he appeared for breakfast in jeans and a sweater. "My shower overflowed yesterday. Aunt Pauly told me to use Uncle Bill's."

Neither of us mentioned it again, but I couldn't forget the black hair that ran from his chest to the towel at his waist.

After that, whenever I knew Carly had used Daddy's bathroom, I went in to straighten up, knowing it would irk Daddy if he saw a mess. I'd thought Carly would be neater because of his military training, but he left a wet floor, soggy towels, the soap in a pool of gunk. I was in there wiping the floor and heard the den door slam. Daddy came in.

"Hey." I pretended not to notice him unzipping his trousers.

"What're you doing in here?"

"There was water on the floor."

He pushed back the shower curtain. "Who's using my bathroom?"

I stuffed the damp towel into the hamper. "Carly's shower overflowed again. The plumber will be here tomorrow, so . . ." I pushed past Daddy.

Mama's heels tapped on the hardwood floor. She came to the door of the bathroom. "William, if you'd fix the plumbing in the rec room, Carly wouldn't have to use your shower."

"I don't have time." Daddy closed the bathroom door and Mama shouted through it.

"You have time to fix things next door." She meant our neighbor Linda Gibson, a blonde divorcée who was always asking Daddy for help. Mama had told Aunt Rita, "Except for calling on William, she never calls at all."

Two days before Christmas, Carly and I sat in the living room, looking through the photo albums we kept on a shelf by the mantel. Halfway through the first one he said, "These are great. Who keeps them up?" The leather album looked small in his big hands.

"Mama."

"I wish Mom would do this. We've got hundreds of pictures just tossed in shoe boxes." He pointed to a photo of Stell, Puddin, and me standing on the pier at Rainbow Lake at Shumont. "That's great." I was knock-kneed and skinny. Puddin, about four in the photo, leaned against my hip. Stell had on her first bathing suit with a bra.

Mary walked through, carrying a broom, and Carly asked, "Could you make a fresh pot of coffee?"

"Yes, sir." She opened the den door to a blast of cold air, propped the broom on the breezeway, and closed the door fast. "Sure has got to be winter. Cream and sugar?"

Carly nodded.

"How long has Safronia worked for y'all?" I asked him.

"Since before I was born. Why?"

"I just wondered. Mary's been with us a long time, too."

Carly turned a page of the album, touched a picture of a small, brown-haired woman in a tailored suit and spectator pumps, carrying a briefcase. "Who's that?"

"Mama's mother. She's dead."

"What's with the briefcase?"

"She was a salesman, a woman salesman."

"I don't see any photos of your granddad."

"He left Grandmother Bentley with two daughters and a son to raise. That's why she went to work."

"Left? For where?"

"The West. Oregon, I think. He had a girlfriend."

"You said two daughters. I didn't know Aunt Pauly had a sister."

I turned a page and pointed to a skinny girl in a clingy striped dress with a white collar, staring straight at the camera. "That's Mama's older sister, Hanna. She died of leukemia when she was twenty-one. Mama was seventeen."

"Gosh, that's awful."

"Yeah. Mama and Uncle Taylor are all that's left of her family."

Mary came into the den with a tray. Two full cups, the cream pitcher and sugar bowl, spoons, napkins. "Here you are," she said to Carly.

"Just put it there." He pointed to an end table.

She said to me, "Fixed you some hot chocolate."

"Thanks, Mary," I said. She left.

Carly poured cream into his coffee, added sugar. "Wow, I've never seen this."

It was a photo of Uncle Stamos and Aunt Rita—hugely pregnant—dated July 1933. "That's right before I was born. They look so young."

Uncle Stamos, skinny as a rail, stood next to his short round wife, one arm around her shoulders, the other hand on her belly. I touched the photo. "Your parents still love each other, don't they?"

"Sometimes it's almost embarrassing."

"I think it's terrific."

He was quiet, then said, "Are your mom and dad—are they still in love?"

"I guess."

I had a hard time getting to sleep that night, trying to think of some way I could talk with Carly about Mary, about the way he spoke to her, acting as if she were no more than a piece of furniture. But he'd become a grown-up and I wasn't sure he'd understand.

After lunch on Christmas Eve, Mama took a turkey from the freezer, wrapped it in a bath towel, and put it on the glass-topped table on the breezeway.

"Are you just going to leave it there?" I asked.

"It'll be out of the way while it thaws, and the neighborhood dogs can't get to it."

Mary came in from the dining room. "The silver's done, Miz Watts, and the curtains is ironed. We don't hang them now, they'll wrinkle."

Mama wiped her hands on her apron. "Jubie, get the cabbage out of the fridge and pop off the bad leaves."

I grated cabbage and carrots for slaw while Mama and Mary threaded the dining room sheers back onto the rods. By the time Mary left for three whole days off, the hampers were empty and all the beds had fresh sheets. Even the telephone smelled like Pine-Sol and there was a bayberry candle in the guest bathroom.

I sat on the living room sofa, eyes closed, smelling the mulled cider warming on the stove, a pound cake in the oven, the blue spruce tree strung with lights. I wondered if everybody's house smelled this way at Christmas, and whether Carly missed being at home. I opened my eyes and

Mama was standing in the archway to the dining room, holding Davie, his blond curls shiny against the shoulder of her red wool dress. Mama rubbed his back, her nails gleaming from a fresh manicure. She'd pulled her curls into a chignon encircled with a black velvet ribbon. The pearls at her throat made her skin glow.

"You look elegant, Mama."

I could see how pleased she was. "Time to get dressed for the candlelight service. Wear your burgundy jumper. Save the velvet for tomorrow." She straightened an arm cover on the queen chair and left the room.

By noon on Christmas, torn wrapping paper and ribbons littered the living room. Daddy was on the floor with Davie, putting together train tracks. "Jubie, be a lamb and add an inch to my glass." He winked at Mama. "Just an inch."

Mama took the glass from Daddy. "I'll do it, Bill, and have one myself." She went into the dining room. Bottles clinked. She drank something while she stood in front of the liquor cabinet, then poured whiskey into glasses.

Stell leaned back in the queen chair, her feet curled beneath her, sleepy, content. Carols played from the new LP Daddy had given Mama.

"Where's Carly?" I asked.

"Talking to his parents," Mama said.

"In Kentucky?" Puddin called from under the

grand piano, where she was putting pajamas on her Bide-a-Wee doll.

"Yes." Mama handed Daddy his glass and sat next to me on the sofa.

Carly walked in. He was wearing the blue pullover we'd given him for Christmas and was so good-looking I blushed. "Phone, Uncle Bill. It's Meemaw."

Daddy stood, grunting. "I'll be right back."

Davie put down his choo-choo and came to me, holding his arms in the air. "Doobie."

Daddy called from the den, "Pauly, come say hello to Mother."

Mama groaned. She raised her glass to Stell. "I'll be nice."

After Mama got off the phone with Meemaw, she and Daddy sat on the sofa. He put his arm around her and she put her head on his shoulder. A curl of hair hung loose from her chignon and he wrapped it around his finger, tugged it gently, tickled her neck with it. She straightened and moved away.

At dusk we sat in candlelight around the dining room table. Mama carried in the meat platter with the turkey and put it down in front of Daddy. "William, you carve. I'll be right back." She glanced sideways at Carly. A minute later she came through the swinging door, carrying another platter with a baked ham on it, crosshatched and dotted with cloves. "Ta-da!" she sang out and put it in front of Carly.

His face lit up. "I thought I smelled ham cooking."

"I made raisin sauce, too, from Rita's recipe." Mama pointed to a steaming gravy boat and handed Carly a ladle. "Help yourself."

Daddy frowned. "Good lord, Paula. You made enough to feed an army."

Mama put her hand on Carly's shoulder and said, "It won't be as good as your mother's."

"White meat, Pauly?" Daddy asked.

Mama sat down. "And there are scalloped potatoes, biscuits. Apple pie for dessert. Just the same as your mom fixes at Christmas."

Daddy said, "Jubie, hand me your mother's plate."

On the Sunday Carly was leaving to go back to West Point, I was in the kitchen, doing the lunch dishes, listening to Mama and Daddy talk as they lingered in the dining room over coffee.

"The next time Cordelia needs help, you and I'll have to go," Mama said.

Daddy mumbled something.

"You have to face it. We need to be thinking about an old folks' home."

"She's not that bad yet."

"That's your opinion. Going up there for a week or two is just putting a finger in the dike."

Carly came through the back door in his uniform, carrying his hat and gloves. "I'm ready to go. Where's everybody?"

I touched the braid on his sleeve. He resembled a soldier in an old photograph, dressed for battle. I never had talked to him about Mary and now he was leaving. I said, "Mama and Daddy are in the dining room with Davie. Stell and Puddin are upstairs. I'll call them."

"Carly?" Daddy walked into the kitchen. "You're leaving?"

"Yes, sir."

Mama came in carrying Davie. "Be sure to let us know when you get there."

"Mom and Dad'll call you." He put on his hat and touched Davie's cheek. "Good-bye, Davie."

Stell came in the kitchen, still in her Sunday best. She stood on tiptoe to kiss Carly's cheek. He put one arm around her, the other around me, and pulled us to him. The brass buttons on his chest were cold to my cheek. My face almost touched Stell's as he held us close.

CHAPTER 16

After we packed up to leave Pensacola, Uncle Taylor and Mama stood by the car talking. She shook her head and pushed him away, her face splotched from crying. He took a couple of steps back and said something, then reached for her and held her for a long time before she got into the car.

Mama put the key in the ignition. "I wish we could stay here."

"Uncle Taylor invited us to," I said.

"I mean forever."

"Why don't we just go straight to Pawleys Island?" Stell asked. Carter was going to meet us at Pawleys, and Stell could hardly wait to see him.

"I told you. I want to buy fruitcakes." Mama blew her nose and turned on the radio to a breakfast club, where a man and woman were talking about blueberry waffles. "Fresh blueberries make all the difference," the woman said, a smile in her voice.

Stell said, "I don't get what's so special about Claxton fruitcakes."

"They're the best." Mama turned up the volume.

Puddin said, "Mama, let's sing something."

"Claxton is out of the way," Stell said. "I looked at the map."

"Hush. I'm listening to this show."

Mary took Puddin's hand in the way she had of saying *Your mama's upset, baby.*

181

• • •

A few miles west of the Chattahoochee River, Mama tapped the gas gauge the way she always did when it was low. At the river we saw a sign saying the bridge was out, that there was ferry service, courtesy of the State of Georgia. Cars were lined up and Mama told me to walk down to the dock to see how long it would take to get across.

"Mind if I go, too, Miz Watts? Stretch my legs."

Davie reached for Mary, and Mama lifted him from his seat.

Mary put Davie down between us. I counted the cars as we walked along the shoulder at Davie's pace. I could feel people staring at us—the colored woman, the toddler, the tall girl.

"Can't carry but ten vehicles," said a man at the dock. "How far back are you?"

"There's nine cars and a pickup ahead of us." I was proud of myself for having counted.

"Tell your mother it'll be at least forty-five minutes 'fore she can cross. She's best off waiting. There's a bridge north and one south, but it's a good thirty miles to either."

"We're almost out of gas."

"Stop the motor. Roll down the hill. She can gas up at Donalsonville, ten miles the other side of the river."

An hour later we drove onto the ferry and stopped at the prow. "We'll be the first ones off,"

Mama said. "Thank God." Davie stood in the front seat as the boat began to move, saying, "Boat. Oh, boat," over and over. Halfway across I got out of the car. Something seemed almost not possible about a boat carrying such a load with a motor so small it putt-putted. The only thing keeping us going straight was a hemp rope, thick around as my arm. The ferry rode so low my sandals got splashed when the swirling water lapped over the side, and I knew from the pull against the guy rope that if I fell overboard, I'd be carried around the next bend before anyone could throw out a life preserver. A damp, diesel-smelling breeze cooled my face.

I got back in the car at the landing. As soon as the prow gate was lowered, Mama started the engine. With the front wheels on the landing and the back wheels on the ferry, the motor quit.

I asked, "Are we out of—"

"Shit!" Mama said, hitting the steering wheel with both hands.

"Mama!" said Stell.

"Shut up." Mama ground the ignition, but the car wouldn't start.

Horns honked behind us.

The boatman walked up. "What's the problem, ma'am?"

"I'm afraid we've run out of gas."

"You're kidding, right, little lady?" The man leaned down, his face close to Mama's.

Mama looked straight ahead. "No."

The man called toward the dock, "Need some help here; lady's out of gas." More horns honked.

A pickup was in back of us on the ferry. The man driving it got out. "Can't give you a push. My bumper's too high."

Four men got behind the car and tried to push us off the ferry, but the landing sloped uphill and the car was too heavy, even with everybody out except Mama.

"I be goddamn," the boatman said when they gave up.

A woman stuck behind the pickup said we could siphon gas from her car. The boatman got a can and a hose from a shed on the dock. After they poured the gas in our tank, the boatman signaled Mama.

"Easy, now, don't pump it. Push the pedal down, hold it, turn the key."

I saw Mama's foot going up and down on the gas pedal. "He said not to do that."

"I guess I know my own car." She turned the key. The motor ground and ground but wouldn't turn over. Her face was so red I thought she might start crying.

The boatman lifted the hood. "She's flooded. They ain't nothing to do but wait till she dries out, ten, maybe fifteen minutes."

Mama got out of the car, rummaged around in the trunk for a book she'd been reading at Uncle

Taylor's. She got in the front seat, settled back against the driver's door, and propped her feet on the dashboard. She opened her book and began to read. With her sunglasses on and her skirt hiked up showing her curvy legs, she looked like a movie star.

The truck driver stepped up to the car. "Wisht I could of pushed you."

Mama went on reading as if she'd gone stone deaf.

The boatman said, "Turn your key off, ma'am, so's you don't drain the battery."

Mama turned a page.

Mary said, "I'll take the children up into the trees where it's shady."

Mama didn't answer.

Davie was sleepy and fussy. Mary carried him and took Puddin by the hand to the shade. She sat under a tree with her legs spread so her skirt made a cloth for Davie to sit on. Puddin sat in the grass beside Mary, leaning against her.

Stell and I sat nearby. The grass felt good on my legs. Stell said, "We have a crazy mother."

I stretched out. "Uh-huh."

"Did you hear the word she said?"

"She's sad about leaving Uncle Taylor's."

Stell Ann lay back in the grass with her arm over her eyes. "I don't want to talk."

CHAPTER 17

In Albany, Georgia, well after sunset, Mama pulled into a motel, one long building with rooms opening onto the parking lot. She went into the office to register us. When she got back to the car, she drove to the end of the building.

"What about Mary?" I asked.

"I ordered a rollaway, and I didn't mention her." Mama set the brake and said to Mary, "Go on in. As long as no one sees you, it'll be fine."

We left before dawn and I fell asleep in the car, slumped against Mary. When I woke I saw that spit had dribbled from my mouth, leaving a streak on the sleeve of her dress.

She smoothed my hair. "You sleep good?"

Puddin was asleep, too, with Davie wedged between us, looking out the window, his hand in my lap, fingers curled. "Doobie."

"Hey, Davie-do."

"Doobie sleep." He closed his eyes.

A thin forest of scraggly pine trees passed by, behind a wide black-water ditch, its surface still and shiny as wet tar.

Puddin opened her eyes. "I need to use the bathroom."

"Tee-tee," said Davie.

Mama said, "We'll stop when we find a decent place."

That meant Esso, because they cleaned their restrooms every day. Texaco was next best because it put opera on the radio every Saturday.

"Mama, I really have to."

"Ye gods! If I pulled over now, you'd have to pee in the swamp."

"Pee," said Davie.

Puddin bounced in her seat, then scrunched her fists in her lap, rocking.

Davie laughed. "Tinkle."

A sign appeared in the distance on the right.

"Red star at one o'clock!" I called out.

Mama pulled into the Texaco. "One o'clock, my fanny."

Puddin jumped out and ran. "I see the restroom," she called over her shoulder.

The heat wrapped itself around me when we left the car. Mary smoothed my shorts in back, pulling the legs down. "Your whole self is wrinkled. I reckon I'm not much better." But she was. Except for wet circles under her arms, she looked like she'd just gotten dressed and fixed her hair, not like she'd been stuck for hours in the backseat of a car with three kids.

Mama gave me a five-dollar bill and told me to go to the grill next to the gas station. "Lunch. French fries. Hot dogs, no onions for Puddin and Davie."

I walked up to the order window and hollered through the screen, "Hello?" The whole world smelled like onion rings.

A teenaged girl came from a back room, wiping her hands on a towel. "Yeah?"

She got to work before I finished the order, putting buns in a steamer, lowering a basket of slivered potatoes into boiling oil, dropping wieners onto a sizzling griddle.

Her pink peasant blouse was cut so low the tops of her bosoms showed, and her white shorts had ketchup on the pocket. She looked past me. "Where y'all from?"

"Charlotte, North Carolina."

"Where you going to?" Her yellow hair was tied back with an orange ribbon. Stell would have said the ribbon was a mistake because you shouldn't mix clashing colors, and orange is tacky like purple.

"Pawleys Island, South Carolina."

"Someday I'm going to see the ocean." She put a grilled wiener in the middle of each bun.

"You work here all the time?"

"Except for school. I'll go full-time soon's I'm married." She ladled chili.

"You're getting married?"

"Next summer. My boyfriend drives army tanks in Berlin, Germany."

"Golly. How old are you?"

"Turned fifteen last week." She sprinkled chopped onions.

To show I wasn't shocked, I said, "Your hair's great."

"It's the same color as Jane Powell's." There was lipstick on her teeth. "Y'all gonna eat here?" She pointed to a picnic table, under trees behind the Texaco.

"To go, please."

She wrapped everything in newspaper and put it in a grocery bag. "The two without onions is on top. That's three dollars."

Mama walked up behind me. "C'mon, Jubie, we're losing time. What'd you get?"

"Six orders of French fries and eight hot dogs."

"Eight?"

"Anybody who's still hungry can—"

"Anybody like you?"

"Yes."

"Better watch for when you stop growing up and start growing out." As we walked back to the car, Mama said, "That girl ought to cover herself and wash her face."

"Her hair is the same color as Jane Powell's."

"Jane Powell would shave her head if she had such hair."

"She's getting married next summer."

"She'll have three kids before she's twenty."

"But she's engaged to a soldier who—"

"June, don't admire such a life!"

We got back in the car. Even with lunch to look forward to, I dreaded more time scrunched in the backseat. Mama had put the key in the ignition when I shouted, "Puddin!"

Mama turned. "Ye gods, where's she gone now?"

I ran to the filling station. Puddin wasn't in the restroom, not in the tiny office, not in the empty service bays. Mama stood by the gas pump hollering, "Carolina Wendy Watts! Come here right now!"

I ran around back. She was sitting in the weeds, leaning against the block wall of the station, crying.

"Puddin-tane! What's wrong?"

"Mama wouldn't stop. I wet myself." She howled.

Mama came around the other side of the building. "What's going on?"

I helped Puddin up. "Puddin damped her panties."

Mama's face was a mix of *I'm really mad* and *oh, well.* "C'mon, Puddin, let's get fresh undies from the trunk." The *oh, well* won.

Mary picked the onions off her hot dog, a look on her face that said for me not to notice. She took a bite and I remembered her indigestion.

As soon as Mama finished eating we were back on the road.

Stell wiped her fingers and stuffed the napkin in the trash bag. "Only three weeks till school. I can hardly wait."

"Yuk." I hated to think about the end of summer vacation.

"I'm excited," Stell said, "because of the new Pledge of Allegiance."

I had no idea what she meant.

"Congress added the words 'Under God.'"

"Where?"

She said, in her most religious voice, "'One nation under God, indivisible.' It's so wonderful."

"Hmph." Mary crossed her arms on her chest.

I asked her, "Don't you think it's a good thing, adding God to the pledge?"

"Putting God in the pledge and on money— that's like a sign in the sky saying 'air.'" Sometimes Mary surprised me, the things she thought about.

Mama raised the volume on the radio and fiddled with the dial, picking up snatches of *Young Dr. Malone*. The static was so bad she turned it off. "I've got a headache that won't let up."

Stell said, "Mama, please let me drive. You can sleep for a while."

Mama pulled off the road and walked around the car, stopping to stretch, her hands on the small of her back. She got in the passenger seat. "You get a ticket, you're grounded."

Stell looked in the rearview mirror. I waved at her. She stuck out her tongue, then adjusted the mirror by the wing window. "All set." She pulled onto the highway. A tractor-trailer truck came right up on our bumper, air horn blasting. Stell jumped.

"Stell!" Mama gasped. "You pulled out in front of him."

"He's speeding."

The truck zoomed around us and the car rocked, but Stell kept it in the road. Mama slumped against the window.

For the next hour, Mama slept and Stell drove at a steady fifty-five. We passed a group of Burma-Shave signs. I read them aloud: "Substitutes are like a girdle. They find some jobs they just can't hurdle. Burma-Shave." I thought about Mama struggling to pull up the stiff elastic sheath, attaching her stockings to it, announcing she was nearly ready by saying, "I've got my girdle on." I vowed I'd never wear one.

On the outskirts of Claxton, we passed farms, cotton processors, feed and grain mills. Highway 280 changed to Main Street, and Stell slowed down. Daddy said small towns were speed traps.

Davie climbed onto my lap, his body a hot water bottle.

"No." I pushed him away.

"Doobie," he whined, "badge." He held out the cap from a Coke bottle.

"Quiet down back there," Mama said.

He collapsed against me, hot and damp. I said no again, trying to whisper and be firm at the same time.

"Badge," he shouted.

Mama swung her left arm over the seat in a slapping motion.

Stell glanced back at me. "What's going on?"

Afterward I said I'd known at that moment that

it was going to happen. I said it so much I was pretty sure it was true.

A shadow loomed. There was a screeching crunch and our car spun and tilted. We slid across the seats on top of each other. The car hung on two wheels, slammed back down. Metal hit the pavement.

Davie broke the silence, crying, "Oooh-h-h-h. Oooh-h-h-h."

"Is everybody okay?" Mama's voice shook.

"Jesus bless us," said Mary.

Mama said, "Puddin?"

"I'm here," Puddin said, her voice shaking. "Under Jubie."

Davie wailed again.

"You okay, Davie-do?" I put his palm to my lips and felt wet on my face.

"No!" His hand was bleeding.

Stell opened the driver's door and stood by the car, looking dazed.

"C'mon," Mary said. "Let's get out."

The battered old truck that hit us was across the street, its front tires on the sidewalk.

Mama took Davie and uncurled his fist, peeling back his fingers one by one. "Oh, Davie. You've got a cut shaped like a bottle cap, isn't that funny?"

Davie hiccupped and looked at his hand.

Puddin said, "You're bleeding, Jubie." I tasted blood where I had bitten my lip.

"Jesus H. Christ," somebody said. A crowd had

gathered. People stared, gestured, talked to each other.

"Let me see. Not too bad." Mama pulled a Kleenex from her pocket, pressed it against my lip. Blood had splattered the front of my new T-shirt. Mama looked at the cut. "You don't need stitches, Jubie."

I held the tissue against my lip, looking around for Mary. She was standing by the back of the car, rubbing her head. "Are you hurt, Mary?" I asked.

"No. Bumped around a bit." She looked at the car and shook her head. "Gone take some fixing."

I walked around the Packard. The right front fender was bashed in and the car was turned around, heading west again. A steady drip from the front grille made a puddle in the street.

Puddin said to Mama, "I bumped my head."

Mama parted Puddin's hair to examine her scalp. "You're getting a goose egg. Everything else okay?"

"Yes, ma'am."

"Stell Ann?"

"I hit my head, too."

Mama tipped Stell's chin and looked into her eyes, "Look up. Down. Side to side. How many fingers?" Mama held up three fingers.

"Three."

"Sit over there in the grass and be real still."

A woman said, "Whoo-ee! Bobby Joe done it again."

A man in a white jacket stepped out of a Rexall on the corner. "I'm a pharmacist. Be glad to help, if I can."

Mama nodded.

He looked at Davie's hand. "I've got just the thing for that." He went in the Rexall and returned with a bottle of Mercurochrome. When the man tried to touch him, Davie screamed, turning his face to Mama's bosom. She held his hand out to the pharmacist. When he'd finished, the man put a Band-Aid on the cut and gave Davie a cherry lollipop. "Got a candy for you being such a good boy."

Davie sniffled and put the sucker in his mouth. Mama kissed his head.

A man was checking out our car, getting down on his knees and peering underneath. He had on sunglasses, and his hair was so long it hung down under his straw hat.

Mama handed Davie to me. He put his face against my neck, which made me want to cry. I began to shake. I sat on a bench outside the Rexall, trying not to throw up, swallowing over and over until the sick feeling went away.

The man who'd been checking the car spoke to Mama. "Name's Jake Stirewalt."

"I'm Mrs. Watts, Mrs. William Watts."

"S'my place over there." He pointed to a garage. "Be happy to try to fix 'er, Mrs. Watts. You might need a rade-yater. And I ain't got one."

"Can you get one?"

"Hafta check the Packard dealers. Savannah, Augusta. Might could take a while."

"Oh," said Mama. "Well."

Stell Ann was sitting in a patch of grass across the street. Mary stood at the edge of the crowd, holding Puddin's hand. She waved when she saw me looking at her.

A siren sounded a block away, then a sheriff's car pulled up. A man in a uniform got out and spoke to Mama. "I'm Deputy Hinson. Is anybody hurt?"

"My son's hand is cut, and my daughter's lip. Everybody bumped heads, but I think we're okay."

He called across the street. "Bobby Joe? Walk on over here."

The truck driver lolled against his fender. The front of his truck was crumpled, but he didn't seem to care. He pushed himself away from the truck and wobbled into the street.

"Off the wagon, Bobby Joe?"

The man nodded and folded himself into the sheriff's car.

"I have my way, you never gonna drive again." Inside the car the man slumped against the window, his hair making a flat gray circle on the glass.

The deputy's leather holster was high on his hip, the gun black and square like Daddy's. Had the deputy ever used it?

He called out, "Anybody see what happened here?"

Stell stood and walked over to Mama.

A man stepped up. "Bobby Joe Tart came barreling out of Grady. Didn't even slow down at the stop sign. Hit this young lady's car. She was on Main, going toward town."

"Is that right?" the deputy asked Stell.

Mama said, "It happened so fast."

Mr. Stirewalt walked up. "Okay if we push the car to my shop?"

"Yeah, go ahead," the deputy said.

Mama said, "Don't work on it until I've talked to my husband."

Mr. Stirewalt handed Mama a piece of paper. "Here's my number. J and J's Garage. The best in Claxton. You ask anybody."

People walked away. Talking, looking back at us like they didn't want to let go of the excitement. The deputy asked Mama a few more questions and wrote things down.

Davie held out his hand, palm up, showing me the Band-Aid. "Davie hurt."

"Yes, but it's fixed now."

"Kiss it." He put his hand to my mouth. I caught the dry rubber smell of the Band-Aid mixed with cherry lollipop.

Mary began taking the luggage from the trunk. I put Davie down next to Puddin so I could help Mary pile our stuff on the sidewalk. Mr. Stirewalt and two men pushed our car to the garage across the street.

"Guess we're stuck." Puddin put her head against my shoulder.

Mr. Stirewalt walked back to Mama. "You'll want to stay at the motel park a couple blocks from here. You can call me tomorrow." He turned and hollered, "Gaither?"

"Yeah?" answered one of the men who'd pushed our car.

"Take Mrs. Watts and her kids over to Sally's."

"Will the motel have a place for our colored girl?"

"That's a problem." Mr. Stirewalt took off his hat, leaving a dent in his greasy hair.

The man named Gaither said, "They's a nigger hauls our trash. You can't find a place for your girl, I'll ask him." There were damp rings under his arms. His gray work pants were too short for his lanky height, leaving his knobby ankles bare. "Somebody'll keep her." He smiled at Mary, but his eyes were hard.

An old pickup rattled to a stop beside us. The passenger windshield was cracked. The boy driving it hopped out and handed the keys to Gaither, who tossed our luggage over the tailgate, bumping against me when he turned to pick up another suitcase. He stank from cigarettes and foul sweat.

Mary moved to help with our bags and Gaither said, "I can handle this, girl."

She backed away, looking down.

He ran his fingers through his thick brown hair, swept back in an oily ducktail.

Mama and Stell Ann got in the cab. Mama settled Davie on her lap, then called through the window, "Get in the back." Puddin and I climbed in.

Mary handed me her pocketbook. She grabbed the sidewall of the truck and put one foot on the bumper, then pulled herself up, holding her skirt against her knees as she stepped over the tailgate. Puddin and Mary each sat on a piece of luggage, and I sat on a toolbox. The truck smelled like our basement when the sewer backed up.

Gaither drove slowly down the street. Claxton looked friendly, the streets swept, store windows shining in the afternoon light. Gleaming railroad tracks ran parallel to Main Street. A woman in a yellow print dress watered flowers in hanging pots in front of a millinery store. Men sat in chairs outside a barbershop. A sign in the window said MY GRANDMOTHER'S FRUIT-CAKES FOR SALE. INQUIRE WITHIN. The barber in his white coat leaned against the doorjamb beneath a red, white, and blue barber pole turning around and around, the stripes spiraling out through the top.

The truck turned in a driveway at a sign: SALLY'S MOTEL PARK. CABINS. POOL. VACANCY, and pulled up beside a brick house with the word OFFICE on the front door. Gray stone paths connected the cabins, dividing the green lawn into squares and triangles. I couldn't see the pool.

Gaither got out, cleared his throat, coughed.

A woman came from the office, shading her eyes with her hand. Her short brown hair was finger-waved in tight rows.

"Hey, Sally," said Gaither.

"Hey, Gaither."

"These folks had a wreck. Jake's got they car." Gaither unrolled a pack of cigarettes from his shirtsleeve. "This here's Sally Bishop."

"Hello, Miss Bishop," said Mama. "We need rooms. At least one night."

"It's Mrs. Bishop." The woman looked at Mary. "That your girl?"

"Yes."

She walked away, her hand to her mouth, the other hand in a fist on her hip. She turned. "You and one of the kids could stay in Cabin Two"—she pointed—"a double bed. The others in Cabin Four—two double beds, a kitchenette, with a cot for your girl."

"How much?" Mama asked.

"Four a night for the small cabin, ten a night for the big one. In advance, daily."

"My goodness."

"Take it or leave it. No place else'll have her, not around here."

"Do you have a phone I could use?"

200

Mama and Mrs. Bishop went into the office. A sign by the door said, FRESH BAKED FRUITCAKES. MORE CHERRIES, NO CITRON.

Mama's voice came through the open office window, leaving a message with Daddy's secretary. After she hung up, she said to the motel woman, "My husband's not available. I need to make one more call." She spoke into the phone, giving the operator Uncle Taylor's number. "Person to person, collect, please."

She waited a couple of minutes, then said, "Oh, Taylor, thank God you're there. We had a wreck. Everybody's okay, but the car . . ." She blew her nose. "God knows where Bill is. I left a message." She said something I couldn't hear, then, "Yes, but I need him. I feel so overwhelmed."

After Mama hung up, I said to Stell, "I hope we stay here. I want to swim."

"I hope they have a bathtub, not just a shower."

Mama came back outside and said, "Carry my suitcase over there." She pointed to Cabin Two. "And take the rest to yours, Cabin Four."

Mrs. Bishop came outside. "There's another thing." Her voice was strident. "I could get in trouble for letting your girl stay here, but I can see you're in a mess, so I'm making an exception."

"We're grateful," Mama said.

"But there are rules. She's got to use the outhouse, not either of y'all's bathrooms. Behind Cabin Six, through those trees." She pointed.

201

"What about bathing?" Mama asked.

"She can't use the pool."

"I meant washing herself."

"There's a pump behind Cabin Four." She coughed and touched her hair. "That's the best I can do. I could lose business if word gets out. There are folks around here . . ." She turned and walked toward the office.

"Yes," Mama said under her breath. "There are always folks."

I climbed into the back of the truck and handed our suitcases over to Mary. When I was getting out, Gaither walked up and took my hand to help me. His hand was gritty. I jumped from the bumper and moved away.

"See you around." Gaither flicked his cigarette onto the lawn. He coughed and cleared his throat again as he got in the truck.

We were unpacking in our cabin when the motel lady brought a folding cot for Mary, a wooden frame with green canvas slung from it, like the one I slept on at Girl Scout camp. She gave Mary a faded bedspread, two sheets, and a pillow. "You won't need a blanket, hot as it is."

We set the cot up under the window in the kitchenette—a double-burner hot plate, a tiny refrigerator, and a sink. A note on a tattered index card was Scotch-taped to the wall: *Tables under bed.* I looked and found four small folding tables.

Mama was going to have to eat her words about never having supper on TV trays.

"This one's mine." Stell sat on one of the beds. "You and Puddin can have the other one."

Ever since we left Charlotte, Stell had made it known that she wasn't sleeping with Puddin. Maybe because they shared a bedroom at home and Stell wanted a break from her.

Mama came to our cabin to check it out. She looked into the bathroom. "Mary, help yourself to the toilet and the shower. I'm sure the girls don't mind. If that Sally woman says anything, send her to me."

Mary nodded.

Mrs. Bishop knocked at the door. "Phone, Mrs. Watts. I believe it's your husband." I hoped she hadn't heard what Mama said to Mary.

Mama's mouth twisted. "Y'all get settled while I talk with your father."

CHAPTER 18

I found the swimming pool through the trees behind the motel cabins. It was small, with chairs and lounges crowding the concrete apron. The piddling diving board had almost no spring and was barely high enough to dive from. I stretched out on it in my bathing suit, rubbing my shoulder blades against the torn hemp runner. Traffic on the boulevard swooshed faintly in the background. A car door slammed shut, and somebody shouted, "See you!" I scratched my back on the ragged hemp, stared at the cloudless sky, and thought about Leesum. If he was as good a diver as he was a swimmer, he'd know what a stupid board this was.

The boards Daddy had built for Charlotte Municipal Swimming Pool were for real divers, like Daddy might have been if he'd had coaching. He could still do a jackknife.

The City of Charlotte had held a dedication for the new boards last Memorial Day weekend, when Municipal Pool opened for the summer. We'd been running late and Mama drove fast, but the parking lot was jammed when we got there. She pulled in behind Daddy's car, laughing. "I've got him hemmed in."

People were sitting on portable bleachers around the pool, the mayor, friends from the country club, men from Watts Concrete Fabrications. Daddy stood near the high dive, in his blue seersucker suit, wearing a straw fedora with a stained band. He said something to Uncle Stamos, who seemed to fade into the background the way he always did when the two of them were together.

Stell and I sat on one side of Mama, Puddin on the other. Davie kept twisting in Mama's lap. She snapped at him to be still, then glanced around to see if anyone had heard her. She smiled at the mayor's brother, who we knew from the club.

The air smelled of chlorine, cigarettes, and suntan oil. The pool was turquoise glass under the hot sun and I wanted to jump into it, make waves and shout. The still blue water needed breaking up.

"Testing, one, two, three, four" came from the loudspeakers. The squeal of feedback brought a groan from the crowd. "Turn it down, Pete," a man hollered. Stell Ann raised her eyebrows, put her hand over her mouth, muffling a snicker. Puddin looked bored.

The mayor spoke into the mike. "Good afternoon! I'm happy to have y'all here. Hope you brought your suits!" Everybody laughed as though he'd said something really funny.

"We need this great facility for our young athletes. Can't expect them to train without first-class equipment. Charlotte is now the largest city in the Carolinas, and we have every hope of being represented in the Olympic Games before too long." There was scattered applause among the crowd. "First order of business is entertainment. Let's hear it for the Myers Park High School Marching Band!"

A drum cadence started. The gates swung open in the chain-link fence surrounding the pool, and the head majorette high-stepped through. The crowd laughed as the band marched in wearing plumed hats, boots, and bathing suits. They halted and marched in place on the pool deck. The cadence changed to a repeated slow beat on the snare drums. A flute played the refrain from "Dixie." The crowd rose to its feet and sang. I got chill bumps singing about old times that were not forgotten. At the end of the chorus, people started to sit back down, but one of the majorettes stepped up to the mike and sang a verse I'd never heard:

Ole Missus marry Will the weaver.
Willum was a gay deceiver.
Look away! Look away! Look away! Dixie Land!
But if she want to drive 'way sorrow,
She can sing this song tomorrow.
Look away! Look away! Look away! Dixie Land!

Her voice hung in the air. Then everyone sang the chorus again, more fiercely than before. After the band marched out and the drum cadence faded, the mayor said, "I'm going to turn the mike over to the man who made all this possible.

William Watts is president of Watts Concrete Fabrications, the company that built these fine diving boards. A proud husband and father of four, he has his family here with him today." The mayor tipped his hat to us, then continued. "Two of the Watts girls are already great competitive swimmers, and Bill is often seen at their meets." Stell touched my arm. I kept my eyes down, wondering if I should look up. The mayor went on. "The Watts family are active members of Selwyn Avenue Methodist Church and Myers Park Country Club, where Bill is on the board of directors, and where he recently achieved elite status by shooting a hole in one on the back nine. Let's have a hand for William Watts!"

The crowd applauded. Daddy handed his glasses to Uncle Stamos and walked to the base of the diving boards.

"Why's he wearing that old hat?" I asked Mama.

"Shh. He's going to speak."

Mama seemed puffed up with the importance of the occasion, maybe because Daddy had become someone in Charlotte, a respected businessman. I sat up straighter.

Daddy waved away the microphone. "Can everybody hear me okay?" he yelled, and the crowd called back, "Yes!"

Daddy shouted, "What's essential about concrete?"

Somebody hollered, "What?"

"It's gotta be hard!" Daddy jumped up and down on the pavement and people roared with laughter, every eye on him. He stood at the deep end of the pool, his reflection beside a mirror image of the high dive. "Our shop's just a local outfit, a bunch of guys working on small jobs. When we won the bid for the pool deck and base for the diving boards, I had to hire more crew and go back to school." He kicked off his loafers and put his foot on the first rung of the ladder to the high dive. "Had to learn the latest about compressive strength, hardening time, accelerators, L-bolts . . ." He stood at the top of the ladder and touched the base his company had built. "This is one of the biggest structures we've poured to date." He lifted his hat from his head and saluted the crowd. The red stone in his ring glittered. Then with a flick of his wrist, he sailed his hat into the air, grinning as it spun around and landed in the middle of the pool. Laughter filled the air again. Mama shook her head. "That's why he wore his old hat."

The sun glinted off Daddy's hair. "We designed the base ourselves to support these springboards." He stepped off the ladder and walked out onto the board. "They have to be anchored with precision or divers won't get all the bounce they need"—he took two steps and the board bent beneath his weight—"for a half gainer with a triple twist." Daddy flexed his knees and the board went down, rose up. I was proud that he knew what a gainer was. He turned his back to the pool and put his feet at the end of the board, heels lined up with the edge. "Even the simplest dive needs good spring."

He was silent for a minute and the crowd waited. "A trained diver knows all boards are different, but his stride is the same." Daddy lifted one foot and seemed to go off balance, spreading his arms to steady himself. I was sure he was pretending. He took four steps back toward the ladder. "The diver takes four paces from the end, then turns." Daddy pivoted.

"How high is three meters?" He looked puzzled. "Most Americans need a slide rule for that one." He was tall and solid above the white base, so handsome. I was proud to be his daughter. "Three meters is nine point seventy-five feet, about the height of the gutter on a one-story house. So a three-meter board is ten feet off the water." He kneeled and put his hand on a bar underneath the board. "The secret to spring is the fulcrum, this bar. As you can see, it's adjustable." He pointed to a crank. "Proper placement of the fulcrum keeps the bounce under control." He stood and pointed backward, toward the ladder. "If we moved it that way, the bounce would throw the diver into the next county." He stood on his tiptoes, arms wide. I looked away, embarrassed by the damp circles at his armpits. He lowered his heels and stood flat-footed again.

"A diver marks his pace from the end of the

board so he knows where to start his approach."
He took three long, fast steps and his arms carved
circles, then his hands came together and rose
above his head. His left leg came up into a tight
knee bend, then slammed down on the board and
he leaped into the air. His hands came down to
meet his feet in a perfect jackknife. For an instant
he hung in the air, then his head and hands fell and
his legs snapped up. He split the water in a straight
vertical, almost no splash. The crowd gasped,
exploded with applause.

Mama said, "What a show-off."

Daddy surfaced arms first, rising like Esther
Williams in a water ballet. He slicked his wet hair
off his forehead as he climbed the ladder, his
seersucker suit clinging to his broad shoulders and
long legs.

Puddin jumped into the motel pool, splashing me.
I rolled off into the water. She swam over to me in
a jerky stroke that wasn't much better than a dog
paddle. "Guess what? Daddy's coming!"

I went under and grabbed her feet, heard her
muffled shriek through the water. "When?" I
sputtered as I came back to the surface.

"Tomorrow. Mama's glad."

I swam to the side of the pool. Mary came
through the gate, carrying Davie on her hip.

"Your daddy be here tomorrow."

"Puddin told me."

She put Davie down. "He want to be sure your mama's car get fixed right."

Davie walked to the side of the pool, holding out his hands. "Doobie, water."

"You take him in the pool, you got to keep the Band-Aid dry."

I got out and walked with Davie to the shallow end. We sat on the steps and Davie kicked the water.

Mary pulled a Kleenex from her pocket and wiped her face. I wished she could come in the pool with us and I wished that Daddy would stay in Charlotte.

CHAPTER 19

"Stell, Jubie, let's go buy fruitcakes." Mama stood in the door of our cabin.

Stell was brushing her hair, the glossy brown shimmering in a shaft of morning sunlight through the open window. "Ten minutes, okay?"

Mama nodded. She had her hand on the screen door when Mary spoke. "I want to buy some fruitcakes myself."

"Then we'd have to take Puddin and Davie," Mama said.

"I'll keep them out of your way," said Mary. "I can get the cakes for you. How about that?"

"Yes, ma'am. Want three fruitcakes."

"Is that all? No problem whatsoever."

"With citron, those yellow pieces that has such a fine sharp taste."

"I know what citron is." Mama started out the door again.

"Not all fruitcakes has citron. I particularly favors it."

"Most of them do."

"No, Mama," I said. "Some signs say 'No Citron.'"

"Oh-h-h-h." Mama turned to leave. "Let's not get things too complicated."

• • •

At Claxton Fruit Cake Company, Mama ordered ten tube cakes, five pounds each, in holiday tins, and arranged to have them shipped.

"Okay, girls, let's go."

"Mama!" She'd forgotten.

"Yes?"

"Mary's cakes."

"Oh, my goodness. Thanks, Jubie." She turned back to the man behind the counter. "Three one-pound cakes, please, in a bag. We'll take them with us."

I asked, "Are you sure she doesn't want bigger ones?"

"I wouldn't think so."

Mama was in a hurry to get back to the motel, in case Daddy had gotten there; she walked way ahead of me and Stell. We took our time.

From the truck the store displays had looked full of interesting things to buy. Up close, the windows were streaked, the merchandise faded and dusty. The leaves of the dying flowers hanging outside the millinery store had bug bites in them. There were only five things in the display case: two white straw picture hats, a pink cloche, a blue beret, a yellow pillbox.

Burnett's Grocery, with baskets of produce on the sidewalk, had a hand-lettered poster in the window:

TENT REVIVAL!
Friday, August 13, 8 PM.
The Reverend Brian Samuel Cureton preaching.
The Campground at
New Smyrna AME Zion Church.
COME TO JESUS!

"I want to see a tent meeting," said Stell Ann. Mama was almost a block ahead of us.

"You're crazy. Mama and Daddy wouldn't be caught dead in a colored church."

"I wasn't going to invite them."

"They won't let us go alone."

Stell walked up to a man who was napping in a chair in front of the barbershop. "Sir?"

The man's eyes popped open.

"Could you tell me how to get to New Smyrna AME Zion?"

"That's a Nigra church."

"Our girl wants to know." Stell lied smoothly.

"It's a ways out Zion Church Creek Road."

"Could she walk there?"

"Easy. It's not but maybe a mile." He closed his eyes and sat back in his chair as we walked away.

"Mary will take us," Stell said. It was settled.

Mary, Davie, and Puddin were at the swing set in the courtyard. I ran to Mary. "Hey! We got your cakes!"

Mama came up behind me. "With citron, just what you wanted. Two dollars and forty cents. Do you want to pay me or should I take it out—"

"No, ma'am, I'll pay you." She looked in the bag. "Oh."

"I'm going over to my cabin. You can give the money to Jubie."

"All right."

"What's the matter?" I asked her.

Mama turned around.

"Nothing. They just so little."

"Well, Mary," said Mama, "the big ones are awfully expensive."

"Yes, ma'am. These're fine."

"Good," Mama said brightly, and went to her cabin.

I sat in one of the swings. "Okay, so what's wrong? Really."

"I was going to give one to my friend for a present. One for our church party, one for me and the kids. Thought they'd be big, not them weedy things."

"I'm so sorry."

"It's all right."

I jumped to my feet. "I've got it! We can go to the fruitcake store tomorrow morning. Stell will stay with Puddin and Davie if we explain to her. You can get all the cakes you want."

She grinned, the gold on her front tooth gleaming. "That'd be real fine."

• • •

I was in our cabin, searching for my *Wonder Woman* comic to read by the pool, when a car door thumped shut. Puddin yelled, "It's Daddy!"

I peeked through a gap in the Venetian blinds where a slat had broken. Daddy had Davie, swinging him high, talking to him. Mrs. Bishop from the motel office was in her driveway, looking toward Daddy and smiling. His hair was sun-streaked and he had a good tan, like he'd been playing golf regularly and fishing at Lake Wylie. He propped Davie on his shoulders, which were so broad Davie looked like a doll. Stell stood several feet away from him. I was sure she was thinking about Aunt Lily. Daddy turned to her, and the sun glinted off his glasses. She shrugged at something he said and pointed toward Mama's cabin.

I backed away from the window. With the blinds closed, the cabin was hot and dim; the only light came through the screen door. I didn't want to say hello to Daddy, because I would have to act tickled to see him. I wanted it to be as if he had been with us all along, so we wouldn't have to make over each other. I was sitting on the bed when Mary came in with Davie, bringing the sunlight with her. The screen door clattered shut.

"Why's this place closed up, hot as it is?"

"I shut the blinds so I could put on my bathing suit."

"Why didn't you put it on?"

"Daddy's here."

"Your daddy never seen you in a bathing suit?" She sat beside me, rocking Davie. He had his thumb in his mouth and his eyelids drooped. Perspiration dotted the curve of his nose, and I touched it with the back of my finger. He put his head on Mary's shoulder and closed his eyes. She rocked, humming, rubbing his back. I smelled Davie's baby powder and her soap. My eyes got heavy. Maybe we'd all fall asleep and Daddy wouldn't want to wake us.

Mary stopped rocking. "He gone to sleep?"

"Uh-huh."

She lowered Davie to the bed, putting him down on his back, smoothing out the cotton bedspread under him. She unglued his hair from his damp forehead and picked up a magazine from the floor. "You didn't come say hey to your daddy."

"I will, after he sees Mama. Did he ask about me?"

She fanned Davie. "I said you was swimming. Thought you was."

The screen door opened. Daddy stood in the doorway, blocking the light.

I got up. "Hey, Daddy."

He hugged me. "Hey, Junebug." He held me at arm's length and looked at me. "You've grown another foot."

"Nope, I've still only got two."

He laughed. "Mary told me you were swimming."

"I will be, soon's I get my suit on."

He touched me on the shoulder. "You doing okay?"

"Yes, sir."

Daddy rubbed Davie's tummy. "I wish I could sleep like that."

"Bill?" Mama called from the yard.

"Hey, Pauly!" Daddy's face lit up. He went outside. Mama stood by his car, her arms folded across her bosom. Daddy reached in his pants pocket and offered her a gift-wrapped box. "Wanted to bring some joy back in your life."

Mama took the gift, not looking at Daddy. She tore it open. "Joy!" Mama's favorite perfume. She shook her head.

"We've got to get past this, Paula." Did he mean Aunt Lily?

"I need time."

"It's almost a year." He put his arm around her shoulders and she didn't pull away. As they turned to walk toward Mama's cabin, he asked, "The Packard, is it a mess?"

"It's a mess."

I went into the bathroom to change so I wouldn't be naked in front of Mary. When I took off my blouse, I thought about what Mama would say if she noticed the hair in my armpits. There wasn't much, and it was so light sometimes I thought it was my imagination, but I knew Mama would make me shave, just as she'd made me wear Stell

Ann's old training bras as soon as I started getting bosoms. I put on my suit and draped a towel around my shoulders, the way lifeguards do in the movies, and left the bathroom.

Mary looked up. "That a new swimsuit?"

"What do you think?" I twirled, trailing the towel.

"I think you growed up while I wasn't looking."

A pencil of sunlight coming through the broken blind played across my thighs and I looked down at the same time Mary did. She put out her hand and smoothed my upper legs as if to wipe away the faint blue and yellow marks.

I'd seen Davie with my comic, so I went to see if it was in Mama and Daddy's cabin. I opened the door and smelled Daddy's aftershave. The bed was made, with the tufted spread hanging just to the dust ruffle. I knew if I looked under the pillow on Mama's side, I'd find her pink nightgown. I tripped over Daddy's white ducks. His seersucker jacket was on the chair back, his khaki slacks folded over the arm. My comic wasn't with Davie's things. Not on the bedside table or on the dresser with Daddy's pocketknife and change. I looked under the dresser and saw Daddy's Zippo gleaming in the dusty shadows. I pushed it behind a leg of the dresser and left it there.

In the bathroom, his Dopp kit was by the sink, and Mama's slippers were on the floor, but no

Wonder Woman. I stood in the middle of the cabin, ready to give up and go to the pool, when I saw a Tinkertoy beside the night table. I lifted the dust ruffle and there was my comic book, pushed against the wall behind Daddy's brown leather suitcase. I crawled under the bed, grabbed it, and heard Mama and Daddy on the path outside.

"Oh, Pauly, she just wanted to look at the new paint job on the breezeway."

"Linda Gibson has her eyes on you, and you don't discourage her."

"I'm only being neighborly."

The cabin door opened. I pulled my feet up so that I was lying on my side, wrapped around Daddy's suitcase.

"You stare at her breasts."

"The day I don't notice a nice figure, you can put me under."

"I wish that's all you did. You don't even bother to be discreet. Ye gods, my brother's wife . . ."

"Let it go, Paula, my love. I've missed you."

Mama sighed. "Me, too, Bill."

The grit on the floor was sandpaper on my shoulder.

"C'mon, sweetheart." Daddy's voice was soft.

"What if the kids come looking for us?"

I made myself lie so still I felt my breathing stop.

"Let's lock them out." A click. "Come here, Paula." Daddy sat down and the bed sank to within inches of my face. My right arm was folded under me, the comic in my hand. The floor felt like a hot iron on my elbow. I held my hand over my nose to keep the dust out. "I'll never get enough of you," Daddy said.

They were quiet, then something fell beside the bed. Daddy's shirt. Mama's sandals landed near my face, her sundress slid to the floor. Daddy said, "Sit up, let me do it." His shoes dropped off the end of the bed, followed by Mama's bra and panties.

I decided I would kill myself if they found me. It got so quiet I was afraid to breathe. The mattress sank over me, almost touching my face. Mama started making sounds, not words. Daddy growled. The metal bed springs moved up and down, up and down, touching my cheek, then rising again. I pushed one ear against the floor, put my finger in the other one to shut out the sounds. Some of Mama's noises got through. The dust made me want to sneeze and I pinched my nose until tears filled my eyes. One of the hooks holding the bed springs stretched away from the frame. I stared at it, certain it would give way and the mattress would fall on me. I watched it hard, making it not slip any more. Just when I was sure it was going to fail, Daddy shouted something so loud I jumped, certain he'd seen me.

Mama moaned. "Bill, oh, God, Bill."

The mattress moved, grew still. They panted like they'd been running. Mama sighed and they got quiet. I waited and waited, listening until their breathing slowed. My right leg cramped. Were they asleep? They had to be—then Mama's feet touched the floor beside my head. She walked into the bathroom and closed the door. In the stillness that followed, Daddy's regular breaths turned into snores. Sounds came from the bathroom, water running, the toilet flushing, the echoing gargling noise of Mama brushing her teeth. I pictured her holding the bridge with her false tooth in it. The bathroom door opened and Mama padded barefoot to pick up her bra and panties. She slid into her sandals. Her clothes rustled. I heard the snapping of her hair as she brushed it, the soft pop of her lipstick tube, the click of the bolt lock. She opened the front door. Daddy mumbled, "Zat?"

"Sleep well, honey." Mama's Zippo clinked.

Daddy began to snore again. I wriggled out from under the bed and onto my back. Daddy's foot hung over my face, his big toe almost touching my nose. I slid away and got to my feet, tiptoed away from the bed. Daddy turned onto his back. His thing lay across the bushy hair at the bottom of his belly.

I opened the screen door slowly, but the rusty springs creaked. I had one foot on the front stoop, my back to the room, when his snoring stopped. A fly buzzed near my ear. Daddy coughed. "Jubie?"

"Sir?" My voice cracked.

I heard him moving in the bed. "What are you doing?"

"I just wanted—"

"What?"

"My *Wonder Woman*. Davie had it and I wanted to take it to the pool, so I came—"

"Look at me."

I couldn't turn around to his nakedness. I held out the comic book.

"June!" His voice was stern. I turned. He had covered himself. The fly landed on my shoulder and I let it sit there, tickling me.

"Tell your mother I'm going to nap for a while."

"Yes, sir." The screen door clattered behind me. I ran into the yard and down toward the pool.

I slowed to a walk on the path through the pines, sick with relief. I had a stitch in my side and I rubbed it with my balled-up fist, choking to keep from crying.

At the pool I peeled the comic book off my sweaty hand, hurled it to the pavement, and dove into the deep end, barely missing Stell, who was hanging on the side. I went all the way to the bottom and hooked my fingers through the drain to hold me down in the cold, clear water.

CHAPTER 20

Daddy said he'd heard that Georgia barbecue, like fruitcakes, shouldn't be missed. I added it to my list of favorite foods, along with onion rings and pecan pie.

Mama took a bite, closed her eyes, breathed deeply. "Delicious." She'd said, "Bill, oh, God, Bill," in that same tone of voice. I had to look away.

"Have you talked with Carter?" Mama asked Stell.

"Yes. He and his family are going on to Pawleys today."

"And the people we rented from, will he tell them about our delay?"

Stell nodded. "He'll get the key and directions to our place. I told him I'd call when we leave Claxton, maybe Monday. He'll wait for us at the pier, no matter how late."

"That is just so nice of him," said Mama.

Stell said, "He's a nice boy." She ate a hush puppy. "There's a tent meeting tonight."

Daddy said, "So?"

Stell said, "As you know, I have a great interest in religion."

Oh, brother, I thought.

Daddy rolled his eyes.

Stell wiped her mouth with a napkin. "I've

always wanted to go to a revival. You remember when we went to see Daddy Grace and I—"

"Where's this meeting?" Daddy asked.

"Just outside town. We can walk. I'm sure Mary would like to go."

Mama looked at Daddy. "Or they could use the Chrysler."

"Not on your life," Daddy said. "She already wrecked the Packard."

"That wasn't my fault!" Stell shrieked.

Daddy looked sorry. "What time's this thing?"

Stell smirked at me. "Not until eight, and it's only five thirty."

I watched my feet while we walked, trying to keep my tennis shoes from getting too dirty before we got to the meeting. Stell had polished her white patent leather flats with Vaseline; they were glopped with a paste of grease and red dust.

I remembered something I saw in a newspaper in Claxton. I wanted to ask Mary about it but wasn't sure how. School would be starting soon, and there was all sorts of speculation about how we'd be affected by something called *Brown versus Board of Education*. The Supreme Court. Colored and white kids going to school together. I'd seen a picture in the paper of a Negro girl in Washington who was going to a white school because the Court said she could. The girl stood in front of her house with her mama and daddy. The words under the

225

picture said it was little Alysha Alderman, but she didn't look little to me. Her skinny arms dangled from the sleeves of her dress, and she was almost as tall as her father.

"Mary, did you go to school when you were a girl?"

"How else you think I came to read and write?"

"Your mama could have taught you."

"Mama never read nor wrote, not in her life."

"Where'd you go to school?"

"In what used to be a house, till the land around it got farmed out. The people moved on, leaving a rotten barn and a decent farmhouse."

"Who was your teacher?"

"We had first one, then another. Wore them out because all of us was in the same room, even ones too young to be in school, but they had to be someplace while they mamas would go clean houses, do mill work. Then they was us older ones. I kept going till I was fifteen and had to go do houses my own self."

"You know those signs we keep seeing, 'No Browns in Our Schools'?"

"I know about that."

"That's because of *Brown versus Board of Education*," Stell said. I'd never thought to ask her.

"That's it," said Mary. "But I s'pect your mama's right. Won't see Negro children going to school with white children here. Not for a while. But it'll happen. Just people needs to register, vote. Take time, but we do it."

She meant her people, not us.

The rest of the way to the tent meeting, my mind was filled with thoughts of what it would be like to go to school with coloreds. Would they sit beside me? Were they smart enough to learn? Mary was. Leesum was. The way Mama and Daddy talked, mixing blacks and whites in school would be horrible, but maybe they were wrong.

We saw a lake in a field, a rowboat tied to a pier. A platform with a stub of a diving board floated out in the middle, and two colored boys sprawled on the float. A girl stood at the end of the board, holding her arms over her head, hands together, pointing toward the sky. She leaned over the end of the board until she fell in, then climbed up and did the same thing again. I could have showed her a thing or two about diving. At the far end of the pond, a woman was fishing, the float on her line making rings on the water.

Long before we got to the tent we could see it, a huge khaki box growing out of the grass. A man and three children trotted down the road.

"We gone be late, Daddy," said one of the children.

"Naw we ain't," said the man, "if you runs fast." He touched his hand to his hat as he passed us.

At the path that led to the tent, Stell brushed the dust from her legs. Mary smoothed down the skirt of her dress, straightening till she seemed a foot taller.

In the dusk, the tent glowed, with yellow light pouring from every opening. As we approached, I heard a jumble of voices, a girl giggling. A man shouted something I didn't understand. Whatever he said made the girl laugh so hard she choked.

Mary spoke to a man standing by the entrance, smoking. "Evenin'."

"Yes'm, yes'm." He nodded to us.

"We comin' to de meetin'," Mary said.

"Yes'm, you and the young misses?"

"That right. That right." Her head bobbed up and down. "Have it started?" She sounded like our yard man.

"No'm, and still plenty room."

"Mary, why are you talking—" She grabbed my hand and looked at me in a way that hushed me.

She asked, "It okay we takes a seat?"

His head bobbed back and forth. "Fine, just fine."

Inside the tent the air was warm and damp. Too many bodies too close together. We stood in the aisle. People turned in their seats, looked at us. Silence moved across the tent. An old woman stood and held her hand out to Mary.

"Evening, Sister. You visiting the meeting?"

"Yes'm, me and de girls. I works for dey mama."

"We welcome you." She motioned to some empty chairs three rows from the back. "Help yourself."

We took seats on the wide aisle. A center pole

raised the canvas high off the floor. Support poles formed a vast square room, with flaps tied back at each corner to let in air. People sat on folding wooden chairs, ladder-backs and stools, metal porch chairs, wooden rockers. Children sat on fruit crates in the aisle. In less than a week I'd been in two tents—the first one at the carnival where I met Leesum.

The wooden altar had a cross painted on it, with twelve flaming candles set in brass candlesticks around the front and along both sides. A choir in purple robes filled chairs behind the pulpit, sitting silent and still, their faces lit by the flickering light. All I could think about was how hot they must be in their robes.

Stell's shoulder touched mine. She fingered her cross, pulling the chain tight against her neck. Mary opened her purse and took out a fan— cardboard with a wooden handle and a picture of Jesus suffering the little children. "We can share."

A family sat in front of us, a man in overalls and a white shirt, a woman in a flowered dress and hat. Three children, two girls and a boy. The older girl looked at me. She wore pearls and there was a coarse hair caught in the clasp.

Two boys in white robes entered through one of the corners of the tent, carrying flowers they put in front of the choir, which stood humming in unison, then falling into harmony until the hum became a strong chord that faded and grew, soft, loud, soft again. Eyes closed, they swayed side to side.

A fat man in a dark suit walked up the aisle, holding a Bible against his chest. His head was bowed and his eyes were closed, but he never missed a step. When he turned and looked at the congregation, the candles lit his face. His white hair bushed out from his head, and his eyes glittered as he set the Bible on the pulpit, then lifted his hands and said, "Brothers and Sisters, welcome to the house of God."

"Amen!" the congregation responded in many voices. The hum of the choir rose in pitch.

"Welcome to Jesus!" the preacher shouted.

"Jesus! Amen!" the people replied. I heard Mary's voice.

The humming got louder. The preacher lowered his face, closed his eyes. A woman began to sing, her voice strong and rich. *"O my brother, do you know the Savior"*—she stepped away from the pew, raised her arms and sang so loud the tent filled with her voice— *"who is wondrous kind and true? He's the rock of your salvation. There's honey in the rock for you."* The choir echoed her last phrase. *"Oh, there's honey in the rock, my brother, there's honey in the rock for you."*

The singing made the air in the tent even hotter, and I could hardly breathe for the smell of the bodies around me. The woman singing solo raised her arms again, and loose skin swung in arcs to her elbows. Her face glowed.

Stell Ann repeated the words. "There's honey in the rock for you."

The hymn ended and a man behind us said, "Sister Roland, she got the call."

"A voice from God."

Nothing else broke the silence until the preacher shouted, "Repent!"

Stell gasped. Mary sat still, her eyes closed.

"Repent!" the preacher screamed again. "Is there honey in the rock for you? We got to ask ourself this question every day. Not just on Sunday, not just when we in trouble, but every day. Every minute of every day we got to live for Jesus. Elsewise Jesus can't be waiting around for us."

"Can't wait!" a man shouted.

"Amen!" came from several places at once.

"Has you got sin?" asked the preacher.

"Yes, Lord," screamed a woman.

"Yes, yes!"

"Repent!" the preacher shouted.

"Amen! Hallelujah! Praise Jesus!"

"Some of you thinks your sins is forgiven," the preacher said. "You repent. God forgives you. But the Lord don't work in advance. He don't pardon sins you fixing to commit."

"That right, Lord don't work in advance," a woman behind me repeated. Sweat slid from my hair down my neck.

The preacher stared first at one person, then another. "Let the one who has no sin throw a rock at me now." The only sound was the rustling of Mary's sleeve as she fanned herself. "If there's somebody out there who repented last meeting and hasn't sinned in the meantime, come on up here and take my place."

Voices rumbled, "Yes, Reverend. We all sinners. Amen. God's love." Nobody walked forward.

He touched the Bible on the pulpit. "Read the Word, my people! The Good Book will keep you straight. Study on it till it's in your mind, for those times when a Bible ain't handy or you cain't find your glasses." He picked up the Bible, opened it, and recited:

"Enter into his gates with thanksgiving and unto his courts with praise: Be thankful unto him, and bless his name. For the Lord is good, his mercy is everlasting; and his truth endureth to all generations."

He snapped the book shut. "But none of us is ready to enter the Kingdom of Heaven. Not you. Not me. We got to ask Jesus to forgive us. Get down on your knees. Pray till it hurts. Be ready when you're called."

Stell's face glowed. Her lips parted. "Jubie?" She fell against me, then hit the floor, wedged between me and the chairs in front of us.

"Oh, no!" Mary screamed. The preacher paused. People turned to look at us. A big woman rose from her seat across the aisle. She shoved chairs out of her way and bent over Stell Ann, pushing me aside like a chair.

"She be okay, just fell out." The woman picked Stell up as if she weighed nothing and headed down the aisle toward the exit. Mary and I followed.

The preacher started up again, and the congregation turned back to him.

Outside the tent, the woman lowered Stell Ann to the ground and sat down beside her. She grabbed the fan from Mary, clutched it in her beefy hand, and began to fan Stell with a fury. I reached out to pat Stell, but the woman said, "Leave her be. She in the spirit." Like Mary giving me an order. I sat back in the dust. The woman had BO so bad it made me choke. Mary kneeled beside us, her eyes closed, hands folded in prayer.

A mass of gray hair surrounded the woman's fat face. Her purple dress had a collar of white lace, ragged and dirty around her neck. She prayed, her face shining in the light from a nearby torch. "Lord, this white child have fainted for you. Your spirit come over her and she be fill with Jesus. Gentle her, so she come back to us." She took Stell's right hand in both of hers.

Stell's eyelids fluttered. The woman leaned over her and a drop of sweat landed on Stell's forehead. Stell's eyes opened. She looked up into that black perspiring face, inches from her own.

"Hey, honey, you coming back?"

Stell moaned and closed her eyes.

"Oh, Lord, be in her now, give her cease from sorrow."

Mary said, "I believe this child has had about all the Lord she can take for one night. You go get some water."

"Yes'm, that probably do it." The woman put her hand on my shoulder and pushed down hard as she got to her feet.

"Stell Ann? You wake up now, it's time to get on home." Mary rubbed Stell's hands. "Estelle Annette Watts, open your eyes."

Stell looked up at Mary. "What happened?"

"You took off for a while."

The woman was back with a cup of water. Stell sat up and drank.

Mary said, "Stell, can you stand?"

Stell got to her feet. "I'm okay, really."

"You reckon you can walk back to the motel park? It's a good ways."

"Honestly, I'm fine."

There was a clatter of voices inside the tent, and the woman said, "Reverend Cureton taking a break." She reached into a pocket of her dress and took out a watch with a broken wristband. "Dint do but half a hour. He hungry. We always feeds 'em good."

"We be getting on," said Mary. With Stell in the middle, we held hands walking back up Zion Church Creek Road as the moon began to rise.

CHAPTER 21

At the edge of town, Stell directed us down a tree-lined avenue with wide lawns, a shortcut to the motel. We left the rumble of the boulevard. Our footsteps clattered on the sidewalk in the warm night, and our shadows stretched ahead and disappeared in the glow of the next streetlamp.

Mary asked Stell, "Is it okay, us going down this street?"

"It's the quickest way back."

"That's good."

I remembered the curfew signs in Wickens.

We walked a bit, then Stell said, "Reverend Cureton has fervor."

"Um-hum," Mary said.

I said, "He's no Daddy Grace."

Stell snickered. "You've never heard Daddy Grace preach."

Mary chuckled, her gold tooth glinting. "They different, that's for sure. Reverend Cureton preaches in a tent. Daddy Grace, he got a door mat woven from twenty-dollar bills for wiping the mud off his gator shoes."

A car came down the street, slowed as it got to us, sped away.

A mosquito buzzed my ear. The air smelled like fresh-cut grass.

There was a loud pop, the tinkling of breaking

glass. A streetlight went out a block away. Everything was quiet, even the crickets. Mary said, "Some boy got a new BB gun." She walked faster. "I was a member of the House of Prayer from a child, and Daddy Grace was Moses to me. But I saw the light. Now I'm at McDowell Street Baptist."

"Where Leesum is?"

"Yes, with Reverend—"

Another loud pop. A streetlamp near us shattered. Stell gasped.

"Stell, Jubie—" Mary's voice was shrill.

A man spoke behind us. "We gonna get you, girl."

Across the street a porch light came on. A woman shouted, "What's going on?"

"Nothing, ma'am," the man called out. "We're just clearing some niggers outen your neighborhood."

"Help!" I screamed.

The light went out. A door slammed.

"They're after me," Mary said. "Y'all run. Get the police—"

Someone grabbed my hand and wrenched it behind my back, up between my shoulder blades. Another man shoved Stell against a tree, his hand over her mouth. I screamed again.

"Shut up!" The man holding me had rotten cigarette breath and stank of liquor.

A third man said, "What you doing walking in a white neighborhood after dark?"

Mary said, "Going home from the meeting."

The man facing Mary wore a white T-shirt that glowed in the moonlight. He slapped her. "Use your manners, girl."

She didn't say anything.

He socked her. Mary cried out, put her hand to the side of her face. "Please, mister, leave us be."

I yelled for help. The man behind me jerked my hand higher and coughed against my neck. "I said shut up." His foul breath washed across my face and I clamped my teeth so hard my jaw hurt.

The man in the T-shirt hit Mary in the stomach. She doubled over with a horrible groan.

"Go on," the man behind me said. "Hit her again."

"I got a idea about this girl."

"Same idea I got about these li'l white gals?"

Mary struggled to speak. "Dey don't know 'bout pleasin' a man. I can show you boys a good time. All you."

"Nigger gals are born wanting it," said the one holding me.

"Yessuh," Mary said. "Yessuh, yessuh, you right." Talking colored again.

A car came down the street. Brakes squealed and a woman hollered from the car, "Let's get outta here."

The men who held Stell and me shoved us on the sidewalk together, facedown. One of them said, "Put the darkie in the backseat."

Car doors slammed and they pulled away from the curb, tires squealing. The motor grew faint.

The pavement hurt my cheek. Crickets sounded loud again. A screen door banged shut. Stell prayed in a fast whisper, "Jesus, we offer ourselves for your care. Please be with us. Shelter us from our enemies."

"Mary," I said. "Ask God to protect Mary."

"God, please"—she stammered—"what's that?"

I listened, trying to separate the sound from the crickets and tree frogs. Metal clinking, a clicking. "A dog, coming down the sidewalk." I smelled it, felt it snuffling around our legs.

Stell jerked. "It's in my face."

The dog licked my arm and I pushed against its hairy belly. "Shoo!"

Claws clicked on the sidewalk; the dog's collar jangled as it ran away. I sat up.

Stell tugged at my sleeve. "They'll come back." She began to shiver.

I pulled her to me. She was my big sister and I wanted her to be strong. "You're scaring me."

We sat there, Stell shaking and crying in my arms, making me crazy. I touched my elbow where the dog had licked me and my hand came away wet and sticky. "Ugh," I said, wiping my hand on my skirt.

"What?" Stell's voice shook.

"Dog gunk." I touched the spot again. "And I skinned my elbow."

She got to her feet and took my hand, pulling me up. I caught my hem under my shoe and felt the skirt tear away from the bodice.

Stell said, "Mary's dress was caught in the car door. Flapping in the wind."

I put my cheek against her hair and sobbed. "What will they do to her?"

A door opened in a house across the street and a woman stepped out on her porch. "Who are you girls?"

"Help us!" Stell ran toward the woman, pulling me behind her.

A block away a car roared around a corner, came straight at us. Stell froze in the headlights. I pushed her up on the curb as the car stopped and two men jumped out.

"Somebody called the sheriff," a tall man said.

"Thank goodness," Stell said.

"Are you hurt?"

"No," we said together.

The lady came down her front walk. "Sheriff Higgins."

"Mrs. Rainey." The tall man was in slacks and a golf shirt, not a uniform.

"These girls've been making a racket."

"They took Mary," I said.

"She was hurt," said Stell.

Mrs. Rainey looked at my dress. "You should cover yourself."

My stomach showed where I'd ripped my dress.

"Go after them," I said to the sheriff, "before they kill Mary."

"Who's this Mary?"

"Our maid," Stell Ann said.

"She colored?" asked the skinny man who was with the sheriff.

"Yes, sir."

"What happened to her?"

"Some men beat her up. They put her in their car and took her away. They were talking about—"

"About what?" the sheriff asked.

"Tell him," I said to Stell.

"He, the biggest man, he said he wanted to—that he was going to—attack her."

"Sounds like they already did that," the second man said. He was shorter than the sheriff, with a scratchy voice.

"Assault her," Stell murmured.

"I'm sorry to ask you this, missy, but do you mean rape her?"

Stell looked down. "Yes, sir, that's what they meant."

"Oh, my," said Mrs. Rainey. "If y'all don't need me, I believe I'll go back inside." Her front door closed and the porch light went off.

"How old's this darkie?" the short man asked.

"Her name is Mary Luther and she's forty-seven," I said.

The sheriff looked at me over the rim of his glasses. "Did she provoke them? Did she talk back?"

240

I said, "She's too smart for that."

"A smart nigger?" The short man snorted.

"Mary *is* smart, and she's not—" Stell said.

"Don't pay any mind to Ray there," Sheriff Higgins said. "Where you girls from?"

"Charlotte, North Carolina."

"What y'all doing in Georgia?"

"We're on vacation."

"Y'all the ones had that wreck yesterday at Grady and Main?"

"Yes, sir."

"Where are you staying?"

"At Sally's Motel Park," I said, "with our family."

"We'll let you call your parents from the station. It's late for y'all to be out alone."

"We weren't alone." I couldn't swallow around the rock in the back of my throat. "We were with Mary."

241

CHAPTER 22

The sheriff's office was in a building smaller than our garage. A man in uniform behind the front desk looked up as we walked in.

"These girls need to call their parents," Sheriff Higgins said.

"Yes, sir." The man scrambled to move the phone to the front edge of the desk. "You need the book?" Stell nodded. He handed her a flimsy directory.

The sheriff went to a coffeepot in the corner and poured himself a cup. "Could I get you some water?" he asked me. "Too late to send out for Co-Cola."

I shook my head. I kept taking deep breaths, tried to stop trembling. Where was Mary now? What were they doing to her?

Stell hung up. "Daddy'll be here in ten minutes."

"Come on in my office," said the sheriff. "We'll be done by the time he gets here."

He sat behind his desk, pointing Stell and me to two metal chairs. The one window was open, but the room was too warm. "Give me a second." The sheriff pulled out several desk drawers, looking for something. "Here it is; knew I had one." He handed me a safety pin. "You ripped your . . ."

He looked out the window while I pinned the skirt of my dress to the bodice. "Everything'll be okay, sooner or later."

How could he know that?

A jittery fluorescent light buzzed overhead. He wrote something on a pad, then swiveled his chair and picked up three sheets of paper, sandwiched carbon paper between them, and rolled them into the typewriter beside his desk. "August 13, 1954, ten-oh-five p.m.," he said, typing. "Lillington Avenue at Cameron." Plick-plick-pling, using two fingers, looking down at the keys, then over his glasses at what he'd typed. He glanced back at Stell. "I need your full name and age."

"Estelle Annette Watts. Sixteen and a half."

"One six." He typed the numbers. "Birth date?"

"February 11, 1938."

"And you?"

"June Bentley Watts. Thirteen. October 4, 1940."

He typed again. "And your girl's name? What'd you say it is?"

Stell said, "Mary Luther," and I said, "Mary Constance Culpepper Luther."

The sheriff typed some more and I added, "She'll be forty-eight next month." I wished I could remember her exact birthday.

"The men who took your maid, how many were there?"

"Three," I said.

"Plus the girl driving the car," Stell said.

"Did you get a good look at them?"

Stell said, "The one who—he shoved me against

a tree. I couldn't see Jubie and Mary." Tears welled in her eyes, rolled down her face. "And they shot out the streetlights. A BB gun or something."

He made notes on the pad, then looked at me. "How about you? Anything that sticks in your mind."

I thought of rotten breath, the smell of liquor, cigarettes, and BO. "Tall," I said. "The one who held me was taller than I am, skinny and strong."

"How tall are you?"

"Five-nine. He'd been drinking."

"How do you know?"

"I know the smell."

His lips pushed into a thin line. He looked at Stell Ann. "The fella who had you, what can you tell me?"

"His hands are calloused." She closed her eyes. "He's big like a football player, or maybe just fat."

"Do you know what kind of car—"

"The one who beat up Mary had on a white T-shirt," I said, remembering.

"Good girl." The sheriff made a note.

Stell said, "A four-door Chevy, with white sidewalls and a loose muffler."

"Stell!" I was proud of her.

"You sure?"

"I heard the muffler dragging. I looked up as they drove off and—"

"But you said the streetlights—"

"Full moon, or almost."

"You're right." His pen moved on the pad. "What color was the car?"

Stell shook her head. "Light blue or gray."

The sheriff stood. "Be right back." He went into the outer office.

Stell took my hand. "They'll find her. She'll be all right."

"What if they don't?"

We sat in silence.

The sheriff came back, sat down behind his desk. "Y'all got a picture of your girl?"

"No," said Stell.

"I do." Stell looked at me. "I *do*. From Uncle Stamos' birthday party."

"Mary wasn't in any of those."

"I kept the ones Mama tossed out. One was just Mary and me. I've got it at the motel."

"That'll help," said the sheriff. "Coloreds look so much alike."

"No, they don't," Stell said.

The sheriff said, "Hmph." Like Mary.

I asked him, "When are you going to start looking for her?"

"We already are. Ray's driving around town, asking questions. We just radioed him a description of the car."

I hoped someone would find Mary before Ray did.

The door swung open, banging against the wall. "Par'me, Sheriff, but they's a man out here making a ruckus."

Daddy's voice boomed from the front office. "I want my daughters, damn it! Are they hurt?" I slid down in my chair.

Somebody said something I couldn't hear. Daddy yelled, "Where in hell are they?"

The sheriff said, "Bring him on in."

Daddy burst into the sheriff's office. "God, I'm glad you're okay. You are okay, aren't you?"

"Yes, sir," we both said at once.

"We're about done here, Mr. Watts."

Daddy shook the sheriff's hand. "Just want to take my girls to their mother." He looked at Stell. "I guess you got enough religion."

She stared at the floor.

We answered a few more questions. When Sheriff Higgins said he was finished, I asked, "Is Mary okay? Do you think she's okay?"

He looked at Daddy, down at his desk. "I'm sure she is. We'll see."

We left his office with Daddy holding our hands. We were almost to the Chrysler when he shoved Stell so hard she fell against the car.

"Daddy!" she cried out.

I couldn't move. I'd never seen him raise a hand to anyone but me.

"It's all your fault, you and that goddamn religious stuff you're always pushing at us. Jesus this and Jesus that!" He kicked one of the tires.

"It's not my fault." Stell stood by the car, her

face white in the moonlight. I wanted to warn her to be quiet.

Daddy drew back his hand as if he were going to hit her.

"Go ahead. You're only a hundred pounds heavier, so it'll be fair. I'll scream if you touch me."

He stood there, his glasses two disks of reflected light. "Get in the car."

I couldn't get to sleep. The heat was in bed with me, and there was no cool side to the pillow. Every time I closed my eyes, I could hear the men beating Mary. I kept wanting to grunt and moan. After a long time of trying to get comfortable, I got up. I bumped into Mary's cot on my way to the door. If she'd been there, I would have gone to my knees and put my head on her chest. I wanted her strong brown arms around me so bad my bones hurt. I went outside and stood in the grass and cried, hoping someone would hear me and afraid someone would. The stoop light came on at Mama and Daddy's cabin. The screen door opened and Mama came out, ghostly in her nightgown. I waited for her to say something, but she just stood there rubbing her arms. I finally said, "Mama?" my voice so shaky I didn't sound like me.

"Jubie? What are you doing out here?"

"I can't sleep. I'm worried about Mary."

"Let's sit." She pointed to the swing set. She sat

in one swing and I sat in the other, smelling the rusty chains, feeling the splintery boards through my pajamas. Mosquitoes bit my legs, but I was too sad to swat them. The air was filled with the heavy sweet smell of Mrs. Bishop's gardenias. Silent tears rolled down my cheeks. I wanted Mama to hug me or hold me the way Mary did, but if she tried, we'd feel strange.

Mama said, "They'll find her. Of course they will."

I tried to believe her. We swung for a while, me sniffling, Mama slapping at bugs, not saying anything. The night sounds got louder, like the crickets and frogs had been waiting for us to stop talking so they could get going again. That morning, I'd seen two dead frogs floating in the pool, white bellies up. Did they die from the chlorine or get so worn out from treading water that their hearts just quit? A man lying on a lounge had said, "Sometimes there's half a dozen of them. Strange how dead things don't sink."

The swings moved in unison.

Mama said, "It's going to be all right, you'll see."

"Mama, they beat her so bad. She needs a doctor." A yowling rose from my chest.

"You're going to wake everybody in the park."

"Not Mary," I wailed.

A screen door opened, Daddy called out, "Pauly? What's that racket?"

Lights came on in the office where Mrs. Bishop's apartment was. Mama took my hand and pulled me up. "We've got to go inside."

Daddy was in front of his and Mama's cabin, hands on his hips, the light behind him. "It's the middle of the night."

"Jubie's upset about Mary. I was just trying to calm her down."

She was just listening to me cry.

"C'mere, Junebug," Daddy said. I fell into the dusty tobacco smell of him. He held me close, rubbed my back.

Mama kissed my cheek, her cigarette breath enveloping me. "I'll go back in, then."

I cried into Daddy's chest until the horrible ache inside me was numb. When I got quiet, he said, "C'mon, Jujube, I'll walk you home." At the cabin, he said, "The police'll catch those guys and bring Mary back. Don't you worry."

"Daddy, that man at the front desk said there wasn't any use looking for her at night because she'd be so hard to see."

"He's not in charge, honey. Sheriff Higgins is heading the search, a good man."

"The men who took her have to kill her. She knows what they look like."

"They probably think kidnapping a darkie isn't much of a crime. Might as well let her go."

In the cabin, I folded back the spread on Mary's cot and fluffed the pillow so her bed would be

249

waiting for her when she came in. I stood, touching her pillow, then wiggled in under the top sheet. If she got back before morning, she'd have to wake me. Knowing that, I fell asleep.

That night Mary spoke to me. If I was awake or asleep, it happened, and it wasn't a dream. She said, "Jubie, you're a fine girl, and I'm a fine girl, too."

I woke to whispers and giggles. Puddin, Stell Ann, and Davie were all in bed together, Davie under the sheets and Stell and Puddin poking at him, playing with him. Acting normal. I sat up. "Mary?" I asked.

The cabin got quiet. Stell shook her head.

"Nothing at all?"

"Nothing." I saw the strain on her face. She was just keeping up a good front for Puddin and Davie.

I got dressed and took Davie to Mama's cabin. She was sitting on the bed in her nightgown, sipping from a mug, letting her toenails dry. Pieces of cotton stuck out between each toe. The room was filled with sunshine, the smell of coffee, nail polish, cigarettes. I dumped Davie on the bed next to Mama, and she pulled him to her, cooing, "Hey, Davie-do, how's my boy this morning?"

He patted her face. "Mary?"

Mama looked at me, tears in her eyes.

"Wouldn't they have found her by now, if they were going to?"

"I don't know, Jubie. I just don't know. But it doesn't look good."

I felt empty and hard inside. "Where's Daddy?"

"Gone to talk to the sheriff and see about the Packard."

There was a knock at the door. "See who that is, honey."

"It's just me, Mrs. Watts, come to find out what happened to your girl." Mrs. Bishop pushed open the screen door. Her finger waves looked painted on. She reached for the ladderback chair by the door.

Mama said, "Please have a seat."

"Thank you." Mrs. Bishop sat, crossing her legs. She swung her foot and dangled her wedgy until it was barely hooked on her toe. "I was afraid your girls might have trouble."

"What do you mean?"

"Going off to that colored revival. Anybody knows they shouldn't have done that."

Mama sat up straight.

"Them being teenagers and walking after dark with a nigger."

"We do not use that word."

"You one of those integrators? I wouldn't have thought you'd be political, being such a lady."

Mama stood, stern and dignified, even in her nightgown with cotton between her toes. "I am not political, but I don't use foul language."

Davie began to cry.

"Mrs. Watts, please, I didn't mean to offend."

I picked up Davie.

Mama opened the door. "As soon as our car is fixed, we'll be on our way."

Mrs. Bishop went out, closing the screen carefully.

I couldn't believe what I'd heard. "We're leaving?"

"When the car—"

"Without Mary?" I wanted to hit her.

She took my hand and patted the bed. "Sit with me a minute." We sat. I shifted Davie to my lap and bounced him with my leg.

Mama said, "Bill's urging the sheriff to do everything possible. The car isn't as bad as we thought, and it might be ready Monday." Davie began to fuss and I moved my leg faster and faster.

"If Mary hasn't turned up by then—" Mama said, "I'm sure she will, but if she doesn't . . ."

"We'll leave?" I choked back tears.

"We can't stay indefinitely, honey. We're doing everything we can, but sooner or later—"

Davie screamed.

"Check his diaper," Mama said. "I've got to shower." She stood and took her robe from the back of a chair.

"Mama!"

"What?" She sounded exasperated.

I rubbed Davie's back. "We can't leave without knowing. . . ." Davie howled in my ear.

Mama tested one of her toenails, then pulled the cotton out. She went into the bathroom and closed the door. The shower came on.

I hugged Davie. "Shhh, shhh." I walked around and around, holding him close until his crying slowed, breathing through my mouth because his britches smelled so bad. I grabbed a diaper from the stack on the dresser and sat on the bed with him, rocking him back and forth, then lowering him to the spread. "Hush, hush, sweet boy. Gone change your diaper." I sounded like Mary.

Mama came out of the bathroom in her robe, her hair in a towel turban. A cloud of soapy-smelling steam followed her. She handed me a warm washcloth. "Wipe him good."

I pulled the diaper off Davie. "What's an integrator?"

"People who want to send you to school with colored children."

I wadded up the diaper, dropped it on the floor, and cleaned Davie's bottom, sprinkling him with baby powder. He kicked his legs happily.

Mama straightened. "And the word is 'integrationists,' not 'integrators.' Some people are prejudiced and ignorant to boot." She went in the bathroom, closing the door behind her.

Davie clapped his hands and reached for me. "Doobie."

By next week, he wouldn't remember Mary.

CHAPTER 23

Stell Ann was as sad as I was, but her way of handling it was to get busy. When I got to our cabin, she was straightening it, putting dirty clothes in a pillowcase. I wished I could be that way. "Where's Puddin?" I asked.

"I don't know." Stell's eyes were swollen. She hadn't combed her hair or washed her face, so unlike her.

"Does she know about Mary?"

Stell shrugged.

I ran outside, saw a speck of pink through the trees. Puddin's favorite T-shirt. She sat in a carpet of pine needles beside the outhouse, staring into the distance.

"Puddin?"

"Nobody told me." She scratched her knee. "Is she dead?"

I dropped down beside her, trying not to breathe in the odor coming from the outhouse.

"She must be dead or she'd come home," Puddin said.

I put my arms around her, held her. We walked together back to our cabin.

Stell and Mama took the kids to lunch. I wasn't hungry and Mama didn't insist. I put on my bathing suit and went out into the hot noon sun.

The concrete apron at the pool burned my feet. I dove in and breaststroked to the far wall before I came up. A woman was settling herself into one of the lounges. "You sure are a good swimmer."

"Thanks." I ducked my head, slicking back my hair.

"Are you on a swimming team?"

"Back home." I swam the length again, coming up near where the woman sat.

"Where's home?"

"Charlotte, North Carolina."

"Oh, goodness, you must be one of the girls got attacked on Lillington Avenue."

"How'd you know?"

She reached for her Coppertone. "I live just around the corner from where it happened. Sally said y'all were from Charlotte."

She had kind eyes and curly hair going from red to gray. Old as Meemaw, but thin and healthy, which made all the difference. She rubbed oil on her shoulders. "That bruise on your arm—from last night?"

For a second I was confused. Had Daddy hit me? Didn't matter, my answer would be the same. "Yes, ma'am."

"Do you know who attacked you?"

"Some men." I wanted her to hush.

"And—was it your sister, too?"

"Yes, ma'am, but we're okay."

"I'm glad you're all right."

I needed to say something out loud. "Mary, our maid, she's missing."

"Oh, yes, the Nigra girl who was with you." She poured Coppertone on her shins. "I'm sure Sheriff Higgins is doing what he can."

I ducked under and swam away fast. At the other end I climbed out and ran back to the cabin.

I had to find somebody who'd know how much Mary mattered, somebody who would do something, go looking for her. Out where the tent meeting was, lots of coloreds lived around there.

I trudged back up Zion Church Creek Road through afternoon shadows that striped the red clay. A man and three children stood in a circle in the field, holding fishing poles, heads bowed as if they were praying. Was it the same family from yesterday, the girl who was diving from the float? The wind carried a rusty smell like Rainbow Lake at Shumont. Birds flew up from the tall grass. Wires stretched between phone poles along the road and down a driveway to a brick house with sagging shutters, a vegetable garden in the front yard. A small, round colored woman was cutting corn off the stalks, dropping the ears into a bucket. The mailbox by the driveway said Ezra Travis. I walked toward the house, past corn plants rattling in the afternoon breeze.

I stopped by a thick azalea shrub between the garden and the house. The woman looked at me.

She was darker than Mary, shorter, fatter. A white apron covered her pink print dress. She slid her knife into the pocket of her apron. "Yes?"

"Are the Travises at home?"

"I'm Mrs. Travis."

"I'm trying to find—"

The woman said, "And you are?"

"Oh. June Watts."

She took off her gardening gloves. "Hello, Miss Watts. And who're you trying to find?"

"Somebody who could have been at the tent meeting last night." When she didn't say anything, I added, "A religious colored person might be able to help me."

Her face relaxed into a half smile. She smoothed her apron. "Would you like to come in? You look about to drop."

"That'd be nice." Chipped terra-cotta pots of pansies and geraniums lined the wide porch. I followed her up the steps, wiping my hands on my shorts. An overhead fan hummed rhythmically in the front room.

"Please have a seat," she said. "I'll be right back."

I sat on the edge of the sofa.

There were crocheted antimacassars on the worn sofa arms, newspapers on the floor by a rocking chair, a book open on a table. A vase of chrysanthemums on an upright piano caught the slanted light coming in the windows. Shelves lined the walls, floor to ceiling, crowded with books. The smell of fried chicken and baked apples made my mouth water.

I sank back into the throw pillows on the sofa. My eyes felt gritty and my lips tasted of salt.

Mrs. Travis returned with glasses and a pitcher on a tray that she put on an end table. She handed me a wet washcloth. "To wipe your face, cool down."

I covered my face with the cloth, breathed in the sharp smell of soap, wiped my neck and arms. Mrs. Travis pointed at the tray. "Just put it there and help yourself." I poured a glass of lemonade and took a long swallow.

She sat in the rocker. "How is it that a religious colored person might help you?"

"My sister and I went to the tent meeting last night."

Her eyebrows rose. "Two white girls all the way out here?"

"Our maid was with us."

"I see."

I drank until there was nothing left but ice.

"Help yourself."

I filled my glass again. "We were on our way home and some men attacked us."

"Oh!" She sat up straight in the rocker. "Are you all right?"

"My sister and I are, but our girl's gone. The men took her."

"I take it she is Negro."

"Yes." I had an urge to say, "Yes, ma'am," although I'd never said "ma'am" to a colored woman in my life.

"Is she from Claxton?"

"Mary works for us in Charlotte, North Carolina. Mama brought her on our vacation to help out."

"Do your folks know where you are now?"

I shook my head, feeling guilty. "I was at the motel pool, talking to a lady about what happened. She didn't understand about Mary. So I was trying to find somebody. Somebody who—" I couldn't think of anything else to say.

"Somebody who would understand?"

"Uh-huh." I clenched my hands to keep from crying. We sat there, me staring at my fists and her rocking. At first the silence was awkward, but then it got easier just to sit, tears spotting my shirt. There was only the sound of my hiccupping breaths, the creak of her rocker on the wood floor, the whir of the ceiling fan. I was still crying when the screen door opened. I looked up to see a man standing just inside the door, his eyes like lights in his ebony face. He was carrying a briefcase and wearing a suit and tie, as if he were dressed for church.

"What's going on?" he asked.

Mrs. Travis stood. "Ezra, this is Miss June Watts." She handed me a Kleenex. "June, this is my husband. Mr. Travis is an attorney."

The man sat on the other end of the sofa and laid his briefcase between us.

Mrs. Travis poured him a glass of lemonade. "You look worn out."

Mr. Travis loosened his tie. He asked me, "What brings you out this way?"

I talked and he listened, running his thumb up and down the side of his glass. When he finally spoke, his voice was full of pain. "I have some sad news."

"About Mary?"

"I believe so."

Mrs. Travis sat with her head bowed, her chin resting in her hand.

"I heard about what happened last evening, Mrs. Luther's disappearance." He pulled a handkerchief from his pocket, wiped his forehead. "They found a Negro woman a while ago. She'd been—she was—" He folded the handkerchief and put it away.

I stood.

"In the field near the pond, just down the road a bit. Sam Bradford was fishing with his children. . . ." His voice drifted off.

"I just passed the pond," I said.

"Sheriff's car was there when I rode by on my way home." Mr. Travis looked out the window.

"It's some other girl. All coloreds look alike. The sheriff said so." I was shaking so hard I thought my teeth would crack.

Mrs. Travis rose and put her hand on my shoulder, gently pushing me back onto the sofa. "Ezra, would you fetch the quilt from the linen chest?"

Mr. Travis covered me with a quilt, tucking it around me. I wanted to leave my body and never return to the cold knowing.

Mrs. Travis asked, "How can we reach your folks, June?"

"Sally's Motel Park."

Mr. Travis dialed, standing in the doorway between the kitchen and the living room, the phone to his ear. He asked for Daddy and waited. "Hello?" Mr. Travis said who he was and why he was calling. He listened. "Yes, I believe so," he said. "No, I don't know if—" He looked at Mrs. Travis and shook his head. "Apparently she just walked out to where we live."

He nodded to the phone. "My wife and I told her. She's quite upset. It might be best if you would— no, I'm not telling you what to do."

He held the receiver away from his ear, then said, "Mrs. Travis and I can bring June to the motel, or you can come get her, whichever suits."

He gave Daddy directions, then hung up. "Your father is naturally upset."

I turned my face to the sofa cushions and closed my eyes. Mr. Travis' voice faded.

Daddy said something I couldn't understand. I opened my eyes. I was alone in the Travises' living

261

room. Daddy and Mr. Travis were on the front porch, silhouettes in the fading daylight. Mr. Travis shorter, thicker in the middle. Daddy broader in the shoulders. A match flared as Daddy lit a cigarette.

I heard the click of a phone hanging up, Mama's quick high-heeled steps in the kitchen. I closed my eyes again, keeping my face buried in the sofa.

Mr. Travis said something, his voice calm.

Daddy answered, loud and sharp, "You've got no right to question me."

Someone gasped. Mama.

Mr. Travis said, "Anything we say now is irrelevant to Mrs. Luther's death."

Death. Mary was dead.

"Jubie?" Mama said. I felt her hand on my back. "Wake up, Jubie."

I opened my eyes. Mama was bending over me, her face splotched, the fan turning above her. Her hair had come loose on one side and hung down her neck.

She wiped my face with the damp cloth, smoothing my hair off my forehead.

"Hey, Mama."

"We were sick with worry about you."

"I'm all right."

"I'm not," said Mama. "I'm undone about Mary." Her eyes were tired. She kneeled on the rug beside the sofa, patting my shoulder, my head.

She stood. "Bill, I think we can leave now."

"You okay, June?" Daddy towered over me, his hand trailing smoke.

"Yes, sir."

"Then let's go."

On the porch, I turned back to Mrs. Travis, who stood in the doorway. "Thank you for your—for the lemonade."

On the front walk, Daddy dropped his cigarette and smashed it under his shoe, leaving the butt and a black smear.

An article in the Sunday paper identified Mary as a colored housemaid from Charlotte, North Carolina, who'd been assaulted and beaten to death. Her body would be sent home. There were no suspects.

I sat on the stoop of our cabin and watched Davie pull his toy train through the dirt. I wanted to dive to the bottom of the pool to let the pressure push my headache away. I held out my hands. "Let's go to the pool."

"Choo-choo." Davie put pebbles on a flatcar. "Choo-choo."

I knocked over his train with the toe of my sandal. Stones tumbled from the flatcar and Davie began to scream.

I bent to pick him up. "C'mon."

"No-o-o-o." His body went limp and he slid through my hands, pushing at me. "Mary!"

"Stop it." I stamped my foot. He turned over on

the ground. The Band-Aid on his hand was filthy. I kneeled. "Please, Davie, let's go to the pool."

Tears made tracks on his dirty face. "Mary?"

"Mary's gone." Mama had said not to tell him Mary was dead because he wouldn't know what that meant. I pulled him into my arms, putting my lips to his hair. "Mary's gone, Davie-do."

He let his head rest on my chest, sobbing, "Mary! Mary!"

The words slipped out. "Mary's dead, Davie."

He stopped crying, arched his back so he could look at my face. He put his thumb in his mouth and dropped his head back down.

Daddy told us they'd bought a coffin. "It's the least we can do."

"I wish we'd gotten the one with satin padding." Mama stood by the Chrysler, smoking. She had on a sundress, her hat, her slingback sandals. She held her straw clutch in one hand.

Daddy jingled the car keys. "Hey, kiddo, wanna go get the Packard? They're meeting us at the garage on a Sunday afternoon. Can't beat that for service!" He was trying hard to cheer me up.

"Okay, Daddy."

"And your mama needs to tend to business while we see about the Packard. You can drive."

That got through to me. "Drive? Me?"

"You. Stell's staying with the kids."

"What if the police—"

He smiled the smile that always melted Mama. "You have a South Carolina license," he winked, "but you can't find it, remember?"

I opened the driver's door. Daddy said, "Sit in the back, Pauly, me girl. Miss June Watts is your chauffeur."

"Bill, this is not a good idea."

"Oh, c'mon. She knows how." Daddy got in front with me, Mama in back. I adjusted the seat and mirrors, switched on the ignition, and drove out of Sally's Motel Park, remembering to put on the turn signals as Daddy had taught me. I hit the brakes too hard, making him brace himself against the dashboard, but he didn't say anything. We let Mama out downtown. I was pretty sure she was heading for the colored funeral parlor. She didn't want me to see her go in there because it would upset me.

J and J's Garage had a rubber hose running across the parking lot, and bells rang as I drove over it. I didn't see the Packard. Daddy told me to park in front. "I'll find out what's going on." A plate-glass window was painted in bold black letters: J AND J'S GARAGE, ESTABLISHED 1946. Through the window I saw Daddy talking to Jake Stirewalt. When Daddy sat down, I knew it would be a while. I walked over to one of the empty bays and looked at the grease pit. Small steps led into it. In the bottom was a pink rag, a broken fan belt, a wrench. Wouldn't anybody who worked in a grease pit want to be someplace else? And what sort of person built coffins? I turned away from the smell of gasoline and creosote, and walked into the sunlight to see Mr. Stirewalt driving our Packard around the building.

Daddy stood outside. "Hey, Jubie, look there."

Mr. Stirewalt handed Daddy the keys. "She's running good. The motor warn't messed up much. You might need a new rade-yater sooner later." He looked at the mashed fender. "Wisht we'd of had time for that."

"We'll take care of it in Charlotte. The motor sounds great, don't you think so, Jubie?"

He was showing off, being a good father. "Yes, sir." I wished he could really care instead of just pretending. I felt tears rising, blinked my eyes, looked away from him. If he saw how sad I was, he ignored it.

"Now all I've got to do is pay for it, right?" Daddy pulled out his checkbook.

"That's right, Mr. Watts." They walked back inside.

I sat on a bench, turning my face to the sun. One sentence jumped out sharply from the rumble of voices in the garage office. "Then again, the only good nigger is a dead nigger, right, Mr. Watts?"

Daddy said, "So I make this out to J and J's Garage?" He should have told Mr. Stirewalt how wrong it was to say such a thing.

"No, to Jake Stirewalt."

266

We got in the Chrysler. Daddy drove.

Mama was waiting on the same corner where we'd left her. She looked like she'd been crying, but when she got in the car, she just said, "Is the Packard ready? Please tell me it's ready."

"It's ready," Daddy said. He patted her shoulder but didn't say anything about her swollen eyes.

"The train is at nine fifteen in the morning. I can have us packed to go right after that."

"What train?" I asked.

They looked at each other, then Mama said, "We have to send Mary back to Charlotte. There are regulations about embalming and shipping bodies. I was seeing to it."

I thought about Link and Young Mary, how sad they must be. "Have you talked with her kids?" I asked Mama.

"Last night, yes." Mama stared out the window. "They're distraught."

"Do you know when the service is? We could go."

Daddy said, "No."

We rode in silence back to J and J's. Daddy handed Mama the keys to the Packard. "We'll see you at the motel." I opened the car door and stepped out onto the hot pavement.

"You riding with your mother?" Daddy asked.

"I'm walking."

"Get back in this car, young lady." Daddy's voice was dangerous.

"No." I didn't look back.

CHAPTER 24

Just after nine on Monday morning, Mama, Daddy, and I watched as three men wheeled a flat hand truck through the train station, loaded with a long box that looked more like a shipping crate than a coffin. M. LUTHER was stenciled in black on the raw pine boards. We followed the hand truck past benches where half a dozen people sat dozing or reading papers, and past a closed door with a sign: NEGRO WAITING ROOM.

The men tilted the coffin to get it into the boxcar and I imagined Mary sliding inside; I hoped her head was at the top so she'd slide feetfirst. Mama walked to the end of the platform and stared down the tracks.

They pushed the coffin across the floor to the back of the car, where light didn't reach. Daddy put his hand on my shoulder and I caught a whiff of cigarettes and aftershave. The boxcar door slammed shut with a thunderclap. Mama's heels clicked on the concrete as she came back to us. Her gray dress and hat made her look sad and plain.

"Let's go," she said.

"It's horrible in that boxcar. Dark and horrible."

"Mary's not suffering anymore, Jubie." Mama reached toward me with her gloved hand.

I turned away. "When is her funeral?"

Daddy said, "A day or so. No more than two, not in this heat."

"Then we have time to get there."

Mama and Daddy looked at each other.

I walked over to the train. I wanted to climb in and ride with Mary. The rusty door of the boxcar was rough to my touch. "I want to go to the funeral. I—"

Mama said, "Bill, we could go back to Charlotte for Mary's service, then to Pawleys for a few more days of vacation."

Daddy shook his head. "We're not driving five hundred miles—from here to Charlotte to Pawleys—for an hour-long funeral. As soon as we're packed, we'll go on to the beach."

The engine chugged to life. The train began to move, clanking slowly out of the station, gathering speed. I watched until the caboose was a red smudge far down the tracks.

Mama pulled me away from the edge of the platform.

We walked back through the train station. A colored man was sweeping the floor in the waiting room, singing, *"Tum-te-dee diddle-de-dee tum-teedy-ay."* He stopped sweeping to let us pass, standing with his broom at his side like a soldier at attention. As we left the station, the swish of his broom started back up, and his singing, *"Tum-te-dee, diddle-de-dee . . ."*

• • •

Before we left our cabin, I checked beneath the beds to make sure we hadn't left anything and found Mary's terry cloth slippers. I stuffed them into the bottom of my suitcase.

Stell, Puddin, and I rode in the Packard. Mama, Daddy, and Davie led the way in the Chrysler. As soon as we got out of Claxton, Daddy pulled way ahead. He put his hand out and waved, urging Stell to speed up, but she drove as if the speedometer were stuck on fifty-five.

I stretched out across the backseat with my bare feet on the ledge of the open window, wiggling my toes in the rushing air. All I could see were the tops of pine trees and the clouds. It was too early to fall asleep, even with the tires humming and the wind lifting my skirt, but I closed my eyes anyway, trying to hum in the same pitch as the tires. Leesum would be settled in Charlotte by now, living at the preacher's house, wearing the new clothes Uncle Taylor had bought him. I kept thinking about writing to him, wanting to tell him how much I missed Mary. He would understand.

I sank into the seat where she'd sat for all those miles, tall and straight in her cotton dresses. I pressed my face into the upholstery and thought about her until I felt her bosom against my cheek, smelled her. My throat hurt with a knot that got bigger and bigger until I let the tears come, sliding from the corners of my eyes into my hair and ears. The car hit a pothole. Mary was gone.

"What in the world?" Stell asked.

I sat up, wiping my eyes. Daddy had pulled onto the shoulder and was waving us around. Stell slowed to a crawl. Daddy hollered, "Go on ahead. We'll be along in a minute."

"Huh." Stell accelerated back up to fifty-five.

I looked out the rear window. The Chrysler pulled onto the road, got large fast. When it was a few feet behind us, Daddy honked.

"What is he doing?" Stell screamed.

Daddy blew the horn in short blasts, his arm out the window waving in a forward motion.

"He wants you to speed up."

I stared at the Chrysler. Mama's face was set, turned to the passenger window.

Stell hit the brake, and Daddy swerved to miss us. Mama slid against Daddy and he steered with one hand, pushing her away, his mouth moving, his face angry. I thought of Davie bouncing around on the backseat.

Puddin whimpered. "Shush." I reached up front to pat her shoulder. She'd been so brave about Mary.

Daddy laid on his horn. I wished Stell would speed up, anything to get him off our tail. She slowed down even more. I looked at the speedometer. Forty.

The Chrysler whooshed around us, spraying grit,

as Daddy hollered through Mama's open window, "Get a move on!"

Stell got back to fifty-five and stayed there. The Chrysler disappeared around a curve.

"They're leaving us," Puddin cried.

"Don't worry," Stell said. "I can get to Pawleys Island. And he knows it."

"I want Mama," Puddin whined.

Stell said, "Cut it out. Find us the map for North and South Carolina."

Puddin sniffled and opened the glove compartment. Maps spilled onto the floor. She sorted through them, sounding out words under her breath. "I got it!" She held up the map.

"Let Jubie help you find the road we're on."

Puddin tossed the map onto the backseat and followed it, sliding over on top of me. Her elbow jabbed me in the stomach. I gasped.

"Damn it, Puddin."

"Bad word. I'll tell Daddy."

"You won't, you brat."

She put her arms around my neck. "I won't, Jubes, not for anything." She felt bony and sweet.

Stell said, "Jubie, we're on Highway 17. We just crossed the Savannah River into South Carolina."

I sat up and studied the map. "Take Alternate 17 at Limehouse. From there it's a hundred and seventy miles to Georgetown, fourteen miles to Pawleys."

"Ha!" shouted Stell Ann. "We'll show the old poop."

I searched the map for the highways leading to Charlotte. "Stell? Don't you want to go to Mary's funeral?"

"Yes."

"Then why aren't we going?"

"Mama and Daddy want things back to normal. For us to get over it." Stell moved her hands on the steering wheel. "Besides, I'm not sure her family wants us there."

"Why not?"

"She was working for us when she died."

"But she was our friend."

"We paid her to be."

When we got to Pawleys Island, we saw the Chrysler parked in the glare of a pole lamp at the pier, Daddy in the driver's seat, a cigarette in one hand, his flask in the other. Mama stood outside the car, talking to Carter beside his blue Ford coupe.

"Ooh-h-h," Stell squealed under her breath, looking at herself in the rearview mirror. She ran her fingers through her hair and pinched her cheeks to make them pink, as if Carter would notice in the dark. "How do I look?"

Her hair needed combing, her shorts were wrinkled, and she looked like a kid. "Fine."

We got out and Carter walked up. He took Stell's hand. "Your letters are great."

"Yours, too."

"Hey, Jubie," he said. "You all right?"

"I'm okay." I got a whiff of Aqua Velva.

"That's great." The last time I saw him was in the tree house. Was he thinking about that? "Where'd your dad go?"

Mama stood beside the Chrysler, holding Davie, Puddin leaning against her. "He'll be right back." She touched my cheek. "Such a long face."

"I've had a headache all day."

"I'll look for aspirin when we unpack."

Daddy came from under the pier, zipping his fly. "Let's go." His eyes shone in the streetlamp. He was already tipsy.

Carter held out a key to Daddy. "Y'all's house is real nice, right on the beach."

"Hop in your car," Daddy said. "Lead the way."

We parked behind a weathered two-story house set off by itself at the end of the island. A wraparound porch was filled with rockers. The hinges on the screen doors needed oiling and the floorboards creaked under our feet.

Carter said, "I'll help Mr. Watts with the luggage. Maybe y'all could open some windows."

"And, Carter?" Mama said. "The flowered bag in the trunk of the Packard?"

"Yes, ma'am?"

"Don't bring it in." She walked around inside the house while Stell and I opened windows.

Daddy came through the front door with suitcases. "Pauly?"

Mama stood in the kitchen doorway, Davie on her hip.

Daddy asked, "Where's this stuff go?"

"You, me, and Davie down. Jubie, Stell, Puddin up." Mama held Davie as if she didn't know what to do with him. The light from the bare bulb over her head turned her hair into a halo. Davie whimpered when she shifted him in her arms. Mary would have put him to bed.

I dragged Puddin's bag and my suitcase up to our room. I was lucky to be sleeping with her. Davie kicked, but Puddin never moved after she got to sleep. The café curtains in our bedroom, white cotton with yellow and green apples, looked like they'd come out of somebody's kitchen. Our mattress drooped in the middle and the throw rugs felt sandy. When I went to hang my toothbrush, I saw that the toilet and sink had rust stains. Mama would have gotten Mary to scrub them with Dutch cleanser.

After Carter helped empty the cars, he and Stell Ann unpacked the kitchen things and Mama said, "We've got to get ice first thing in the morning."

While I was making our bed, Mama came in with a black fan and set it on the dresser. She handed me a bottle of mosquito repellent that smelled like turpentine. "When you're ready for bed, rub this on you and Puddin."

I was in the kitchen taking aspirin when Daddy crossed the front room, a bottle of bourbon in his hand. He let the screen door bang behind him.

"I'm going with Daddy," I called over my shoulder, racing down the porch steps before Mama could stop me.

The dunes were pale hills in the moonlight, the salty wind cool. Daddy was nowhere in sight. A path led to a cut in the dunes and as I came to the rise, I saw him sprawled in the sand, lifting the bottle. He took a long drink.

I called out, "Hey, Daddy."

"Hey. C'mon down."

I sat beside him.

He pointed at the moon with his index finger, his thumb up, like he was holding a pistol.

"What're you doing?"

He took another gulp, propped his bottle in the sand. "Gonna shoot the moon, Jubie girl."

I looked up. "Mary said when it's not quite full, it's a 'give-us' moon. Like in the Lord's prayer."

Daddy snorted. "Gibbous."

Was he making fun of Mary? "You can't shoot it anyway, it's too far away."

"Browning said, 'A man's reach should exceed his grasp, or what's a heaven for?' "

"What about a woman's reach?"

"The only thing a woman has to reach for is a man." He took aim with his make-believe gun, his ring glittering in the moonlight.

I put my hand on his arm. "Leave the moon alone, Daddy. Let's go back to the house."

He staggered when he got up, and I put out my hand to help him. We walked back over the dunes, arm in arm.

Mama stood in the living room, Davie asleep on her shoulder. "Jubie, it's time for bed."

Daddy brushed past her to the kitchen. The icebox door opened and closed, followed by the sound of a church key cutting the top of a beer can.

Mama went to the kitchen. "Bill, please . . ."

His voice became low and husky. "Aw, honey, just put the boy down and come on to bed."

Mama said something I couldn't hear and Daddy said, "I'm tired of everybody making such a racket about it. We can get another maid." How could he talk about another maid? I ran upstairs and into the bathroom, slamming the door behind me. No one could take Mary's place. I sat on the toilet, crying until there were no more tears, then shuffled down the hall to our room.

Puddin sat on the bed by the window, the breeze ruffling her pink pj's. "Read to me, Jubie?"

"First let me put some mosquito oil on you."

Before I finished, Puddin was curled up asleep, her face soft as a baby's. I stretched out next to her, trying to get comfortable, but the oil burned my skin and the sheets felt stiff. I could hear Stell and Carter in the wooden rockers on the porch, their muffled voices drifting up through the window. The fan whirred back and forth, rippling the sheets, the hum of the motor blending with the pounding surf. My head still ached and my eyes stung, but I couldn't keep them open. I moved my leg so it just touched Puddin's, and thought about Mary in a pine box in a freight train, jolting along the tracks northwest to Charlotte.

I woke, sure Mary was near. I groped the darkness. "Where are you?" I heard her say, "Charlotte," clearly, as if she were standing by my bed. "Mary?" I felt blood whooshing in my ears, heard her singing, *"Amazing grace, how sweet I see, that lost a soul of sound."* The mixed-up words made me shiver. I swung my feet off the bed, whispered, "Mary?" No answer, just the crash of waves on the beach. I stumbled toward the bathroom. Maybe she was there. I stared at myself in the mirror. My hair stood out from my head, my face was creased, my eyes puffy. I knew what I had to do. Mary had told me.

Stell's brush and comb were lined up on the back of the toilet with her deodorant and toothbrush. I used her stuff and my toothbrush, put on jeans and a T-shirt, socks and my Keds. I couldn't find a bra, but I was afraid to turn on the light and wake Puddin.

Every time one of the stairs creaked, I stopped, listening, straining to see in just the night-light in the downstairs hall.

Mama's pocketbook was on the kitchen table. I took twenty dollars from her wallet and the keys to the Packard. I grabbed the keys to Daddy's Chrysler, too, off a hook by the back door, and dropped them in my pocket.

The door stuck. I had to jerk it open, making a scraping sound. I ran down the steps out to where the Packard was parked and drove slowly down the beach road at two in the morning, my eyes darting from the pavement to the speedometer, concentrating on steering as straight as I could. At the fishing pier I pulled over and got out to adjust the seat. My knees almost buckled under me and I had to hold the side of the car. I stood and breathed in the wind off the ocean, looking down the pier to where one light burned at the end. Several fishermen stood beneath it. I opened the trunk, lifted Mary's flowered bag with all her things and the three fruitcakes, and put it in front with me.

CHAPTER 25

The beach highway follows the shoreline, so you have to go east to go west—Daddy said that every time we went home from Pawleys. As I drove up the coast, the road a black ribbon in the moonlight, I thought about how mad Daddy would be when he realized I'd taken the Packard. At least I wouldn't be there when he woke up, sour and brittle until he could mend himself with a toddy. He'd take a sip, sigh with pleasure, and say, "The sun's over the yardarm somewhere in the world." But this time he wouldn't have that morning drink. My foot went down harder on the gas pedal. He'd figure out some way to get the Chrysler started, keys or no keys, and take off after me.

Just south of the state line, I took Highway 9 West, Mama's favorite route, easy because it tracks the border between North and South Carolina almost all the way to Charlotte. I concentrated on the things Daddy had taught me about driving, like braking before a curve and accelerating in it. "A good car loves a curve," he'd told me. "Good drivers do, too." Every time a car came toward me with its high beams on, I remembered to focus on the Packard's hood ornament, lining the swan up with the right side of the road. "If you flash your brights," Daddy said, "you blind two drivers." But

I'd seen him do just that and mutter "son of a bitch" while he kept his high beams on.

One time when the two of us were in our old stick-shift Chevy, he said he'd show me something if I promised not to tell Mama. He got the car going fast, pulled up the hand brake, turned the steering wheel, and in nothing flat we were headed back the way we'd come.

"Goose it, Daddy!" I shouted. He was yee-hawing so loud he didn't hear me.

"The bootlegger's one-eighty," he yelled, and did it again.

Daddy always got the man to check the oil and water when he bought gas, no matter what the gauges said, so I did that when I got to Dillon, ninety miles from Pawleys, almost halfway home. The man who came to the car window peered at me through thick glasses as if he were questioning whether I was old enough to drive. But all he said was, "Fill 'er up?"

"Please, and check the oil, the radiator, the tires . . ."

"I know how to service a car."

After I paid him, I pulled Mary's bag close. I wanted to touch her things. The buckles on the leather straps of her bag were hard to open. I'd seen her struggle with them, tugging against the clasps, forcing the metal picks through the holes, saying, "Got 'er!" when the buckles finally gave.

I spread the edges of the opening apart and was overcome by the smell of Cashmere Bouquet.

Her white Bible wasn't in the bag. Mama must have sent it back with her. Young Mary and Link might want it for the funeral, and Mama would have thought of that. I sat for a long while under the yellow light at the filling station, holding Mary's Fuller Brush wide-toothed comb that Mama had given her. It still had a few hairs in it, long and rough, dark and curly.

I pulled them out and wrapped them around and around my finger.

Just after seven, in broad daylight, I pushed up the door on Mama's side of our garage. It screeched on the springs. I inched the car forward, afraid I would scrape the side, but I couldn't leave it in the driveway for anybody to see. I closed the garage door and sat down on the cold floor, arched my back, pulled off my Keds and rubbed my feet. It felt so good not to be in the car with my hands glued to the steering wheel.

The grass in the backyard, still wet with dew, soothed my feet. The cowbell clanked as I opened the kitchen door, startling me, no matter that it had been hanging there since the day we moved in. The house was too quiet. I stepped on something hard and cold—a Coke bottle cap. The house stank of beer and cigarettes. There were dishes piled on the kitchen counter, empty bottles, overflowing ashtrays. I felt like a stranger coming through the back door for the first time, seeing our mess. Daddy's mess. Mama would have a fit if she saw it this way, and I wondered what had happened to the arrangement she'd made for Young Mary to clean for Daddy.

I wedged the doorstop in place to hold the back door open, went to the hallway, and switched on the attic fan. The fresh air brought in the early morning smell of grass and gardenias. I got the trash can from under the kitchen sink and began to fill it with empties—Coca-Cola, Seven-Up, Kentucky Gentleman, Jim Beam, Budweiser.

I dumped ashtrays, swept the kitchen floor, wiped the counters, filled the dishwasher with crusted plates, rinsed clotted milk from bowls, opened the refrigerator. Daddy's water bottle sat on the first shelf, full, and I stood in front of the open icebox, worn out, and drank. I turned to look at the kitchen and thought how proud Mary would have been that I'd cleaned it without being asked. I walked through Davie's room and into Mama and Daddy's bedroom, feeling strange being there all by myself and able to walk around and look without explaining what I was doing. Their bedroom was worse than the kitchen. I kicked at a pair of Daddy's undershorts lying on the floor.

I left their room as torn up as I'd found it and went upstairs where everything was the same as when Stell, Puddin, and I had carried our suitcases to the car. Our beds were made, our stuff put away, even the rug looked as if it had been vacuumed and nobody had walked on it since.

Downstairs the mantel clock in the living room chimed ten. I looked up McDowell Street Baptist Church in the phone book, dialed the number and waited, my fingers crossed, hoping someone would be there, hoping I hadn't missed the funeral, hoping—a woman answered.

"Hello. I'm calling to find out when the funeral is for Mrs. Mary Luther."

"Hold on."

The woman hollered away from the phone, "Sister Luther that got murdered in Georgia, she at two, that right?" I heard a man's deep voice in the background. The woman spoke to me again. "The visiting's at eleven today at Alexander's, service and burying here at two. You know where the church be?"

"Oh, I—no, I don't."

"On McDowell, couple blocks north of Trade. You won't miss it; all the cars and people gone be here."

I got off the phone and looked in my closet for something to wear. As soon as I saw my navy Easter dress, I knew it was the one. Mary had told me I looked so fine in it. I'd wear Stell's straw hat Mary admired. My short white gloves, my navy flats, and one of Mama's pocketbooks.

I scrubbed myself in the bathtub and lathered my

hair twice, using Stell's Breck shampoo she'd tried to hide in the linen closet. I loved how it made my hair silky. When I was as clean as I've ever been in my life, I sank back in the tub, running more hot water, letting the warmth sink into my bones.

All my underwear was at the beach, so I raided Mama's dresser, knowing her things would fit me better than Stell's. I stood at Mama's full-length mirror and looked at myself in her bra, garter belt, and stockings, before stepping into her panties. The curly blonde hair at the bottom of my belly had filled in, just in the last month or so. I looked like a woman. Mama's bra was pink, lacy, and feminine compared with the white cotton ones Stell and I wore. My bosoms filled it completely.

I padded into the kitchen in my stocking feet and fixed myself a peanut butter sandwich, wishing I had milk. When I opened the pantry door to get a can of apple juice, I tried not to look at the mouse droppings. I turned on the radio, just for the noise, and sat on a bar stool, drinking apple juice and tapping my foot to a song with a hard beat.

While I was looking up the taxi company, the phone rang. I didn't answer. It might be Mama or Daddy trying to find out if I was home. A dozen rings, then it stopped. I grabbed it and dialed the cab number fast, before somebody called again and got a busy signal.

At one thirty, I sat on the living room sofa and waited for the taxi, my gloved hands folded on

Mama's navy clutch, Mary's flowered bag by my feet. I'd see Leesum at the funeral and the thought comforted me.

If the taxi driver thought it was strange to be picking up a teenager on Queens Road West on a Tuesday afternoon, he didn't show it. "Where to?"

"McDowell Street Baptist Church, two blocks north of Trade."

"Right you are. Real scorcher this afternoon." He flipped down a flag on his dashboard and pulled away from the curb. I'd heard that cabbies would take you out of the way to get a bigger fare, but he went straight from Queens Road West to Kings Drive, up Morehead to McDowell, just as I would have. He pulled up beside a parked car and asked, "You going to need a ride home, miss?"

"Yes, sir, but I don't know what time. I'll have to call you." I wasn't sure there'd be a phone I could use, but I'd cross that bridge when I got to it. Like Mary always said.

There was a crowd in front of the church, and cars lined the street for blocks in both directions. The cab driver and I were the only white people in sight.

"You sure this is where you want to be?"

"Yes, sir."

"Your parents know you're here?"

I nodded. "I'm representing our family."

"Okey-dokey," he said, and drove away.

My first thought was to find Leesum. I walked

286

around, carrying Mary's bag. People looked at me as if they couldn't imagine why I was there. A short woman held out her hand. "I believe we've met. It's Miss Watts, isn't it? I'm Harriett Coley."

"Yes, hello. You helped me at the Daddy Grace parade."

"It's nice you could come to Sister Luther's service." She touched the rim of her black hat. "Are you by yourself?"

"My parents can't be here."

"Why don't we go inside, let you pay your respects. Maybe put that case by the coatrack."

"It's Mary's. I want to give it to her children."

"They'll appreciate that." Mrs. Coley led me into the church, stopping at a rack where empty hangers dangled. "You can leave the bag there. Nobody will bother it."

The church was filled with people talking in low voices that hushed as I passed.

"Was it your mother who dressed Sister Luther so nice to send her home?" Mrs. Coley asked. She straightened a gold pin on the lapel of her black suit.

"Beg your pardon?"

"Put Sister Luther in her Sunday best. Had her hair done. That was kind."

So that's what Mama was tending to while Daddy and I went to see about the Packard.

Mrs. Coley led me toward the front of the church, where a coffin was set up on a velvet-covered stand surrounded by flowers. Not the pine box we had shipped Mary home in. I kept right on walking toward it without a thought in the world that I would get to it and look down and Mary would be lying there. I just went on with Mrs. Coley propelling me until I almost bumped into it. Then there she was. Her face was soft and pretty, with her hair combed back the way she liked it, her hands on her chest holding her old white Bible. She looked peaceful, asleep.

I put my hand out. "Mary?" My voice broke.

"She's beyond hearing, child," Mrs. Coley said.

I didn't faint. I never for a second didn't know what was going on, but my legs folded. I sank to the floor beside Mary's coffin, wailing with all the sadness I'd been holding in. Mrs. Coley sat down beside me and pulled me to her, rocking me back and forth. "She's with Jesus, child. Her burden is lifted."

CHAPTER 26

Mrs. Coley helped me to my feet. "C'mon, Miss Watts, let's find a place to sit." When I turned away from the coffin, I saw Young Mary in the front pew, eyes swollen, lipstick as bright as the cherries on her hat. She stared at me. Her brother, Link, sat next to her, stern, thick-necked and broad-shouldered, bigger than I remembered from when he worked in Daddy's warehouse. To either side of Link and Young Mary were women dressed in white. Mrs. Coley spoke to several of them and said to me, "Our Mothers Board." The solemn women regarded me.

Where was Leesum?

Halfway down the aisle, Mrs. Coley stopped beside a crowded pew. I followed her into the pew, inching by knees and stepping on a man's foot. Mrs. Coley spoke to folks as we crowded past them. "Y'all scoot over, make room." We had just gotten seated when a woman began to play an upright piano against the wall near the foot of the coffin. A panel was missing above the keyboard, and I could see the hammers hitting the strings as she played.

The afternoon sun streamed through a window made of vivid chips around a white cross of streaked glass that looked like frozen smoke. Rainbow hues fell on Mary, lighting her face. I thought of her cheeks being rouged by a sunbeam through ruby glass, her gray linen dress looking like she'd spilled fruit salad on it. She had been here when others were buried. She might have sat exactly where I was sitting and seen the brilliant colors splash on other coffins.

A man came down the center aisle, wearing a black flowing robe, with a stole around his neck that hung almost to his knees.

"Reverend Perkins?" I asked Mrs. Coley.

She nodded.

So that was Mary's pastor, the one Leesum was living with.

A choir followed the minister, humming to the music, yellow satin robes swaying. A woman sang a solo line in a high, clear voice. *"There is a balm in Gilead."* The choir responded, *"To make the wounded whole."* Again the one strong voice. *"There is a balm in Gilead."* And the choir. *"To heal the sin-sick soul."* I felt they were singing to me.

The choir came to a stop at folding chairs along the wall next to the piano. Across from them sat a row of men in dark suits. "The deacons," Mrs. Coley whispered. One was George McHone, our yard man, wearing a suit and bow tie like he had in the Daddy Grace parade.

Cardboard fans rustled in the warm air, and folding chairs scraped as the choir settled, still humming. Reverend Perkins put his Bible on an elevated pulpit behind the casket. He turned to face the congregation. He was bald, and so light-skinned he could have passed, except for his flat Negro nose.

Children came down the aisle carrying flowers, young ones in front, teenagers behind. The last one to pass our pew was Leesum. I put out my hand, pulled it back, spoke his name.

He turned, handed his flower to another boy, and left the procession. The man next to me said, "What's going on?"

Leesum never stopped looking at me. "She my friend."

"Not enough room here," said a woman on the other side of Mrs. Coley.

"She my friend." Leesum wedged himself into the pew beside me.

"Now, this ain't right," someone grumbled. Two people got up to find seats less crowded. When the others spread out, Leesum stayed beside me, just as close as before. He took my hand and I wished I didn't have gloves on.

Mrs. Coley peered around me. "What are you doing, boy? You're supposed to be up front."

"Stayin' with my friend."

"I can see that."

Behind us someone said, "Y'all shush."

Now I could pay attention to Mary, to her service. With Leesum holding my hand and Mrs. Coley on my other side, I would be okay.

The children proceeded to the front of the church

and handed out the flowers to the Mothers Board and to Young Mary and Link.

At a signal from Reverend Perkins, one of the deacons stood, walked to the casket, and closed the lid. Were they going to bury Mary's Bible with her? All that family history.

The preacher raised his arms. "There's anger amongst us. Some talk of retribution." He said the last word slowly, emphasizing each syllable.

"Too many has died," a man called out.

"That's right," someone else said. "Too many."

"Yes, Jesus!"

Reverend Perkins said, "We're here for one purpose—to honor Mary Constance Culpepper Luther, who lies before us. She who God has called home."

Someone behind me said, "Lord's will."

"But Sister Luther is not lost," the preacher said.

"Hallelujah," a man answered. A woman said, "Sister with Jesus."

"Mary Luther's path was not easy, but she persevered." Reverend Perkins looked at Young Mary and Link. He stepped from behind the altar and went to Mary's coffin, extending his hands, palms up, as if to raise her from the dead.

He spoke again, his voice so low and sad I strained to hear. "The Sister Luther I knew would not listen to words of anger. She'd turn the other cheek to those who would smite her and pray for God to forgive them."

"She gone to Jesus."

"Praise the Lord!"

The church was filled with the rustle of shifting bodies, the smell of flowers. Fans stirred the air.

The preacher wiped his head with a handkerchief and walked back to the pulpit. He looked out over the congregation, his eyes fastening first one place, then another, then on me. "Mary Luther was a cleaning woman, helped her people get their house in order, then went home at night, made order in her own." I felt pinned to the pew. "Might be midnight before she saw her bed. Next day she'd rise up, go back to her labors. But she was blessed with two fine children, told me how proud she was when her boy got to Howard University on a scholarship." He looked at Young Mary and Link.

"Amen! Praise Jesus!"

"Yes, Lord, yes."

Reverend Perkins cleared his throat, took a sip of water. "Sister Luther's kindness touched everybody in this church, but some got her attention more than others." He looked right at Leesum.

Leesum nodded.

I took a fan from a holder in the pew in front of me, and moved the air with it. The fan had an advertisement for Alexander Funeral Home, where Mary's visitation had been. I wished I could have been there.

"There is no room for anger at the funeral of Mary Luther." Reverend Perkins' voice rose. "She lived for love, she died in love."

One of the deacons stood and said to the preacher's back, "She were beaten down by hate."

"By hate," someone agreed.

"Killed in the street."

The preacher turned to look at the man. "That's the truth, Deacon Hull. Hate killed our sister. But the love she lived will triumph over the sin that took her away."

"Love conquer sin," a voice called out.

"I know you're angry." Reverend Perkins spoke again to the man, who was still standing. "But this is not the time for words of vengeance."

The man sat, then stood back up and spoke to the congregation. "Come to the meeting Friday night, brothers and sisters. Gather here to talk about what happened to Mrs. Luther." He sat down. "That's it for now, Pastor."

Reverend Perkins took a Bible from the podium and moved to stand by Mary's coffin. "Mary Luther—the heart of wisdom—knew her scripture. She'd say turn to it in your anger." He opened the Bible. "Isaiah five speaks of those who do evil."

"Therefore, as the tongue of fire devours the stubble, and as dry grass sinks down in the flame, so their root will be as

rottenness, and their blossom go up like dust; for they have rejected the law of the LORD of hosts. . . ."

He thumped his finger on the open Bible. "They have rejected the law of the Lord!" He flipped pages. "Same thing, all over the good book. Psalm thirty-seven says it clearly."

"Refrain from anger, and forsake wrath! Fret not yourself; it tends only to evil. For the wicked shall be cut off; but those who wait for the LORD shall possess the land."

He closed the book and shouted, "The wicked shall be cut off!"

Responses rose throughout the church: "God's word. Fret not. Wait for the Lord."

He returned to the pulpit, closed his eyes, bowed his head. The church was silent. "Lord?" the preacher called out. "Can you see into our hearts?"

A gasping cry, a woman's voice, "My heart's full of hate."

The preacher's voice became conversational. "Jesus, send down your love as you did for those who put you on that cross. Fill our hearts with love." He paused for responses, continued, "This mother lives in the hearts of her children, in the hearts of everyone in this church. And she will live forever in the love of Jesus. World without end, amen."

Amens rang out.

A skinny old man stood in the choir, his head bald except for a ring of white hair. He walked to the front of Mary's coffin, faced the congregation, and began to sing in a trembling bass voice, *"Steal away. Steal away. Steal away to Jesus."* His voice grew stronger and people around me began to hum with him. *"Steal away. Steal away home. I ain't got long to stay here."* Tears ran down the old man's face. The choir joined in, faster, louder. *"My Lord He calls me. He calls me by the thunder."* On either side of me, Mrs. Coley and Leesum sang with the choir. *"The trumpet sounds within my soul. I ain't got long to stay here."* There were no hymnbooks, but the congregation knew the words. Mrs. Coley swayed against me, moving with the music, the brim of her hat brushing my shoulder. *"Steal away. Steal away home."* Her voice swelled in harmony. *"I ain't got long to stay here."*

A deacon went to the casket and opened it. Reverend Perkins said, "Anybody who hasn't done so may now pay final respects to Sister Luther." Members of the congregation went to the coffin, bowed over it. The only sounds were the shuffling of feet, the creak of the floorboards, sniffles, choked sobs. When all grew still, six men came forward. I wondered if Mary's brother was among them. At a gesture from the preacher, Young Mary walked to the coffin. She kissed her mother's face and took the white Bible. Link closed the coffin, and the six men carried it down the center aisle. People stood and reached out to it as it passed. "Be with Jesus, Sister Luther—God bless you, Sister— Praise the Lord." Hands touched the gleaming wood.

Mrs. Coley, Leesum, and I moved into the crowd that filled the aisle, walking slowly through the heavy air toward the rectangle of light that opened into the afternoon heat. Outside, the congregation broke into twos and threes, following the pallbearers to the cemetery behind the church. Mary's open grave was between a marker for her husband, Pharr Lincoln Luther, who died in 1948, and a stone engraved, "CAROL JANE LUTHER, BORN FEBRUARY 2, DIED APRIL 10, 1946." I was five years old when Mary began working for us. She had a whole life I never knew, a baby who lived and died before I ever met her, a husband whose death I didn't remember.

Leesum stayed by my side. I could hardly believe it had been only ten days since I met him. He seemed like my longtime friend. I hadn't thought of him as being so tall, but he had half a foot on me.

A woman from the choir sang out, *"Precious Lord, take my hand . . ."* and others joined in.

Reverend Perkins said something I didn't understand as Mary's coffin was lowered into the ground. Link and Young Mary tossed clumps of dirt onto it. Young Mary had on shoes the same shiny red as her lipstick and the cherries on her hat; her black dress was trimmed in satin and had a peplum that showed off her tiny waist and high hips. I didn't think her mama would have approved of such a dress at a funeral. She caught my eye, looked away.

I stood by the grave. Mary would never be with me again. There was no one I could turn to for the goodness I got from her. I was standing with my hand on her husband's headstone, when Leesum asked, "Where you folks?"

"They couldn't come."

"That's sumpin, you comin' here alone." He looked down at Mary's coffin. "Miz Luther took care of me, just like she said in Florida. I been stayin' with preacher. I'm a junior usher here at the church." He looked past me. "Hey, Link."

I turned. Link Luther stood next to me, his face closed. "Hello, June."

I looked for Young Mary, didn't see her. "I'm sorry about your . . . about Mary."

He nodded. "Ask your father—" He took a breath. "Ask Mr. Watts about that room behind his warehouse."

"What?"

He walked away.

"Link."

He didn't stop.

"I brought your mother's things, her flowered bag."

He turned.

"There's three fruitcakes in it. She bought one for a church party, one for y'all, and one for her best friend." I was ashamed I didn't know who that was. "It's by the coatrack in the foyer."

For a second his face softened. "I'll get it." He disappeared into the crowd, leaving me with Leesum among the clumps of people standing under trees, talking, glancing at Leesum, barely looking at me. I felt a hand on my shoulder.

Reverend Perkins said, "You all right now, Miss Watts?"

I nodded. "It was a good service."

He touched my hand. "Mrs. Luther told me all about you. All about you. You were . . ." He stopped. "She said you—" He cleared his throat. "She loved you, that's all."

Tears came to my eyes. He put his arm around my shoulders. "You'll find a way to get on without her. Lord doesn't give us more'n we can bear." He looked into my eyes. "You know that?"

"That's what Mary always told me."

"Just you remember it." He spoke to Leesum. "I'll see you later."

"Yessuh."

I said to Leesum, "I have to go. My folks don't know where I am."

He looked like a man, dressed up, serious, as he walked with me to the street. "We sendin' somebody to Georgia. They gone find out what happened to Miz Luther."

"The church is?"

"Yeah, Deacon Hull, the one what spoke up in the service. Maybe one or two others."

"The sheriff's working on it."

"They never try too hard to find out who killed a colored." Colored. Leesum was colored. I kept forgetting what that meant.

A yellow cab drove up, the taxi I'd come in. I took Leesum's hand. "I've got to go now."

He stared at me with his green eyes. "I be thinkin' of you, Jubie."

"Same here. Good-bye, Leesum."

From the backseat of the cab, I watched him standing on the curb.

The driver asked, "How was the funeral?"

"Good. I'm glad I went."

"Reckon you were the only white there."

"Yes."

"Did you forget your tote?"

"Oh, no, that belonged to the woman who . . . I took it to her family."

We passed the House of Prayer for All People and Daddy Grace's red, white, and blue mansion across from the ice house. When we turned left onto Morehead, I scrunched down in the seat in case any of Mama's friends were at the Junior Woman's Club. When I sat up, I asked the driver, "Why'd you come back for me?"

"Got a girl your age. Wouldn't want her in colored town by herself."

I liked him for not saying nigger town. When we pulled up to the house, he said, "That'll be a dollar. You gonna be okay, now?"

I gave him a dollar and a quarter. "Yes, sir. Thank you for your kindness."

My heels tapped on the slates of the front walk as I ran to the house. Back in my room, I sat at my dresser, trying to think what to do. In the mirror my hands went to Stell's straw hat, removed it, put it down on the glass-topped dresser, like a lady in a movie, taking off her hat after a tea party. I put it back in the hatbox exactly as it had been, returning the box to the shelf in Stell's closet. I folded the white cotton gloves Meemaw had given me, which I'd never worn before, and put them in the top drawer of my bureau, putting away a girl I'd never really been. When I pulled my T-shirt over my head and zipped up my jeans, I felt I was myself again. I left my room neat, not like my room at all. If I got the car away from the house, there'd be no way for anybody to tell I'd ever been home. Even the shining kitchen could have been Aunt Rita or Young Mary.

I had backed the car into the driveway and was pulling down the garage door when Linda Gibson hollered from her upstairs window, "Hey, June! When'd y'all get home?" I jumped in the car, pretending I hadn't heard her.

At the corner I turned toward town. Traffic was getting heavy as men came home from work, and I felt nervous driving among so many cars. I turned onto Princeton and pulled into the crowded lot at Freedom Park. A breeze came through the open windows. Boy Scouts and their dads were playing ball in the diamond next to the parking lot, yelling and raising dust.

I stretched out on the front seat to decide what I should do, but all I could think about was Mary in her coffin, in the ground, cold, still—forever. I closed my eyes and tried to talk to her, not praying, just speaking out loud. "Hey, Mary, I went to your funeral, and it was fine. You would have—" I stopped, thinking that she already knew everything, just like when she was alive.

CHAPTER 27

I woke to the sound of laughter. The pole lamps in the picnic areas made the park an island of light in the gathering dusk. People sat in the grass around the lake. A man cooking on a grill beside a nearby station wagon handed a hot dog to a boy. A woman filled tumblers from a thermos. I smelled hamburgers cooking and my mouth watered. I locked the car and walked the five blocks home.

The house was quiet. I wanted to turn on the lights or the attic fan, anything to help me feel I wasn't so alone. I got Daddy's water bottle from the fridge and gulped from it, water dribbling down the front of my T-shirt. The dim light from the fridge danced on the bulletin board where we'd left a handmade card saying, *"Good-bye, Daddy. We'll miss you. See you at Pawleys!"* It had been only a week and a half since I'd taken down the swim meet schedule and pushed the thumbtacks into Daddy's card. All of us had written something personal, even Davie—Mama dipping his hand into green poster paint, pressing it to the card. A piece of paper had been added with a brass thumbtack that was pushed into the palm of Davie's handprint. On the paper was writing that I couldn't read in the dim light, except for the signature, "Mary." I pulled at the note. The tack popped out, hit the floor with a ping.

A car door slammed. I stuffed the note in my pocket. The den door rattled, keys jingled, and Daddy called out, "We'll bring it in later." I backed into the front hallway and opened the basement door, holding my breath, trying to make myself weightless as I tiptoed down the stairs, feeling my way. The basement was musty in spite of everything Mary had done to get rid of the mildew. I fumbled until I found the door into the tiny bathroom under the stairs, used only by Mary and the yard man. There was no lid to the toilet and I sat on the seat, trembling, my arms around my waist holding tight to stop the shaking. Footsteps clumped from the den through the dining room, until they were right over me.

"She's been here." Daddy.

"How do you know?" Uncle Stamos.

"This place was a mess when I left."

"I thought Mary's daughter was coming in."

"That didn't work out."

"You're almost out of bourbon," Uncle Stamos said.

I could hear them clearly. What had Mary heard from down here?

"Do you know how hard it is to get car keys made at Pawleys Island?"

"Why'd you have to do that?"

"Couldn't find mine. If Jubie took them, I'll kill her."

I believed him.

"Where could she be?" Uncle Stamos asked.

"Off on a joy ride. She'll wreck the Packard. Again."

"Stealing her mother's car . . . that just isn't like June."

I loved Uncle Stamos for taking up for me.

"Paula lets the girls get away with too much. Jubie needs a firm hand." A chair scraped the floor. "You gotta crack the whip. Same with the boys in the shop."

Uncle Stamos said, "It's got to be better with David Lacey as foreman. He's a good man."

"To make niggers behave, put a nigger in charge." The tone of Daddy's voice made me shiver. "He's big enough and mean enough. He'll hold them." Ice rattled in a glass. "The problem's not just in the shop."

"You mean the Supreme Court thing?"

"Before you know it, they'll be in our schools."

Uncle Stamos said, "It might not be as bad as you think."

"It'll be worse. But the W.B.A. will delay it, at least in Charlotte."

"I wish you weren't involved in that."

"I wish you were. It's important. There are ramifications—"

Someone knocked at the kitchen door. The cowbell clanged.

"Hello, Linda." Daddy's voice boomed good cheer.

"Hey, Bill. Where's the rest of the family? Jubie acted—"

"You saw Jubie?"

"She drove off in the Packard about four thirty. How'd the fender get smashed?"

"An accident in Georgia. Did she say where she was going?"

"She acted like she didn't hear me."

I sat on the toilet. What would Mary do? I could almost hear her say, "Jubie girl, you in trouble. Get yourself to a better place." I stood and took a few steps away from the toilet, back into the basement, bumping against Daddy's wine rack. The bottles rattled. I froze.

The floorboards groaned above me. "I'm going to the bathroom." Uncle Stamos' footsteps faded toward the den. Daddy said something. Mrs. Gibson laughed.

I groped through the basement, climbed on stacked boxes of canning jars, and shoved open the window on the side of the house. When I pushed off to scoot onto the windowsill, the boxes tumbled, making a terrible racket. My shirt caught on the sill, and the latch scratched my belly as I slid into the yard. My feet tangled in the boxwoods and I got dirt in my mouth, but I was stumbling forward before I stood all the way up, gasping until the back of my throat was hot and dry, headed for the safety of Maggie's house.

At her front walk I stopped, pressing my hand to

the scrape on my belly. The living room door was open onto the screen porch and I heard music, a phone ringing, Mrs. Harold calling, "Tommy? Telephone." I opened the screen door. Their cocker spaniel was asleep on the flowered sofa in a pool of yellow light. There was a basket of yarn beside Mrs. Harold's rocker, a newspaper in Mr. Harold's green easy chair, his pipe in a wooden holder nearby. The room was cramped with mismatched furniture. Mama would say it was tacky. I was never so glad to be anywhere in my life.

"Maggie?" I called out.

"Margaret?" Mr. Harold's voice came from the back of the house. "Someone's at the door for you."

"Jubes!" Maggie ran through the living room and threw her arms around me. Her white blonde hair smelled of Prell and felt wonderfully cool to my hot cheeks. "When'd you get home? Cripes, what's going on? Mother!" She yelled over her shoulder and Mrs. Harold hurried into the living room.

"Jubie!" She brushed wisps of gray hair from her flushed face. "Your mum's very worried about you."

"Oh." I collapsed into Mr. Harold's easy chair.

"What's happened to you?" Mrs. Harold stared at my torn shirt.

"I crawled out the basement window."

"Margaret, get a fresh blouse for Jubie." Mrs.

Harold spoke sharply to Maggie, who stood there, her mouth gaping. "Run!"

Maggie flew down the hall.

Mrs. Harold sat on the sofa next to the easy chair, pushing the dog over. She was so fat her arms were dimpled at the elbows. Her chest was flat from when she had cancer. She fished a handkerchief from her empty bodice and dabbed at the scratch on my stomach. "Do you want to tell me what's going on? We really should call your mum."

"Where is she?"

"At your auntie's."

Maggie ran into the living room with her Ship'n Shore blouse, the one I'd helped her pick out.

"That's a girl," said Mrs. Harold. "Jubie, go into the dining room and change. Are you hungry?"

"Yes, ma'am."

"That's something I can fix." She headed down the hall. I went into the dim dining room and pulled my torn shirt over my head.

Mrs. Harold came back as I was buttoning the blouse. She handed me a plate filled with pot roast, corn on the cob, pineapple rings. "It's cold, but it's good." She made room for the plate on the table next to Mr. Harold's chair. Maggie came from the kitchen with a glass of milk, a napkin, utensils. I dug into the food.

Maggie sat near me on the sofa. "I thought y'all were on a trip to the beach."

"Mary got killed," I said, chewing corn.

"Dear Lord," said Mrs. Harold. "Who's Mary?"

"You mean your girl?" Maggie asked.

I nodded, putting down the cob, wiping my fingers. Maggie reached for my hand, her freckled skin pale against my deep tan.

"How did it happen?" asked Mrs. Harold.

"She was kidnapped by some men in Georgia while we were staying there. They beat her to death, and they . . . I took Mama's car and came home for the funeral."

Mrs. Harold said, "You drove home from the beach by yourself?"

"Yes." The phone rang.

"What a remarkable thing to do." I wanted to hug her.

Mr. Harold called out. "Jubie, it's your mum."

I walked into the hallway and sat on the stool tucked into the phone nook. "Hey, Mama."

"Are you all right?"

She didn't sound angry. I was so surprised I couldn't speak.

"Jubie?"

"Yes, ma'am."

"I was so worried about you."

"You were?"

"I didn't know you could drive on the highway."

"I just learned."

Silence, then Mama said, "Your father's upset."

The scratch on my belly stung beneath Maggie's blouse. "I know."

Her voice went sharp. "Have you seen him?"

"I was home, hiding in the basement. He and Uncle Stamos got there, so I left."

"You've really done it this time, Jubie."

"Yes, ma'am." Music played in the background.

"It might be best if you don't see Daddy just yet."

I twisted the phone cord around my finger. "How'd you know where I was?"

"Just a guess. You went to the funeral?"   ·

"Yes, ma'am."

"I wish I'd gone with you."

"You do?"

"Yes, I do. I'm not saying what you did was right, but I'm glad somebody from our family was there. How was it?"

"Sad. Good. I saw Link and Young Mary. And Leesum."

"Who?"

"The boy from Pensacola."

"Oh, yes." Her lighter clinked, she inhaled, exhaled. "Don't worry about your father."

"Okay."

"Where's the Packard? Bill says it's not at home."

"At Freedom Park, in the lot off Princeton."

"I have the spare keys. We'll get it." She paused. "You can stay with Maggie tonight. Or here at Stamos and Rita's."

"I'm sure it'll be okay with Mrs. Harold if I stay here. I need clothes."

"I'll bring some early tomorrow. Everything's going to be all right, Jubie. I promise."

I sagged against the wall of the narrow hallway, so tired I thought I might fall asleep before I found a bed.

In the morning, Mrs. Harold said if I'd give her my dirty clothes, she'd put them in with a load of wash she was going to run. In the kitchen, the washing machine chugged as Mrs. Harold came down the hall to where I sat with Maggie on the living room sofa, wearing Maggie's bathrobe, which was too small but adequate, like Mary's had been for Leesum. Mrs. Harold handed me a wrinkled scrap of paper. "This was in the pocket of your jeans, Jubie. I read it. I'm sorry."

I had no idea what she was talking about. I smoothed out the paper on my knee.

I aint coming back. I am telling what you did. Mary

Mrs. Harold sat down in the easy chair. "What does it mean?"

"I don't know."

When Mama got to Maggie's house, she put her arms around me and held me for a long time, then stood back and smoothed my hair from my forehead. "I still can't believe you drove all the way home."

Mrs. Harold offered tea, and Mama said she would love some. We sat on the sofa together while Maggie went with her mother to the kitchen.

"Here." I shoved the note at Mama. "From Mary. It was on the bulletin board."

Mama read it. "This isn't from Mary."

"She signed it."

"This is not her handwriting. It must be from Young Mary." Mama stared at the note.

CHAPTER 28

Mama and I were fixing lunch when I heard the garage door going up and down. Mama put her hand on my shoulder. "Open the can of tuna for me."

Daddy came into the kitchen. He set a beer on the table with a sharp clack. "What have you got to say for yourself?"

Mama said, "June did what we should have done."

Daddy's eyes went to slits. "She stole your goddamn car!"

Mama turned back to the counter. "I've had enough of your temper." She began chopping onions.

Daddy stared at me across the bar.

Mama said, "Jubie, get the sweet pickle relish from the fridge."

Daddy left the kitchen. Their bedroom door slammed shut.

Mama tried to find a new maid. She talked with her friends, put ads in *The Charlotte Observer* and *The Charlotte News*:

DOMESTIC NEEDED to clean, iron, cook. South Charlotte, No. 3 bus, 8 AM to 6 PM, weekdays. Occasional Saturdays. Lunch provided. Must be healthy. $25 a week. Call Mrs. Watts at 3-5652.

Daddy thought it was excessive to run the ad in both papers, claiming that coloreds only read the *News*. Mama said most of her friends preferred the *Observer*, and they were the likely source for finding a new maid.

Mama had objections to all the maids who answered the ads. One had a lot of experience and several references, but she wanted thirty dollars a week and Mama said that was highway robbery. "Besides, she sounds uppity."

She posted a notice on the bulletin board at Watts Concrete Fabrications, hoping one of the men there would have a wife or daughter who needed a job. Nothing came of that, and Mama thought it was because we had a bad name in the colored community after Mary's death.

Clothes began to pile up on the den sofa, where Mama took them to fold while she watched TV or listened to her programs. The mound of clothes often outlasted the programs and she just left them there. She stopped ironing the sheets and pillowcases, and we had to change our own beds.

One day I found her sitting at the dining room table, crying, holding her damask tablecloth. There was a brown iron-shaped mark in the middle. "I've ruined it," Mama said. "I was on the phone. . . ." Her tears spotted the fabric, and the smell of scorched linen hung in the air. I wanted to comfort her but couldn't think how.

She blew her nose on the ruined damask. "There's just so much to do."

The next morning, Mama got Stell and me to help her move the kitchen table and chairs into the dining room. She put on faded denim Bermudas and tennis shoes, tied a bandana around her hair, and spent the day on her hands and knees with a scrub brush and pails of soapy water, scraping the yellow wax buildup off the linoleum. At supper she showed us her ruined manicure. "I wore rubber gloves, for all the good they did. I'm going to have a nervous breakdown if I don't find help."

A colored woman named Virginia, who was Susan Feaster's maid, helped us for a week while Mrs. Feaster was out of town. After Virginia had been with us a couple of days, Mama said to her, "I don't know what Susie pays you, but I can offer you twenty-eight dollars a week, with lunches."

Virginia turned her down, saying she'd been with Mrs. Feaster for eleven years. Mrs. Feaster was one of Mama's oldest friends, and I wondered if she ever found out about Mama going behind her back.

Mama told Aunt Rita, "I'm just looking for a good Negro, like Mary."

"You'll find someone. There are lots of strong girls who'd make fine domestics." Aunt Rita sliced a ham she and Mama were splitting.

"I've got high standards." Mama took a roll of freezer paper from the pantry. "Mary was smart, a hard worker. I trusted her completely. And the way some of these girls talk makes my skin crawl."

"Mary had decent grammar."

"And she didn't infect the kids with 'ain't' and 'fin uh go' and—"

"Fin uh go?"

"Fixing to go, as in 'Ah'm fin uh go de stoh.'"

"I'd swear you were colored."

Daddy didn't understand why Mama was having such a hard time finding a new maid, so she told him he could look for somebody. He didn't nag her anymore.

I didn't avoid him, but we had little to say to each other when the family sat down to supper or in the den to watch TV. I was uneasy around him and I wished things could get back to the way they'd been before Mary's death. When Daddy walked into a room, I was careful, the way I used to be on the fishing pier at Shumont, where the weathered gray planks looked solid enough until a rotting board gave beneath my feet.

Without Mary, the heart of our home was broken, and hiring a new maid wasn't going to mend it.

CHAPTER 29

Carter called to tell us about the accident. I remembered seeing Richard Daniels on the high dive as we passed Municipal Pool on our way out of town when we left for Pensacola. I imagined him diving, tucking and flipping, the board pulling out of the base, Richard rising from the water, the board falling, Richard's head cracking open like a watermelon.

All I could think about was the board hitting his head. Stell said they drained the pool because of the blood.

Richard was the best diver on the senior team. He spent hours practicing, waiting patiently in line to use the board. While other kids did cannonballs or sloppy swans, he did double flips, slicing the water with a clean entry. People watched when Richard dived.

The house was heavy with silence. Mama, Daddy, and Davie weren't home, and until Carter called, Stell and Puddin and I were as far away from each other as we could get in the quiet house. After the call, we huddled together in Stell and Puddin's room. Puddin kept crying, even though she hardly knew Richard. I held her until she calmed down, leaning against the padded headboard that joined their twin beds. Puddin lay back on the pillows and I stretched out across the foot of the beds, staring at the dead bugs in the glass globe of the ceiling light.

"I talked to Richard last night," Stell said. "He wanted to know if I thought we should have boys on the cheerleading squad."

"Do you?"

"A lot of schools do. With boys you can make pyramids."

"Did Richard want to be a cheerleader?"

She sniffed. "Yeah."

The back doorbell rang. Rang again. The cowbell jangled as the kitchen door opened and Uncle Stamos called out, "Bill? Paula?"

I shouted, "Hey, Uncle Stamos," and ran down the stairs.

He met me in the front hallway. "Where are Bill and Paula?"

"Mama's shopping. I don't know where Daddy is. An awful thing happened. . . ."

"I know. Terrible, horrific," Uncle Stamos said. He couldn't keep his hands still. He looked into the living room, put his hands in his pockets, took them out. "June, I've got to talk with Bill. Tell him to call me." He headed for the kitchen, turned, his face ashen, his eyes brimming. "At the office. As soon as he gets home."

"Yes, sir, I will." Uncle Stamos was gone, the cowbell clanging behind him.

I stared out the window at two birds pecking the

lawn. Stell Ann came into the kitchen. "Puddin cried herself to sleep." She opened the fridge. "You want some tea?"

"I don't want anything except for Richard to be alive."

"I know. I can't stop thinking about him."

A car door slammed, the breezeway screen opened and shut. Mama called out, "Girls?"

She came into the kitchen, carrying two sacks of groceries, Davie holding the hem of her dress. "June, get the rest of the groceries, please."

"Mama, have you—"

"Just bring in the groceries. Then we'll talk."

She'd heard. It took me two trips to carry in all the paper bags, with Mama unloading into the refrigerator and cabinets, Stell helping, nobody saying anything. Davie was in his high chair, banging a spoon on the tray.

"June, get your brother a graham cracker." Mama shook a cigarette from her leather case and sat down next to Davie with an ashtray. She took a deep drag. "Y'all must've heard about Richard Daniels."

Stell put cans of beans on the pantry shelf. I said, "Carter called."

Davie took a bite of graham cracker, said, "Doobie."

"What did he tell you?"

"That the diving board at Municipal fell and hit Richard in the head."

Mama smoked, drumming her fingers on the table. "Is that all?"

"Uncle Stamos came by, looking for Daddy."

"Oh, God." Mama's voice broke. She snubbed out her cigarette and put her head in her hands, crying. "They were talking about it at the store. They said the board . . . that something came apart . . . broke."

Davie threw down the cracker. "Mama!"

She didn't seem to have heard. "Where in hell is your father?"

CHAPTER 30

Richard's picture was on the front page of the *Observer*, with an article covering the details of his death, saying the services were for family only. Mama read it aloud at supper. "I'm sure Mr. and Mrs. Daniels don't want strangers gawking at Richard's grave. I'd feel the same way. People can be callous."

Over the next week, the phone rang and rang. When Mama answered it, she said a cheerful, "Hello?" If it was someone close—Aunt Rita or Uncle Taylor—her voice returned to a flat tiredness.

Daddy went to work and came home. He didn't go to the club or play golf or go fishing at Lake Wiley. He sat at the kitchen table or in the den, picking at the label on his beer bottle, leaving behind him swirling smoke and bits of paper. Mama said on the phone to Aunt Rita that he wasn't drunk and he wasn't sober. One night he and Uncle Stamos closed themselves in the den with a bucket of ice and a fifth of Jim Beam. Stell and I were at the kitchen table, doing homework while Mama put away leftovers after turning on the radio to drown out the rumble of their voices. The den door opened and Daddy went into the dining room. The liquor cabinet door opened, bottles rattled. Uncle Stamos' voice came from the den. "It wasn't the rebar and I won't lie about it. We have to face the music, take whatever . . ."

"No, no," Daddy interrupted him. "We just need to make it look as though . . ." The den door closed and I didn't hear the rest of Daddy's sentence.

I asked Mama, "What's a rebar?"

"They use them in their business." She turned her back to me and wiped around the burners on the stove.

Stell stood. "I need a pedicure." She gave me a sidelong look that told me she wanted me to come with her.

When I got to Stell's room, she was sitting on her bed, polish brush suspended in air, three toes on her left foot still unpainted. "Have you told Mama what Link said at Mary's funeral?"

"No."

"Why not?"

"I'm keeping my head down."

"Tell her." When she tried to spread her stubby toes, they hardly moved. She touched up a spot and blew on the wet polish. "Daddy's in trouble."

"What're you talking about?"

She put the brush to her pinkie. "Sometimes you are so out of it."

"Because nobody ever tells me anything."

"Link told you something."

I breathed in the sharp smell of the polish.

"If Daddy did something wrong, we'll all pay for it." There were tears in her eyes. "Our name will be mud in this town." She put the cap back on the bottle and twisted it tight. "Tell Mama what Link said." She didn't look up.

I washed my face, brushed my teeth, and put on my pajamas. Finally, there was nothing else to do.

Mama was at her dressing table, already in her nightgown, wiping cold cream from her face with a tissue. "What is it, Jubie?"

I sat on the foot of her bed. "At Mary's funeral, Link told me to ask Daddy about a room behind the warehouse."

Mama looked at me in the mirror. "Behind the—there aren't any rooms, just a wall with bays that open to the train tracks."

"Link said to ask Daddy about it."

"Where's your father?"

I stood. "You want me to get him?"

"No, I want to know where he is."

"I guess he's still in the den."

"Close the door."

I shut the bedroom door and sat back down.

Mama lit a cigarette. "Exactly what did Link say?"

"He told me to ask Daddy about a room behind the warehouse."

Mama threw away a tissue, then rearranged her silver comb and brush. "Are you sure Link didn't say 'beside' the warehouse?"

"He said behind or maybe in back of."

She began brushing her hair off her forehead.

"There's a storage shed built onto the side of the building. Maybe that's what he meant." She glanced at me in the mirror, took a drag on her cigarette and put it out. Her face was shiny and she looked tired. "I'll look into it, Jubie. Thanks for telling me." She stood and held out her arms. "Hug good night?"

Her shoulder blades felt like bird bones. I kissed her cheek, which was slightly sticky from the cold cream. "Night, Mama."

The next day, Aunt Rita came over. She looked nervous and uncomfortable.

I was scraping carrots for supper. Mama poured coffee for the two of them and told me to scram. "Put the carrots in water. We won't be long."

As I filled a bowl with water, Aunt Rita said, "I've talked with Stamos and he—"

"Jubie?" Mama looked at me. They weren't going to say anything until I left. I went through the swinging door into the front hall, then tiptoed down the basement steps to Mary's bathroom, where I could hear Mama clear as a bell.

"Stamos knew about it, then."

"Not about the pedestal for the diving board. He'd have closed it down."

"What did he know?"

A cup clinked in a saucer. "I just wish Bill hadn't fired Joe Templeton," Aunt Rita said.

"Joe was embezzling, for God sakes."

"But that's when Stamos took over the books and found out what was going on."

"What? Found out what?" Mama was almost shouting.

"Do you know what rebar is?"

"The rods they use to reinforce concrete."

"I think Bill was buying it cheap, putting it on the books as expensive, and using the money to support the W.B.A." I remembered Daddy and Uncle Stamos talking about the W.B.A., how I'd wondered what it was.

"You think?"

"Stamos let something slip, then clammed up. He's loyal to Bill, Pauly; he follows wherever his brother leads. But he's been bothered for a long time about how Bill runs things. When Stamos took over the books, he was shocked at some of the—"

"Ye gods!" Mama's voice was shrill. "They've taken the books. Those inspector people."

Aunt Rita sounded like she was crying, and her voice was so low I could hardly hear her. "Stamos did tell me that. He feels responsible. He's so guilty about the Daniels boy, so deeply distressed. I keep trying to soothe him, to reassure him." I heard the rasp of a lighter. "He knew the books weren't right. But he couldn't have known about the diving board. He's not that kind of man."

"Not like Bill, you mean."

"I didn't say that."

Mama said, "Jubie told me something last night. That's why I called you." A chair scraped the kitchen floor. "Mary's son, Link, worked at the warehouse for two summers, remember?"

"Sure."

"Jubie saw him at Mary's funeral. He told her to ask Bill about a room behind the warehouse."

"There isn't any—"

Mama interrupted. "I think he meant the storage shed that's on the side of the building toward the train tracks. Might seem like the back."

The phone rang and Mama answered it. "It's Safronia."

Aunt Rita said, "Yes, Safronia, what is it?" There was a long silence. "Just calm down . . . yes, I'll come home. Have you called Mr. Watts? Okay, okay, just stop crying."

Mama said, "What's wrong? I've never heard such carrying on."

"That girl will be the death of me. She says to come home right now, just come 'tireckly' home." She sighed. "I wish I could find someone like Mary."

"I wish I could, too."

Uncle Stamos had left for work on time that morning, but he went back home after Aunt Rita came to our house. Safronia got to work at eleven and found him on the floor in the laundry room, a bath towel around his head. The gun he'd used was near his hand.

Later, Mama said she was sure he did it in the laundry room so any mess he made would be easy to clean. I couldn't stop thinking about Uncle Stamos lying on the floor, wearing a bloody turban. What was he thinking just as he pulled the trigger? When I began to feel the terror he must have felt, I'd say "No!" out loud to stop my thoughts.

He'd put the muzzle of the gun in his mouth. I remembered Daddy saying that most people did it wrong. "Shooting yourself in the temple is no guarantee, but up through the roof of the mouth will do the trick." Had he told his brother that?

When Aunt Rita got home, Safronia met her at the door and told her not to go in the laundry room. So of course that's the first thing she did. She opened the door and cried, "Oh, Stamos! Oh, sweetheart." She sat on the floor beside him and put his bloody head in her lap. For an hour she rocked him, moaning aloud, while Safronia sat in the kitchen, crying.

Then Aunt Rita stood, smoothing her blood-stained dress. "Safronia, we've got to get my husband into the bedroom so I can wash him and prepare his body."

She got trouble from the police about moving him, but they decided that the shock had overcome her. She said shock had nothing to do with it, that her family always tended to the body, washed it and dressed it for burial. Her people didn't believe in embalming, and she wanted Stamos laid out in a coffin in the living room for a visitation, the way her family did in Ohio. Safronia's people did the same sort of thing, so she wanted to help.

When we got to the visitation, Aunt Rita answered the door, and Mama wrapped her in a hug. In the living room, Daddy was sitting in an easy chair near the coffin. Mama said, "Bill," and sat on the sofa. Daddy stood, but when Stell took the place next to Mama, he sat back down. I realized how little he and Mama had said to each other for days.

The house looked the way it always did, neat as a pin. Uncle Stamos used to say that if he finished reading a paper and dropped it, Aunt Rita would catch it before it hit the carpet.

A sweet scent filled the living room from the flowers surrounding the closed bronze casket.

"The flowers are lovely," Mama said when Aunt Rita sat in a chair opposite Daddy's.

"People have been so kind. Enough food for weeks, flowers everywhere." Aunt Rita's eyes were big in her round face, dark circles under them.

Stell leaned toward her. "I'm so sorry about Uncle Stamos." I wished I'd said that, and couldn't think of anything to add.

Slow, heavy footsteps came down the hall, and Mama turned her head to the window. Daddy stood, holding out his hands. "Mother." Meemaw walked in, a black rectangle topped by a round face and neat gray hair in a bun. "Son." She turned her cheek for Daddy's kiss and he led her to the chair where he'd been sitting. She touched the coffin before she sat. Stell scooted closer to Mama so Daddy could share the sofa.

Mama stood and kissed Meemaw's forehead. "Hello, Cordelia."

"Mothers shouldn't outlive their sons." Meemaw's voice was old and weak. She asked Mama, "What'd you do with—I mean, the little ones?"

"A neighbor is staying with them." Mama sank back down on the sofa. "They're too young to . . ." She looked at the casket.

"David is," Meemaw said. "And Carolina—she's what now?"

Mama said, "Seven."

I corrected her. "Eight."

Mama blushed. "Eight. Sorry. She had a birthday. Friday. We haven't had her party yet."

Aunt Rita wiped away a tear. "You tell my sweet Puddin we'll give her a bang-up birthday once all this is over."

"I'll tell her, Rita. She'll like that."

The front door opened and closed. Carly stood in the arched entrance to the living room, tall and somber in his army uniform. He'd flown in from a military post in Germany. "Mom?" He put down his suitcase and held his arms wide. Aunt Rita jumped up and ran to him. "Carly, Carly, I'm so glad you're finally here." They stood there holding each other, Aunt Rita folded in her grown son's arms.

Carly brought a wooden chair in from the hallway and put it next to the coffin. Safronia came into the living room in a starched uniform, carrying a silver service that she put down on the coffee table. "Here's tea and coffee and cookies. Miz Dunn fixed them, and she said you'd pour." She looked at Mama. "Need anything, just holler." She backed out of the room, dusting her white-gloved hands.

"Why in the world—I mean, she's got gloves on," Meemaw said.

"She cut herself Friday," said Aunt Rita. "When she found . . ." Her voice dwindled, then she cleared her throat and continued. "Her left hand is bandaged, so we thought gloves were best."

"I'm amazed she could handle the tray," said Mama.

"Oh, the cut wasn't bad, but her whole hand is wrapped."

Stell picked up the tall pot. "Who wants coffee?" Did she know which pot had coffee in it? She did, as I saw when she poured for Daddy. "Meemaw?"

"Yes, Estelle."

"Excuse me." I went into the bathroom off the

kitchen and sat on the toilet, staring out the window, wondering how long we'd be here, how many sad people I had to see. After a few minutes I left the bathroom by the door into the den, where an oak rolltop desk took up half of one wall. The top was pushed up, with papers scattered everywhere. Aunt Rita couldn't have seen it or she would have tidied things and closed the desk. A curled paper lay on top—a photocopy of the note Uncle Stamos had left for Aunt Rita.

I sat in the oak swivel chair and picked up the stiff paper, my hands shaking.

September 10, 1954
My dearest Rita,

I know you won't understand. I'm not sure I do, either. I cannot face you, Carlisle, or Mother, when you find out what Bill and I did. Even as I write that, I want to defend myself, to say I didn't know. I hope you believe me. When I found out, too late to prevent the Daniels boy's death, I was so ashamed. I should have known. Isn't that what lawyers always say? "He knew or should have known." Well, I should have.

The facts mean nothing now.

There was a smudge on the paper, as if he'd started to write something and changed his mind.

The only truth in all of this is my love for you, which has never wavered. I wish I could have it both ways, face my shame and stay with you. But the one overshadows the other, so I must say good-bye.

By the time you read this note, Cliff Sindell will have received my final documents, which include a letter to Chief Kytle telling him everything I know about what the company did that may have resulted in the boy's death. Cliff will stand by you through all the paperwork and details.

Please ask Carly and Mother to forgive me, as I hope you will be able to do. I love you beyond death, my dearest, sweetest wife.

Stamos

I stared out the window into the backyard, so neat and pretty. Uncle Stamos had loved his garden. A tear fell onto the paper. When I wiped it away, the writing smeared.

I wanted to talk to Leesum. What would he be doing on a Sunday afternoon, living in a preacher's house? McDowell Street Baptist Church didn't have a separate number listed for the rectory, so I called the church. A man answered, and from his voice I knew it was Reverend Perkins.

"Leesum there?" I tried to sound colored.

After a pause, the man said, "Hold the line." Then Leesum said, "Hello?"

"Hey. It's me, Jubie."

"Hey! What you doin' callin' me?"

"Just wanted to talk to you." I felt foolish.

"Glad you did."

"Me, too."

"I got sumpin to tell you. Reverend Perkins and them got together. Three of our elders gone go to Georgia to find out who killed Miz Luther."

"Will you let me know what happens?"

"Of course." There was a pause, then Leesum said, "Just hopes they gets there okay. They drivin' straight through the night, cuz no hotels'll have 'em. It ain't easy right now, not where they be goin."

I remembered about the curfew in Wickens, how hard it was to find a place where Mary could stay, the motel in Albany where we sneaked her in and out. I heard a noise behind me. Carly filled the doorway.

I said into the phone, "I've got to hang up."

I put the receiver down, not wanting to let Leesum go. "A friend," I said to Carly.

But he was reading the note on the desk. By the time he finished, he was crying, too. "Have you seen the laundry room?" he asked.

"No."

"I want to see it."

Aunt Rita found us in the door to the laundry room. I gasped when she touched my shoulder, and felt bad when I saw who it was. But she said, "I don't mind y'all looking. I'm sure everybody wants to."

"Oh, Mom." I thought Carly might start crying again.

"He was thoughtful. Wrapped his head in a towel so there wouldn't be—" She ran her hand over the doorjamb. "After I got him washed and ready for the undertaker, took care of the mess, I prepared to grieve."

She took Carly's hand. "At first I was afraid I would come on a spot I'd missed, when I was looking for the Ajax or something, but now I almost hope I do—a reminder of him, not that I need one, but you know . . ."

I said I did. She looked me in the eyes. "I know you do."

In the car on the way home from the funeral, Mama blew her nose, straightened behind the wheel, took a deep breath. "Let's have dinner at the El Dorado. Pretend we have plenty of money."

Stell said, "Shouldn't we find out what the rest of the family's doing? Aunt Rita and Meemaw and—"

"I'm sick of being sad, and I don't care if I never see Cordelia again." Mama blew her nose.

"What's the W.B.A.?" I asked.

Mama stared out the windshield, not looking at our house when we passed it. She answered in a low voice. "White Businessmen's Association. Who told you about that?"

"Mayor Lindley was talking to Daddy at the funeral."

"What did His Honor say?"

"Something about Daddy trying to get the W.B. A. going in Charlotte with money from the business."

Mama said, "The mayor was in on it. I'm sure he'll say he wasn't."

"The White Businessmen's Association. What does it do?" Stell asked.

"Scares coloreds into giving up on voting, education. Other stuff." Mama turned on the car radio, loud.

At the El Dorado, Mama parked the car and leaned her head on the steering wheel. "I don't know what's going to happen to us." She started to cry. Stell put her arms around her and I reached over the seat and hugged them both; I could feel Mama's shoulders trembling. I wanted her to stop crying, to be strong. Somebody had to be.

Mama wiped her face. "I wish we could move to Taylor's for a while."

CHAPTER 31

The police came to our house a week after Uncle Stamos' funeral. Daddy invited them to have seats in the den, where he settled in his chair, a glass in his hand, the Jim Beam bottle on the table beside him. He'd already called Cliff Sindell, his lawyer, and the police agreed to wait until Mr. Sindell got there.

There were two of them, dressed in suits and ties, looking like ordinary business friends of Daddy's, talking about the best places to fish on Lake Wiley.

Daddy said, "Maybe we could meet out there sometime. You could show me the lures you made."

"We'll see," said the older of the two. He pointed at the Jim Beam. "I hear that's a good bourbon."

"It is," said Daddy. "Made near where I grew up, in Kentucky." He took a sip. "I guess you don't drink on duty."

"No, that's right." The man cleared his throat. "But there's no prohibition on ice tea."

Daddy looked at me.

I went to the kitchen.

When I returned with a tray of glasses and a pitcher of ice tea, Cliff Sindell was there. Daddy had already fixed him a drink. He nodded. "Hello, June."

"Hey, Mr. Sindell."

Daddy said, "Jubie, you can leave us now."

I closed the door behind me, knowing I'd find out soon enough what was going on. Mama was through with secrets.

Having the police in the house hit Mama hard. The next morning, she said to Daddy, "They've got something on you. What else are you hiding?" He left and was gone for three days. When he came back, she wouldn't speak to him, not even hello. After a week of her silence, he moved to a fishing cabin on Lake Wiley. The next day, Mama walked around in her nightgown, drinking coffee and chain-smoking. At lunch she sat at the table, a cigarette in her hand, stabbing a half-eaten tomato with her fork, then picking it up and throwing it against the wall. It slid down the wallpaper, leaving a slick trail of pulp and seeds.

I went for paper towels. Mama snatched them from me and put out her cigarette in her plate, which I'd never known her to do. She scrubbed the wall and collapsed on the floor crying, wiping her face with her nightgown.

Mail piled up on the hall table. I took the unopened bills to Mama, who went to the desk in the den and sat with the checkbook, staring out at the magnolia Daddy had planted when we moved in. An hour later I went back to the den and she was still sitting there in a swirl of smoke. "Mama?"

"Why isn't *he* paying the bills, balancing the checkbook, getting the Packard serviced? Doing what a man's supposed to do." She looked up at me. "I swear to God, Jubie, I wish I'd never met him."

"I'm glad you did, Mama."

Amusement lit her face for the first time in days. "Yes, I guess you are."

Davie called from his bedroom. "Mama!" She stood. "Nap time's over." She handled Davie as well as Mary ever had, and I thought if Mary walked in the door, she'd be a stranger to him. Mama felt smaller to me, and I realized it was because she mostly wore flats or loafers. Carrying a toddler around doesn't go with high heels.

I came home from school to find Mama at the dining room table, holding a sheet of paper, a torn envelope on the floor. She said, "You'll want to read this."

I saw the letterhead centered at the top of the page and sank into a chair.

October 8, 1954
Dear Mrs. Watts:
Confirming our telephone conversation of Saturday last: one Gaither Mowbry, Jr., aged 19 years, was arrested on October 6, 1954, for multiple infractions, not the least of which was a state of advanced inebriation while in command of an automobile.

I remembered the man named Gaither who took us to Sally's Motel Park, his sweat-soaked shirt, how he smoked, coughed, cleared his throat.

Further, Mr. Mowbry attempted to evade the pursuing Patrol car and forcibly resisted arrest to the extent of battering an Officer of the Law. He was placed in my custody, whereupon he was relieved of his possessions and incarcerated for his own and the public's safety. Among the items found in his possession was the ring about which I called you.

I looked at Mama. "Why didn't you tell us the sheriff called?"

She picked up the envelope, folded it in half. "I didn't want to upset you."

She was beyond my understanding. I looked back at the letter.

As per our phone call, the inscription of the ring is PLL to MCC 1925. It is my compelling belief that the ring was the property of the dead Negro woman who was in your employ, one Mary Constance Culpepper Luther. Apparently, Gaither Mowbry thought the ring to be of value, though he was mistaken. It is gold, but skimpy, and has little beyond sentimental worth.

Under the process of the Law, I will keep the wedding band as evidence. There are also details about the Mowbry car that lead us to believe it was used to transport your maid. Certainly I will advise you once the facts in this matter are concluded. Although the outcome should be foregone, there are no guarantees. I remain

Yours truly

Jeremiah Higgins

Sheriff, etc.
P.S. When it is no longer needed as evidence, I will return the girl's ring to you for conveyance to her family or as is appropriate. I should also advise that I have written to the contingent of Negroes who came to Claxton to inquire about the investigation, advising them the same as is conveyed above.

So Leesum and the elders from McDowell Street Baptist—they knew. And the ring would go to Link and Young Mary. I wished I could hold it just once, squint my eyes to read the tiny letters that Mary had told me were as the sheriff described.

"I should have noticed her ring was gone." Orange dots appeared on Mama's yellow blouse.

340

She was crying. "At the funeral parlor in Claxton. I never looked at her hands."

"Oh, Mama, that's when you got her hair done, powder and lipstick, her dress . . ."

"How'd you know?"

"Mrs. Coley, a woman at the funeral—she thanked me for what we'd done for Mary."

Mama wiped her eyes. "I treated her like any old maid, but she wasn't, you know?"

"I know."

"When I woke at the beach and you'd taken the car, I knew where you'd gone. I wanted to be with you so bad. The least thing I could have done is be at her funeral. The very least thing. Fixing her up wasn't enough."

I took Mama's hand, sure she would pull away, but she didn't.

"When you and Puddin got the mumps, Mary brought me a bottle of home remedy."

"Did it cure us?"

"I flushed it down the toilet." Mama shook her hankie, blew her nose. "She was so great when I went into labor with Davie, timing the pains, distracting me. I miss her!"

I was sitting in the den, doing homework, when the door opened and there was Daddy, tall and not so tan, grayer than I remembered and paunchier. I stood up fast.

"Daddy! I didn't hear the garage door."

"Not sure I have the right to park there now." He hugged me hard. "How's my girl?"

"What do you want?" At Mama's voice, Daddy let me go.

"Hey to you, too, Paula."

"Take whatever it is you came for."

He pushed past her, heading for their room. She went after him and I followed, a shadow with ears.

Drawers opened and closed in their bedroom.

"Where's my other suitcase?" Daddy asked.

"The attic."

Silence. Feet stomping. Then Daddy said, "What is it *you* want, Paula?"

"The house. The Packard. Alimony. Child support."

A door slammed. "Talk to Cliff Sindell."

"We're not sharing a lawyer."

Were they getting divorced? I'd been hoping they'd make up, that things would be back the way they were before Mary, Richard, Uncle Stamos. I felt cold and scared and relieved.

Daddy came from the bedroom with suits over one arm, shirts and underwear bunched in the other, passing me as though he didn't see me. He piled everything on the kitchen table, got grocery bags from the pantry and stuffed them with his clothes. Mama handed him a business card. "Give that to Cliff."

Daddy read the card. "P. Hollis Burns, Attorney at Law. Where'd you find him?"

"Her."

"Ha!" Daddy said.

"I know about you and Young Mary."

I froze in the hallway.

Daddy spoke sharply. "What are you talking about?"

"She left a note on the bulletin board."

There was a silence so total I thought they'd hear me breathing. "C'mon, Pauly. All I did was make a pass at her. She was asking for it, swishing around in shorts, dancing to jive."

"She's *seventeen.*"

The den door slammed behind Daddy. I raced out the kitchen door to catch up with him, knowing Mama would hear the cowbell, would know I'd run after him. I didn't care.

He was in the driveway. "Daddy?"

"I guess you heard all that."

"Yes, sir." We looked at each other. "Are you living at Lake Wiley?"

He took out his handkerchief and polished his glasses. "I am, for now." He put his glasses back on, fitting the earpieces one at a time.

"Then what?"

"Back to Kentucky. Live with Mother for a while. Start over."

I looked down to hide my face. "The diving board, Daddy."

He dug in his shirt pocket with two fingers, pulled out a rumpled pack of cigarettes and a book of matches. "I lost my Zippo in Claxton." He lit a cigarette, inhaled, let the smoke out slowly. "We made a mistake. I was going to fix it, but . . ." He put his hand on my shoulder. "Jubie."

"Sir?"

"I'll come back." He kissed my cheek. I thought there were tears in his eyes but couldn't be sure through the glare on his glasses.

After his car pulled out of the driveway, I went to my bed, put the pillows over my head, and sobbed.

That night I dreamed Mama and Daddy and I were going to a party at Uncle Stamos and Aunt Rita's in honor of Carly and his fiancée. Mama and Daddy left for the party first and told me to come along later. While they were gone, I picked stuff from Mrs. Gibson's garden, including some warped volunteer tomatoes—small, red, delicious-looking.

Mama and Daddy came home from the party bitterly disillusioned. They weren't dressed up enough, and Mama thought Rita should have warned them. The other guests were in cocktail clothes, sequins, silks. Mama and Daddy were in their movie clothes, dressed for the evening but not for show.

"We were beneath ourselves," said Mama.

"It's about time," said Mary, and went to the basement.

CHAPTER 32

Stell tossed *The Charlotte News* on the bar. "Hurricane Hazel page one, William Watts page two."

"Let me see." Mama dropped the cup she was rinsing. It clattered in the sink.

"The findings of the commission. They're saying Watts Concrete Fabrications messed up some bolts. Daddy might be criminally negligent."

Mama opened the newspaper and reached for a cigarette.

I looked over her shoulder.

She pushed me away. "You can read it when I'm done."

"Charges will be brought," Stell said.

"Estelle Annette, be quiet."

Stell left the kitchen. If it were possible to slam a swinging door, she'd have done it.

Mama ripped off the first page, balled it up and threw it away, letting the lid of the trash can bang shut. "I almost feel sorry for him."

"Mama, I wanted to read it."

"You know where it is." She went into the dining room, stopped at the liquor cabinet, and fixed a drink. The den door opened and closed. The glider squeaked on the breezeway.

The balled-up sheet of newspaper sat on a mound of coffee grounds, a stain spreading through it. I scooped it from the pail and opened it on the bar. The damp paper began to tear through Daddy's photo—his face brown from the coffee grounds—a formal picture he'd had made when he joined the Thomas Belk Men's Club. The wet paper clung to the Formica as I pushed the pieces back together. There was a caption under the photo: "William Watts, civic leader, former President of the Charlotte Junior Chamber of Commerce." The article was titled in bold words: LOCAL BUSINESS RESPONSIBLE IN DIVER'S DEATH.

A commission formed by the City Council of Charlotte to investigate the death of Richard Llewelyn Daniels, 17, reported its findings yesterday to Mayor Watson Lindley and to Chief Hurston Kytle of the Charlotte Police Department. The commission holds that Watts Concrete Fabrications, Inc., in constructing a base for the diving boards at Charlotte Municipal Swimming Pool, failed to prime the L-bolts that secured the diving boards to the base. The report read, in part, "William Dennis Watts, President of Watts Concrete Fabrications, and his brother, the late Stamos Caton Watts, Vice President, knew or should have known that unprimed L-bolts used in the construction would fail.

The city will bring civil charges against the company and its principals. If William Watts is found to be criminally negligent, further charges will be brought."

The commission is also investigating rumors that the Watts brothers diverted corporate funds to support a recently formed White Businessmen's Association (W.B.A.), with the intent of restraining Negroes from registering to vote. Although no names have been released, there are apparently a number of Charlotte professionals who were members of the W.B.A., which met in a storage room beside Watts Concrete Fabrications. Duplicate sets of financial records are being audited to determine the extent of any fraud. William Watts, a well-known civic leader and father of four, was not available for comment.

The glider clanked back and forth on the breezeway. Maybe Mama hadn't built the diving board that caused Richard's death, but she loved the Packard, the country club, her charge account at Montaldo's. And she was looking a little shabby, like the house. Suddenly I couldn't stand the sound of the glider on its rusty slides. It needed oiling, like the bills needed paying and the hedges needed trimming. The glider squeaked and squeaked. I put my hands on the damp newsprint, one on either side of Daddy's picture, and pressed and pulled until the paper tore through the bridge of his glasses, down his nose, splitting his smile. I left the paper sticking to the bar and went to the breezeway, where Mama sat in the glider, drinking and rocking and smoking. A strong wind blew through the screens.

"It's your fault, too," I screamed.

"Oh, Jubie, calm down." She took a drag from her cigarette.

"What did Daddy do to Young Mary?"

"I don't really know. I was bluffing."

"You're right, what you did for Mary *wasn't* enough." I grabbed the glass from her hand and threw it on the slate floor, where it shattered. The smell of Scotch filled the breezeway.

I yanked open the screen door. The wind caught it and slammed it back against the wall.

I ran through the grass and climbed over the redwood fence into Mrs. Gibson's backyard, inching past the thorny pyracantha to sit in her garden with the marble angel, beside the burning bush, everything drab and gray in the diluted light of the approaching storm.

I gazed into a cave created by the branches of a giant magnolia, where shadow shapes formed as the wind picked up, bringing on rain. All around me, tree limbs and flowers swayed, the red and orange berries of holly and pyracantha, dying mums and marigolds. Pansies that bobbed like drunken clowns. I read the tattered tag hanging from a gardenia bush that still had a few drooping flowers: CARE AND FEEDING OF GARDENIAS: FULL SUN WITH SHADE IN SUMMER. MOIST SOIL, NEVER SOGGY. HEAVY FEEDING. Why didn't people come with instructions?

I was so mad at Mama, at Daddy, even at Uncle Stamos, who knew or should have known—those words stuck in my mind. I sat there getting soaked as the rain and wind battered me. The edge of Hurricane Hazel. Bedraggled daisies lashed my legs and I snatched one from the ground. Even half dead, it was stronger than anything that grew wild by the road. You could do loves-me-loves-me-not on the petals of Mrs. Gibson's daisies and get at the truth. I cupped my hands around it and sniffed the sour citrusy scent that smelled like Mary when she'd been working all day, an odor I sometimes had, too, and never minded. When Mama caught Mary smelling that way, she went to her bedroom to put a touch of perfume on her upper lip. The more I thought about the small meanness of that, the sadder I got, until I was crying all over the limp daisy. Daddy was gone. He'd wind up in jail or an outcast—that was the word that came to me. No matter what, he would never be back with Mama, with us.

The rain pounded me, needles stinging my face, a downpour driven by the wind until it was horizontal. Through the boards of the fence I saw the lights in our house go out. If Hazel stood still, we'd be without power for days. Why did hurricanes only have female names? I'd have to find out about that. Before I left the garden, I picked the last of the gardenias to give Mama.

What I had was Mama and Stell and Puddin and Davie. Maybe they didn't know that as clearly as I did, but I could tell them.

CHAPTER 33

In January of 1955, I woke in my pink bedroom for the last time, in a sleeping bag on the floor, the sun streaming through the open Venetian blinds. The harsh morning light made me feel ready to move out of this bedroom I'd been sleeping in for two and a half years, now strange and empty. I unzipped the bag. I couldn't imagine Mama spending the night on the floor, but when I'd asked her if she minded, she said, "Oh, pooh, it's just this once." I looked behind the door, where a piece of carpet had come loose months ago. Last night I'd tucked a handwritten note under it, then pushed it back in place. Someday when the carpeting was pulled up, someone would find a small paper, folded many times: *To Whom It May Concern. My name is June Bentley Watts and I lived here from September 1952 to January 1955. I dedicate this room to the memory of Mary Constance Culpepper Luther, 1906–1954.*

I got dressed and stuffed my pajamas into my sleeping bag, along with Mary's slippers, which I'd taken to wearing around the house. Mama had looked at them when I came down for breakfast one morning, but she hadn't said anything.

Stell was sitting on the floor in her bedroom, her sleeping bag rolled up and ready to go. The honey-colored carpet was indented where the furniture

351

had been. Would the marks disappear when Stanley Steemer cleaned the rugs and drapes?

I sat beside her and took the ragged stuffed animal she was holding. "Where'd you find him?"

"The top shelf in my closet, where I hid him from Puddin."

"She cried for days, I remember." Our voices bounced off the walls.

Stell flipped one of the filthy ears. "Can you believe Mama ever let her suck on those?"

"I'd forgotten." The ears felt stiff and papery.

"Sweet Bunny, they called it, the ears coated with sugar."

"Yuk!" I tossed the crusty rabbit. It landed in a square of light under the front window.

"Are we still going to be members of the club?" I asked.

"Grow up. We'll be lucky to have groceries."

"Mama's going to get a job."

Stell picked up the rabbit. "Who'd hire her? She's never worked."

"Girls?" Mama's voice echoed up the stairwell.

"Coming!" Stell called down. She walked into her closet and tossed the bunny onto the top shelf. "Back where he's lived these many years. A Cuthbert will find him and commit him to eternal rest." She closed the closet door.

"Have you met them?"

"Only Lucy, at school."

"Maybe she'll have this room."

"Who cares." Stell headed downstairs.

"I'll be right there." I walked back to my room, which felt enormous without furniture. The dusty rose carpet was pock-marked the same as Stell's. A path of my footprints had worn the rug between the bed and dresser, the bureau and closet. I picked up a bobby pin from the floor by the side window and looked out. Carter was dribbling a basketball in his driveway. He threw the ball toward the hoop on his garage. Swish.

I picked up my bedroll and went downstairs. Mama called from her room, "Jubie, the paper bags in the kitchen need to go to the car."

"Yes, ma'am." I got the bulging sacks and went out the kitchen door, which was oddly quiet without the cowbell.

Carter held the basketball at his hip, sweat trickling down his freckled face. "Y'all leaving now?"

"Yeah."

He twirled the ball on his index finger. "I'm glad your dad's not going to jail."

I put down my bedroll, shifted the bags. "He sold his business to pay the fine."

"Stell told me." He bounced the ball.

"See you at school."

He nodded.

By late afternoon, everything was done. Mama was in the kitchen, moving her hand back and forth on the bar as if she were wiping it. She'd taken off her wedding band and there was a mark on her finger like the dents in the rugs. "A small kitchen will be a relief," she said. "Let's go."

Stell stood by the Packard with Carter, who kissed her on the cheek and said, "I'll see you in a couple of days, okay?"

She put her head on his chest for a moment, then got in the front seat of the Packard. I sat in the back, next to piles of clothes. No one spoke as we pulled out of the driveway. When we turned onto Queens Road West, Mama said, "Rita's bringing Puddin and Davie over after supper. We need to get their beds ready. The linens and pillows are on the floor by the beds, towels and washcloths in the bathrooms. Get used to living without a maid."

"We already are," Stell said.

"I mean permanently. And no yard man. There are leaves left over from the fall, a lot of work." Mama drove with one hand while she rooted in her purse. I heard a familiar sound and Mama laughed. "The cowbell. I forgot it was in my bag." She cracked the wing window and lit a cigarette. "I've got a job. I interviewed last Thursday and I'm going back Monday to meet the staff."

"Mama, that's great," I said. "Where?" Cold air and cigarette smoke wafted into the backseat.

"The Center for Rehabilitation, off East Morehead, as a receptionist in the free clinic."

"What'll you do?" Stell asked.

"Answer the phone, open the mail, make

appointments. The free clinic is for people who don't have insurance." Mama took a drag from her cigarette.

I thought about Leesum. Surely he didn't have insurance. Who would pay if he got sick?

Mama flicked the cigarette out the window. "I have no illusions about the job, but at least someone hired me."

From then on we called it the center for the disillusioned.

On Selwyn Avenue we drove into the sunset, passing the road to the house in the woods where we lived when Mary came to work for us. Right after we moved there, Mama had talked about getting a job. Daddy hit the roof and Mama never mentioned the idea again.

She set the brake in the steep driveway of the yellow house. "If we weren't just renting, I'd paint it. The color is revolting."

"I think it's cheerful," I said.

Mama sniffed. "Don't go in without carrying something."

The house was tall and narrow, on a skinny lot that sloped down to Sugar Creek. The neighbors had warned us not to plant anything in the backyard because the creek would rise in the spring.

Mama opened the front door, turning on the outside light over the tiny porch. I carried my clothes up to the room I'd be sharing with Davie. "Just until I get his ready," Mama had promised.

I went back downstairs. Stell was standing by the front door, her hands on her hips. "Mama?" she called toward the kitchen. "Where are the dinner table and chairs?"

"I sold them." Mama walked into the living room. "We'll use the dinette from now on."

"I can't believe we don't have a dinner table."

I went through the kitchen and out onto the back stoop. The grass was hidden by leaves that had been rotting there since fall. I couldn't imagine how we'd get rid of them. Mama opened the back door and hung the cowbell on it, then said, reading my thoughts, "We'll rake them into the creek, no big deal."

Lately Mama had answers for everything.

ACKNOWLEDGMENTS

At age forty-five, I left my hometown of Charlotte, North Carolina, for the backwoods of Chatham County, seeking perspective: I couldn't write about Charlotte until I left it. That providential relocation resulted in my friendship with novelist Laurel Goldman, a fine teacher who is both a tough critic and an admiring fan; this skilled combination has brought out the best in the many writers who've studied with her for the past thirty years, including current and past members of her amazing Thursday morning writing group: Cindy Paris, Fabienne Worth, Melissa Delbridge, Mia Bray, Cat Warren, Eve Rizzo, Carter Perry, Christina Askounis, Jackie Arial, James Ingram, Carolyn Muehlhause, Maureen Sladen, Mary Michael, Phaedra Greenwood, Charles Gates, Betty Reigot, Mary Caldwell, and the late Wilton Mason and Knut Schmidt-Nielsen.

Thank you, Lee Smith, Angela Davis-Gardner, and Peggy Payne for your critical feedback and generosity of time. I'll pay it forward.

And the writers on whom I cut my teeth in Charlotte, NC: J. R. McHone (water brother),

Dennis Smirl, Dick Bowman, Jerry Meredith, David Frye, Greg West, and Bill Barfield—to you, I say: "Aardvarks forever!"

In New York: John Scognamiglio, my editor at Kensington Books, who guided me with care and consideration through the publication process, and my agent, Robert Guinsler, who continued to believe in my book when I'd all but given up. Thanks to you both for taking a chance on a seventy-one-year-old first-time novelist. Now there's a marketing angle!

Pat French, confidante and mother-confessor, thanks for hiking with Jean-Michel and checking on him when I'm away, for not telling me what you think I should do unless I ask you, and for sharing your editorial talents. I'll never forget your call from the airport when you finished reading my manuscript.

Thank you, Diana Hales, for packing your bags when I holler, "Road trip!"

Institutions: The North Carolina Writer's Network, for keeping wordsmiths connected in the Old North State; The Weymouth Center, for providing the peace and solitude scribblers need; The Carolina Room at the Public Library of Charlotte and Mecklenburg County, and the Orange County Main Library, Hillsborough, NC.

For careful reading and critique: Kay Bishop, Robin and Mae Langford, Penny Austen, Kathryn Milam, Traci Woody, Tiffany Wright, Sofia Samatar, Richard Hoey-Bey, Gwendolyn Y. Fortune, Nancy Rosebaugh, Aimee Tattersall, and Daphne Wiggins-Obie. I'm grateful to Bob Conrow and Jamie Long, who gave me the use of their lake home, where my embryonic novel matured into a newborn. And to Taylin, the precocious strawberry-blonde angel who patiently asked me, in the locker room at SportsPlex, when she was eight, then nine, then ten, "When can I see your book?" She never doubted that she *would* see it in print someday.

Other writers from whom I learn so much, on Tuesday mornings: Mary Harrison, John Manuel, Leslie Nydick, Patricia Owens, and James Protzman; on Tuesday evenings: Beverly Meek, Jennie Ratcliffe, Sally Schauman, Virginia Tyler, and Cynthia Zava; on Wednesday mornings: Gabe Cuddahee, David Halperin, Ron Jackson, Susan Payne, and Sarah Wilkins; also to Joyce Allen, Poppy Brite, Sidney Cruze, Ray Harold, John Rhodes, and Mary-Russell Roberson.

My gratitude to the women who brought order to our home when I was a child, and when I matured into an inept housekeeper: Mary Leeper, Elizabeth Cureton, Verta Price, and Atlanta Feaster.

Family is all. Thank you, my children—Homer Jackson Faw III, Teresa Colleen Faw, and Scott Mayhew Pharr—for your everlasting acceptance of the oddities that make me a writer, for putting up with my inattention and vacant stares, for accepting my absences when I'm off somewhere musing. I am likewise deeply grateful for the ongoing faith and support of my sisters: Mary Jane Mayhew Burns, Linda Mayhew Gore, and Susan Mayhew Devine.

Jean-Michel, you rock!

Q&A WITH
ANNA JEAN MAYHEW

Q. Was there any one thing that compelled you to write the novel?

A. In 1957, something happened that changed the way I saw things; thirty years passed before I could write about the feelings it evoked in me. I was seventeen, working as a lifeguard during the summer, and had a deep tan (my hair was bleached almost white by the sun, and my eyes are pale blue; there's no mistaking my Caucasian genes). When the "color line" was removed from the Charlotte city buses, my parents told me that if "one of them" (a person of color) got on the bus and sat next to me, I should get off or at least move to another seat. One day a black woman sat down beside me, and my parents' words flashed through my mind. But I felt riveted to my seat, like it would have been so rude to move. So I sat there and eventually looked down to where our arms rested side by side. My skin was a lot darker than hers. That made a lasting impression on me.

Q. How long did it take you to write your novel?

A. Eighteen years from conception to final draft; while I wrote, I was working full-time as well, but I believe the novel would have taken me many years, regardless of the circumstances. It had to percolate, to find its center, and I had to be patient. I did not know, when I started writing the book, how it would end; I didn't know most of the characters, and only knew a few of the events.

Q. Were you writing in isolation, or did you have support from other writers?

A. Tremendous support from writers in a small group I've been in since I began the novel in 1987. Several books have been published by other members of the group, and in one of them (*The Dream of the Stone*, Christina Askounis, Farrar Straus Giroux, 1993) the acknowledgments say, "This book might have taken half as long to complete without the help of writers in Laurel Goldman's Thursday-morning group, who drew the best from me through draft after draft. . . ." That's true for me as well.

Q. Did you start with an idea, with a character, setting?

A. Character, first and last. The narrator, June Bentley Watts, aka Jubie, was in my head long before I began the book. She's a year younger than

I was in 1954, so readers might assume she's me at that age. Perhaps she was to begin with, but she quickly took on her own personality and led me through the story, as long as I was willing to listen to her. The false notes occurred when I stopped paying attention to Jubie or tried to write my own story. When I lost her voice, the book lost its heart, and I got back on the right path only by paying attention to her.

Q. Your protagonist is thirteen years old. Is your novel young-adult fiction?

A. My novel is literary fiction; however, I hope young adults will read it, because it's set in a time long before their lives and can give them a look into history through the eyes of someone their age. I didn't want the book marketed as young adult because I didn't want it limited by that.

Q. Your book is set in 1954 and is rich with details of that time. Did you have to do a lot of research?

A. Yes. I like to find out about things, to dig for information; I can lose myself, blissfully, in the happy task of research. My husband gave me a 1954 road atlas he found on eBay, so I was able to map the trip the Watts family took through the South. In May 2004, I went to Washington, DC, to exhibits on the fiftieth anniversary of *Brown v.*

Board of Education at the Smithsonian and the Library of Congress. The Carolina Room at the Public Library of Charlotte and Mecklenburg County provided me with online maps of Charlotte in 1954. I bought encyclopedia yearbooks and studied them, also stacks of popular magazines of the time, *The Saturday Evening Post*, *Life*, *Look*, etc. I am still stunned at how white they all are; when writing, I searched period publications for pictures of blacks living their lives and found instead stereotypical stories such as President Eisenhower's golf caddy, and ads for Aunt Jemima pancake mix.

Q. Do you have advice for others who begin writing relatively late in life?

A. Listen to yourself; tell stories you've lived and craft them into fiction. To do that, you must believe that your experiences are valid and of interest to others. Negative thoughts about your talent as a writer will stop you in your tracks. I also suggest getting into a writing group.

DISCUSSION QUESTIONS

1. What do you think about Paula's decision to take Mary on the trip, given the antipathy in the Deep South post *Brown v. Board*?

2. Why does Puddin so often try to hide or run away? What does her behavior say about the family?

3. Why didn't Paula try to stop Bill from beating Jubie?

4. Is Uncle Taylor a racist?

5. Why did the clown at Joyland by the Sea give Jubie a rose?

6. If you'd been Paula (or Bill), what would you have done when Cordelia failed to appear for dinner? How could they have handled that differently?

7. Why does Paula take Bill back after his affair with her brother's wife?

8. Did Bill and Paula act responsibly as parents when they allowed Jubie and Stell to go with Mary to the Daddy Grace parade in Charlotte? The tent meeting in Claxton?

9. Why didn't Paula punish Jubie for stealing the Packard to go to Mary's funeral?

10. What drove Stamos to suicide?

11. Which major character changes the most? The least?

12. Which character in the book did you identify with the most? The least?

13. If you could interview Jubie, what would you ask her? What about Mary? Paula? Bill? Stell?

14. If Bill died at the end of the book, what would his obituary say if Paula wrote it? If Stell wrote it? If Jubie wrote it?

15. Given that there's little hope for Jubie and Leesum to be friends in 1954, what would it be like for them if they met again today?